Jack Vance

The Moon Moth
and Other Stories

Jack Vance

The
Moon
Moth
AND OTHER
STORIES

Jack Vance

Spatterlight Press Signature Series, Volume 31

The New Prime © 1951, 2002
The Men Return © 1957, 2002
Ullward's Retreat © 1958, 2002
Dodkin's Job © 1959, 2002
The Moon Moth © 1961, 2002
Green Magic © 1963, 2002
Alfred's Ark © 1965, 2002
Sulwen's Planet © 1968, 2002
Rumfuddle © 1973, 2002
by Jack Vance

Published by Spatterlight Press

Cover art by Howard Kistler

ISBN 978-1-61947-152-8

Spatterlight Press LLC

Spatterlight
P R E S S

340 S. Lemon Ave #1916
Walnut, CA 91789
www.jackvance.com

CONTENTS

The New Prime

Music, carnival lights, the slide of feet on waxed oak, perfume, muffled talk and laughter.

Arthur Caversham of 20th-century Boston felt air along his skin, and discovered himself to be stark naked.

It was at Janice Paget's coming out party: three hundred guests in formal evening-wear surrounded him.

For a moment he felt no emotion beyond vague bewilderment. His presence seemed the outcome of logical events, but his memory was fogged and he could find no definite anchor of certainty.

He stood a little apart from the rest of the stag line, facing the red and gold calliope where the orchestra sat. The buffet, the punch-bowl, the champagne wagons, tended by clowns, were to his right; to the left, through the open flap of the circus tent, lay the garden, now lit by strings of colored lights, red, green, yellow, blue, and he caught a glimpse of a merry-go-round across the lawn.

Why was he here? He had no recollection, no sense of purpose... The night was warm. The other young men in the full-dress suits must feel rather sticky, he thought... An idea tugged at a corner of his mind, nagged, teased. There was a significant aspect to the affair which he was overlooking. Refusing to surface, the idea lay like an irritant just below the level of his conscious mind.

He noticed that the young men nearby had moved away from him. He heard chortles of amusement, astonished exclamations. A girl dancing past saw him over the arm of her escort; she gave a startled squeak, jerked her eyes away, giggling and blushing.

Something was wrong. These young men and women were startled and amazed by his naked skin to the point of embarrassment. The gnaw of urgency came closer to the surface. He must do something. Taboos felt with such intensity might not be violated without unpleasant consequences; such was his understanding. He was lacking garments; these he must obtain.

He looked about him, inspecting the young men who watched him with ribald delight, disgust or curiosity. To one of these latter he addressed himself.

"Where can I get some clothing?"

The young man shrugged. "Where did you leave it?"

Two heavy-set men in dark blue uniforms entered the tent; Arthur Caversham saw them from the corner of his eye, and his mind worked with desperate intensity.

This young man seemed typical of those around him. What sort of appeal would have meaning for him? Like any other human being, he could be moved to action if the right chord were struck. By what method could he be moved?

Sympathy?

Threats?

The prospect of advantage or profit?

Caversham rejected all of these. By violating the taboo he had forfeited his claim to sympathy. A threat would excite derision, and he had no profit or advantage to offer. The stimulus must be more devious…He reflected that young men customarily banded together in secret societies. In the thousand cultures he had studied this was almost infallibly true. Long-houses, drug-cults, tongs, instruments of sexual initiation — whatever the name, the external aspects were near-identical: painful initiation, secret signs and passwords, uniformity of group conduct, obligation to service. If this young man were a member of such an association, he might react to an appeal to this group-spirit.

Arthur Caversham said, "I've been put in this taboo situation by the brotherhood; in the name of the brotherhood, find me some suitable garments."

The young man stared, taken aback. "Brotherhood?…You mean fraternity?" Enlightenment spread over his face. "Is this some kind of hell-week stunt?" He laughed. "If it is, they sure go all the way."

"Yes," said Arthur Caversham. "My fraternity."

The young man said, "This way then — and hurry, here comes the law. We'll take off under the tent. I'll lend you my topcoat till you make it back to your house."

The two uniformed men, pushing quietly through the dancers, were almost upon them. The young man lifted the flap of the tent, Arthur Caversham ducked under, his friend followed. Together they ran through the many-colored shadows to a little booth painted with gay red and white stripes near the entrance to the tent.

"You stay back, out of sight," said the young man. "I'll check out my coat."

"Fine," said Arthur Caversham.

The young man hesitated. "What's your house? Where do you go to school?"

Arthur Caversham desperately searched his mind for an answer. A single fact reached the surface.

"I'm from Boston."

"Boston U.? Or M.I.T.? Or Harvard?"

"Harvard."

"Ah." The young man nodded. "I'm Washington and Lee myself. What's your house?"

"I'm not supposed to say."

"Oh," said the young man, puzzled but satisfied. "Well — just a minute…"

Bearwald the Halforn halted, numb with despair and exhaustion. The remnants of his platoon sank to the ground around him, and they stared back to where the rim of the night flickered and glowed with fire. Many villages, many wood-gabled farmhouses had been given the torch, and the Brands from Mount Medallion reveled in human blood.

The pulse of a distant drum touched Bearwald's skin, a deep *thrumm-thrumm-thrumm*, almost inaudible. Much closer he heard a hoarse human cry of fright, then exultant killing-calls, not human. The Brands were tall, black, man-shaped but not men. They had eyes like lamps of red glass, bright white teeth, and tonight they seemed bent on slaughtering all the men of the world.

"Down," hissed Kanaw, his right arm-guard, and Bearwald crouched. Across the flaring sky marched a column of tall Brand warriors, rocking jauntily, without fear.

Bearwald said suddenly, "Men—we are thirteen. Fighting arm to arm with these monsters we are helpless. Tonight their total force is down from the mountain; the hive must be near-deserted. What can we lose if we undertake to burn the home-hive of the Brands? Only our lives, and what are these now?"

Kanaw said, "Our lives are nothing; let us be off at once."

"May our vengeance be great," said Broctan the left arm-guard. "May the home-hive of the Brands be white ashes this coming morn…"

Mount Medallion loomed overhead; the oval hive lay in Pangborn Valley. At the mouth of the valley, Bearwald divided the platoon into two halves, and placed Kanaw in the van of the second. "We move silently twenty yards apart; thus if either party rouses a Brand, the other may attack from the rear and so kill the monster before the vale is roused. Do all understand?"

"We understand."

"Forward, then, to the hive."

The valley reeked with an odor like sour leather. From the direction of the hive came a muffled clanging. The ground was soft, covered with runner moss; careful feet made no sound. Crouching low, Bearwald could see the shapes of his men against the sky—here indigo with a violet rim. The angry glare of burning Echevasa lay down the slope to the south.

A sound. Bearwald hissed, and the columns froze. They waited. *Thud thud thud thud* came the steps—then a hoarse cry of rage and alarm.

"Kill, kill the beast!" yelled Bearwald.

The Brand swung his club like a scythe, lifting one man, carrying the body around with the after-swing. Bearwald leapt close, struck with his blade, slicing as he hewed; he felt the tendons part, smelled the hot gush of Brand blood.

The clanging had stopped now, and Brand cries carried across the night.

"Forward," panted Bearwald. "Out with your tinder, strike fire to the hive. Burn, burn, burn—"

Abandoning stealth he ran forward; ahead loomed the dark dome. Immature Brands came surging forth, squeaking and squalling, and with them came the genetrices — twenty-foot monsters crawling on hands and feet, grunting and snapping as they moved.

"Kill!" yelled Bearwald the Halforn. "Kill! Fire, fire, fire!"

He dashed to the hive, crouched, struck spark to tinder, puffed. The rag, soaked with saltpeter, flared; Bearwald fed it straw, thrust it against the hive. The reed-pulp and withe crackled.

He leapt up as a horde of young Brands darted at him. His blade rose and fell; they were cleft, no match for his frenzy. Creeping close came the great Brand genetrices, three of them, swollen of abdomen, exuding an odor vile to his nostrils.

"Out with the fire!" yelled the first. "Fire, out. The Great Mother is tombed within; she lies too fecund to move…Fire, woe, destruction!" And they wailed, "Where are the mighty? Where are our warriors?"

Thrumm-thrumm-thrumm came the sound of skin-drums. Up the valley rolled the echo of hoarse Brand voices.

Bearwald stood back to the blaze. He darted forward, severed the head of a creeping genetrix, jumped back…Where were his men? "Kanaw!" he called. "Laida! Theyat! Gyorg! Broctan!"

He craned his neck, saw the flicker of fires. "Men! Kill the creeping mothers!" And leaping forward once more, he hacked and hewed, and another genetrix sighed and groaned and rolled flat.

The Brand voices changed to alarm; the triumphant drumming halted; the thud of footsteps came loud.

At Bearwald's back the hive burnt with a pleasant heat. Within came a shrill keening, a cry of vast pain.

In the leaping blaze he saw the charging Brand warriors. Their eyes glared like embers, their teeth shone like white sparks. They came forward, swinging their clubs, and Bearwald gripped his sword, too proud to flee.

After grounding his air-sled Ceistan sat a few minutes inspecting the dead city Therlatch: a wall of earthen brick a hundred feet high, a dusty portal, and a few crumbled roofs lifting above the battlements. Behind the city the desert spread across the near, middle and far distance to the hazy shapes of the Altilune Mountains at the horizon, pink in the light of the twin suns Mig and Pag.

Scouting from above he had seen no sign of life, nor had he expected any, after a thousand years of abandonment. Perhaps a few sand-crawlers wallowed in the heat of the ancient bazaar, perhaps a few leobars inhabited the crumbled masonry. Otherwise the streets would feel his presence with great surprise.

Jumping from the air-sled, Ceistan advanced toward the portal. He passed under, stood looking right and left with interest. In the parched air the brick buildings stood almost eternal. The wind smoothed and rounded all harsh angles; the glass had been cracked by the heat of day and chill of night; heaps of sand clogged the passageways.

Three streets led away from the portal and Ceistan could find nothing to choose between them. Each was dusty, narrow, and each twisted out of his line of vision after a hundred yards.

Ceistan rubbed his chin thoughtfully. Somewhere in the city lay a brass-bound coffer, containing the Crown and Shield Parchment. This, according to tradition, set a precedent for the fief-holder's immunity from energy-tax. Glay, who was Ceistan's liege-lord, having cited the parchment as justification for his delinquency, had been challenged to show validity. Now he lay in prison on charge of rebellion, and in the morning he would be nailed to the bottom of an air-sled and sent drifting into the west, unless Ceistan returned with the Parchment.

After a thousand years, there was small cause for optimism, thought Ceistan. However, the lord Glay was a fair man and he would leave no stone unturned... If it existed, the chest presumably would lie in state, in the town's Legalic, or the Mosque, or in the Hall of Relicts, or possibly in the Sumptuar. He would search all of these, allowing two hours per building; the eight hours so used would see the end to the pink daylight.

At random he entered the street in the center and shortly came to a plaza at whose far end rose the Legalic, the Hall of Records and Decisions. At the façade Ceistan paused, for the interior was dim and gloomy. No sound came from the dusty void save the sigh and whisper of the dry wind. He entered.

The great hall was empty. The walls were illuminated with frescoes of red and blue, as bright as if painted yesterday. There were six to each wall, the top half displaying a criminal act and the bottom half the penalty.

Ceistan passed through the hall, into the chambers behind. He found but dust and the smell of dust. Into the crypts he ventured, and these were lit by oubliettes. There was much litter and rubble, but no brass coffer.

Up and out into the clean air he went, and strode across the plaza to the Mosque, where he entered under the massive architrave.

The Nunciator's Confirmatory lay wide and bare and clean, for the tesselated floor was swept by a powerful draft. A thousand apertures opened from the low ceiling, each communicating with a cell overhead; thus arranged so that the devout might seek counsel with the Nunciator as he passed below without disturbing their attitudes of supplication. In the center of the pavilion a disk of glass roofed a recess. Below was a coffer and in the coffer rested a brass-bound chest. Ceistan sprang down the steps in high hopes.

But the chest contained jewels — the tiara of the Old Queen, the chest vellopes of the Gonwand Corps, the great ball, half emerald, half ruby, which in the ancient ages was rolled across the plaza to signify the passage of the old year.

Ceistan tumbled them all back in the coffer. Relicts on this planet of dead cities had no value, and synthetic gems were infinitely superior in luminosity and water.

Leaving the Mosque, he studied the height of the suns. The zenith was past, the moving balls of pink fire leaned to the west. He hesitated, frowning and blinking at the hot earthen walls, considering that not impossibly both coffer and parchment were fable, like so many others regarding dead Therlatch.

A gust of wind swirled across the plaza and Ceistan choked on a dry throat. He spat and an acrid taste bit his tongue. An old fountain opened in the wall nearby; he examined it wistfully, but water was not even a memory along these dead streets.

Once again he cleared his throat, spat, turned across the city toward the Hall of Relicts.

He entered the great nave, past square pillars built of earthen brick. Pink shafts of light struck down from the cracks and gaps in the roof, and he was like a midge in the vast space. To all sides were niches cased in glass, and each held an object of ancient reverence: the Armor in which Plange the Forewarned led the Blue Flags; the coronet of the First Serpent; an array of antique Padang skulls; Princess Thermosteraliam's bridal gown of woven cobweb palladium, as fresh as the day she wore it; the original Tablets of Legality; the great conch throne of an early dynasty; a dozen other objects. But the coffer was not among them.

Ceistan sought for entrance to a possible crypt, but except where the currents of dusty air had channeled grooves in the porphyry, the floor was smooth.

Out once more into the dead streets, and now the suns had passed behind the crumbled roofs, leaving the streets in magenta shadow.

With leaden feet, burning throat and a sense of defeat, Ceistan turned to the Sumptuar, on the citadel. Up the wide steps, under the verdigris-fronted portico into a lobby painted with vivid frescoes. These depicted the maidens of ancient Therlatch at work, at play, amid sorrow and joy: slim creatures with short black hair and glowing ivory skin, as graceful as water-vanes, as round and delectable as chermoyan plums. Ceistan passed through the lobby with many side-glances, thinking sadly that these ancient creatures of delight were now the dust he trod under his feet.

He walked down a corridor which made a circuit of the building, and from which the chambers and apartments of the Sumptuar might be entered. The wisps of a wonderful rug crunched under his feet, and the walls displayed moldy tatters, once tapestries of the finest weave. At the entrance to each chamber a fresco pictured the Sumptuar maiden and the sign she served; at each of these chambers Ceistan paused, made a quick investigation, and so passed on to the next. The beams slanting in through the cracks served him as a gauge of time, and they flattened ever more toward the horizontal.

Chamber after chamber after chamber. There were chests in some, altars in others, cases of manifestos, triptychs, and fonts in others. But never the chest he sought.

And ahead was the lobby where he had entered the building. Three more chambers were to be searched, then the light would be gone.

He came to the first of these, and this was hung with a new curtain.

Pushing it aside, he found himself looking into an outside court, full in the long light of the twin suns. A fountain of water trickled down across steps of apple-green jade into a garden as soft and fresh and green as any in the north. And rising in alarm from a couch was a maiden, as vivid and delightful as any in the frescoes. She had short dark hair, a face as pure and delicate as the great white frangipani she wore over her ear.

For an instant Ceistan and the maiden stared eye to eye; then her alarm faded and she smiled shyly.

"Who are you?" Ceistan asked in wonder. "Are you a ghost or do you live here in the dust?"

"I am real," she said. "My home is to the south, at the Palram Oasis, and this is the period of solitude to which all maidens of the race submit when aspiring for Upper Instruction … So without fear may you come beside me, and rest, and drink of fruit wine and be my companion through the lonely night, for this is my last week of solitude and I am weary of my own aloneness."

Ceistan took a step forward, then hesitated. "I must fulfill my mission. I seek the brass coffer containing the Crown and Shield Parchment. Do you know of this?"

She shook her head. "It is nowhere in the Sumptuar." She rose to her feet, stretching her ivory arms as a kitten stretches. "Abandon your search, and come let me refresh you."

Ceistan looked at her, looked up at the fading light, looked down the corridor to the two doors yet remaining. "First I must complete my search; I owe duty to my lord Glay, who will be nailed under an air-sled and sped west unless I bring him aid."

The maiden said with a pout, "Go then to your dusty chamber; and go with a dry throat. You will find nothing, and if you persist so stubbornly, I will be gone when you return."

"So let it be," said Ceistan.

He turned away, marched down the corridor. The first chamber was bare and dry as a bone. In the second and last, a man's skeleton lay tumbled in a corner; this Ceistan saw in the last rosy light of the twin suns.

There was no brass coffer, no parchment. So Glay must die, and Ceistan's heart hung heavy.

He returned to the chamber where he had found the maiden, but she had departed. The fountain had been stopped, and moisture only filmed the stones.

Ceistan called, "Maiden, where are you? Return; my obligation is at an end..."

There was no response.

Ceistan shrugged, turned to the lobby and so outdoors, to grope his way through the deserted twilight street to the portal and his air-sled.

Dobnor Daksat became aware that the big man in the embroidered black cloak was speaking to him.

Orienting himself to his surroundings, which were at once familiar and strange, he also became aware that the man's voice was condescending, supercilious.

"You are competing in a highly advanced classification," he said. "I marvel at your — ah, confidence." And he eyed Daksat with a gleaming and speculative eye.

Daksat looked down at the floor, frowned at the sight of his clothes. He wore a long cloak of black-purple velvet, swinging like a bell around his ankles. His trousers were of scarlet corduroy, tight at the waist, thigh and calf, with a loose puff of green cloth between calf and ankle. The clothes were his own, obviously: they looked wrong and right at once, as did the carved gold knuckle-guards he wore on his hands.

The big man in the dark cloak continued speaking, looking at a point over Daksat's head, as if Daksat were nonexistent.

"Clauktaba has won Imagist honors over the years. Bel-Washab was the Korsi Victor last month; Tol Morabait is an acknowledged master of the technique. And there is Ghisel Ghang of West Ind, who knows no peer in the creation of fire-stars, and Pulakt Havjorska, the Champion of the Island Realm. So it becomes a matter of skepticism whether you, new, inexperienced, without a fund of images, can do more than embarrass us all with your mental poverty."

Daksat's brain was yet wrestling with his bewilderment, and he could feel no strong resentment at the big man's evident contempt. He said, "Just what is all this? I'm not sure that I understand my position."

The man in the black cloak inspected him quizzically. "So, now you commence to experience trepidation? Justly, I assure you." He sighed, waved his hands. "Well, well — young men will be impetuous, and perhaps you have formed images you considered not discreditable. In any event, the public eye will ignore you for the glories of Clauktaba's geometrics and Ghisel Ghang's star-bursts. Indeed, I counsel you, keep your images small, drab and confined: you will so avoid the faults of bombast and discord…Now, it is time to go to your imagicon. This way, then. Remember, greys, browns, lavenders, perhaps a few tones of ocher and rust; then the spectators will understand that you compete for the schooling alone, and do not actively challenge the masters. This way then…"

He opened a door and led Dobnor Daksat up a stair and so out into the night.

They stood in a great stadium, facing six great screens forty feet high. Behind them in the dark sat tier upon tier of spectators — thousands and thousands, and their sounds came as a soft crush. Daksat turned to see them, but all their faces and their individualities had melted into the entity as a whole.

"Here," said the big man, "this is your apparatus. Seat yourself and I will adjust the ceretemps."

Daksat suffered himself to be placed in a heavy chair, so soft and deep that he felt himself to be floating. Adjustments were made at his head and neck and the bridge of his nose. He felt a sharp prick, a pressure, a throb, and then a soothing warmth. From the distance, a voice called out over the crowd:

"Two minutes to grey mist! Two minutes to grey mist! Attend, imagists, two minutes to grey mist!"

The big man stooped over him. "Can you see well?"

Daksat raised himself a trifle. "Yes… All is clear."

"Very well. At 'grey mist', this little filament will glow. When it dies, then it is your screen, and you must imagine your best."

The far voice said, "One minute to grey mist! The order is Pulakt Havjorska, Tol Morabait, Ghisel Ghang, Dobnor Daksat, Clauktaba and Bel-Washab. There are no handicaps; all colors and shapes are permitted. Relax then, ready your lobes, and now — grey mist!"

The light glowed on the panel of Daksat's chair, and he saw five of the six screens light to a pleasant pearl-grey, swirling a trifle as if agitated, excited. Only the screen before him remained dull. The big man who stood behind him reached down, prodded. "Grey mist, Daksat; are you deaf and blind?"

Daksat thought grey mist, and instantly his screen sprang to life, displaying a cloud of silver-grey, clean and clear.

"Humph," he heard the big man snort. "Somewhat dull and without interest — but I suppose good enough…See how Clauktaba's rings with hints of passion already, quivers with emotion."

And Daksat, noting the screen to his right, saw this to be true. The grey, without actually displaying color, flowed and filmed as if suppressing a vast flood of light.

Now to the far left, on Pulakt Havjorska's screen, color glowed. It was a gambit image, modest and restrained — a green jewel dripping a rain of blue and silver drops which struck a black ground and disappeared in little orange explosions.

Then Tol Morabait's screen glowed; a black and white checkerboard with certain of the squares flashing suddenly green, red, blue and yellow — warm searching colors, pure as shafts from a rainbow. The image disappeared in a flush mingled of rose and blue.

Ghisel Ghang wrought a circle of yellow which quivered, brought forth a green halo, which in turn bulging, gave rise to a larger band of brilliant black and white. In the center formed a complex kaleidoscopic pattern. The pattern suddenly vanished in a brilliant flash of light; on the screen for an instant or two appeared the identical pattern in a complete new suit of colors. A ripple of sound from the spectators greeted this *tour de force*.

The light on Daksat's panel died. Behind him he felt a prod. "Now."

Daksat eyed the screen and his mind was blank of ideas. He ground his teeth. Anything. Anything. A picture…He imagined a view across the meadowlands beside the river Melramy.

"Hm," said the big man behind him. "Pleasant. A pleasant fantasy, and rather original."

Puzzled, Daksat examined the picture on the screen. So far as he could distinguish, it was an uninspired reproduction of a scene he knew well. Fantasy? Was that what was expected? Very well, he'd produce fantasy. He imagined the meadows glowing, molten, white-hot. The vegetation, the old cairns slumped into a viscous seethe. The surface smoothed, became a mirror which reflected the Copper Crags.

Behind him the big man grunted. "A little heavy-handed, that last, and thereby you destroyed the charming effect of those unearthly colors and shapes..."

Daksat slumped back in his chair, frowning, eager for his turn to come again.

Meanwhile Clauktaba created a dainty white blossom with purple stamens on a green stalk. The petals wilted, the stamens discharged a cloud of swirling yellow pollen.

Then Bel-Washab, at the end of the line, painted his screen a luminous underwater green. It rippled, bulged, and a black irregular blot marred the surface. From the center of the blot seeped a trickle of hot gold which quickly meshed and veined the black blot.

Such was the first passage.

There was a pause of several seconds. "Now," breathed the voice behind Daksat, "now the competition begins."

On Pulakt Havjorska's screen appeared an angry sea of color: waves of red, green, blue, an ugly mottling. Dramatically a yellow shape appeared at the lower right, vanquished the chaos. It spread over the screen, the center went lime-green. A black shape appeared, split, bowed softly and easily to both sides. Then turning, the two shapes wandered into the background, twisting, bending with supple grace. Far down a perspective they merged, darted forward like a lance, spread out into a series of lances, formed a slanting pattern of slim black bars.

"Superb!" hissed the big man. "The timing, so just, so exact!"

Tol Morabait replied with a fuscous brown field threaded with crimson lines and blots. Vertical green hatching formed at the left, strode across the screen to the right. The brown field pressed forward, bulged through the green bars, pressed hard, broke, and segments flitted forward to leave the screen. On the black background behind the green hatching, which now faded, lay a human brain, pink, pulsing. The brain sprouted six insect-like legs, scuttled crabwise back into the distance.

Ghisel Ghang brought forth one of his fire-bursts — a small pellet of bright blue exploding in all directions, the tips working and writhing through wonderful patterns in the five colors, blue, violet, white, purple and light green.

Dobnor Daksat, rigid as a bar, sat with hands clenched and teeth grinding into teeth. Now! Was not his brain as excellent as those of the far lands? Now!

On the screen appeared a tree, conventionalized in greens and blues, and each leaf was a tongue of fire. From these fires wisps of smoke arose on high to form a cloud which worked and swirled, then emptied a cone of rain about the tree. The flames vanished and in their places appeared star-shaped white flowers. From the cloud came a bolt of lightning, shattering the tree to agonized fragments of glass. Another bolt into the brittle heap and the screen exploded in a great gout of white, orange and black.

The voice of the big man said doubtfully, "On the whole well done, but mind my warning, and create more modest images, since —"

"Silence!" said Dobnor Daksat in a harsh voice.

So the competition went, round after round of spectacles, some sweet as canmel honey, others as violent as the storms which circle the poles. Color strove with color, patterns evolved and changed, sometimes in glorious cadence, sometimes in the bitter discord necessary to the strength of the image.

And Daksat built dream after dream, while his tension vanished, and he forgot all save the racing pictures in his mind and on the screen, and his images became as complex and subtle as those of the masters.

"One more passage," said the big man behind Daksat, and now the imagists brought forth the master-dreams: Pulakt Havjorska, the growth and decay of a beautiful city; Tol Morabait, a quiet composition of green and white interrupted by a marching army of insects who left a dirty wake, and who were joined in battle by men in painted leather armor and tall hats, armed with short swords and flails. The insects were destroyed and chased off the screen; the dead warriors became bones and faded to twinkling blue dust. Ghisel Ghang created three fire-bursts simultaneously, each different, a gorgeous display.

Daksat imagined a smooth pebble, magnified it to a block of marble, chipped it away to create the head of a beautiful maiden. For a moment she stared forth and varying emotions crossed her face — joy at her sudden existence, pensive thought, and at last fright. Her eyes turned milky opaque blue, the face changed to a laughing sardonic mask, black-cheeked with a fleering mouth. The head tilted, the mouth spat into the air. The head flattened into a black background, the drops of spittle shone like fire, became stars, constellations, and one of these expanded, became a planet with configurations dear to Daksat's heart. The planet hurtled off into darkness, the constellations faded. Dobnor Daksat relaxed. His last image. He sighed, exhausted.

The big man in the black cloak removed the harness in brittle silence. At last he asked, "The planet you imagined in that last screening, was that a creation or a remembrance of actuality? It was none of our system here, and it rang with the clarity of truth."

Dobnor Daksat stared at him puzzled, and the words faltered in his throat. "But it is — home! This world! Was it not this world?"

The big man looked at him strangely, shrugged, turned away. "In a moment now the winner of the contest will be made known and the jeweled brevet awarded."

The day was gusty and overcast, the galley was low and black, manned by the oarsmen of Belaclaw. Ergan stood on the poop, staring across the two miles of bitter sea to the coast of Racland, where he knew the sharp-faced Racs stood watching from the headlands.

A gout of water erupted a few hundred yards astern.

Ergan spoke to the helmsman. "Their guns have better range than we bargained for. Better stand offshore another mile and we'll take our chances with the current."

Even as he spoke, there came a great whistle and he glimpsed a black pointed projectile slanting down at him. It struck the waist of the galley, exploded. Timber, bodies, metal, flew everywhere, and the galley laid its broken back into the water, doubled up and sank.

Ergan, jumping clear, discarded his sword, casque and greaves almost as he hit the chill grey water. Gasping from the shock, he swam in circles, bobbing up and down in the chop; then, finding a length of timber, he clung to it for support.

From the shores of Racland a longboat put forth and approached, bow churning white foam as it rose and fell across the waves. Ergan turned loose the timber and swam as rapidly as possible from the wreck. Better drowning than capture; there would be more mercy from the famine-fish which swarmed the waters than from the pitiless Racs.

So he swam, but the current took him to the shore, and at last, struggling feebly, he was cast upon a pebbly beach.

Here he was discovered by a gang of Rac youths and marched to a nearby command post. He was tied and flung into a cart and so conveyed to the city Korsapan.

In a grey room he was seated facing an intelligence officer of the Rac secret police, a man with the grey skin of a toad, a moist grey mouth, eager, searching eyes.

"You are Ergan," said the officer. "Emissary to the Bargee of Salomdek. What was your mission?"

Ergan stared back eye to eye, hoping that a happy and convincing response would find his lips. None came, and the truth would incite an immediate invasion of both Belaclaw and Salomdek by the tall thin-headed Rac soldiers, who wore black uniforms and black boots.

Ergan said nothing. The officer leaned forward. "I ask you once more; then you will be taken to the room below." He said "Room Below" as if the words were capitalized, and he said it with soft relish.

Ergan, in a cold sweat, for he knew of the Rac torturers, said, "I am not Ergan; my name is Ervard; I am an honest trader in pearls."

"This is untrue," said the Rac. "Your aide was captured and under the compression pump he blurted up your name with his lungs."

"I am Ervard," said Ergan, his bowels quaking.

The Rac signaled. "Take him to the Room Below."

A man's body, which has developed nerves as outposts against danger, seems especially intended for pain, and cooperates wonderfully with the craft of the torturer. These characteristics of the body had been studied by the Rac specialists, and other capabilities of the human nervous system had been blundered upon by accident. It had been found that certain programs of pressure, heat, strain, friction, torque, surge, jerk, sonic and visual shock, vermin, stench and vileness created cumulative effects, whereas a single method, used to excess, lost its stimulation thereby.

All this lore and cleverness was lavished upon Ergan's citadel of nerves, and they inflicted upon him the entire gamut of pain: the sharp twinges, the dull lasting joint-aches which groaned by night, the fiery flashes, the assaults of filth and lechery, together with shocks of occasional tenderness when he would be allowed to glimpse the world he had left.

Then back to the Room Below.

But always: "I am Ervard the trader." And always he tried to goad his mind over the tissue barrier to death, but always the mind hesitated at the last toppling step, and Ergan lived.

The Racs tortured by routine, so that the expectation, the approach of the hour, brought with it as much torment as the act itself. And then the heavy unhurried steps outside the cell, the feeble thrashing around to evade, the harsh laughs when they cornered him and carried him forth, and the harsh laughs when three hours later they threw him sobbing and whimpering back to the pile of straw that was his bed.

"I am Ervard," he said, and trained his mind to believe that this was the truth, so that never would they catch him unaware. "I am Ervard! I am Ervard, I trade in pearls!"

He tried to strangle himself on straw, but a slave watched always, and this was not permitted.

He attempted to die by self-suffocation, and would have been glad to succeed, but always as he sank into blessed numbness, so did his mind relax and his motor nerves take up the mindless business of breathing once more.

He ate nothing, but this meant little to the Racs, as they injected him full of tonics, sustaining drugs and stimulants, so that he might always be keyed to the height of his awareness.

"I am Ervard," said Ergan, and the Racs gritted their teeth angrily. The case was now a challenge; he defied their ingenuity, and they puzzled long and carefully upon refinements and delicacies, new shapes to the iron tools, new types of jerk ropes, new directions for the strains and pressures. Even when it was no longer important whether he was Ergan or Ervard, since war now raged, he was kept and maintained as a problem, an ideal case; so he was guarded and cosseted with even more than usual care, and the Rac torturers mulled over their techniques, making changes here, improvements there.

Then one day the Belaclaw galleys landed and the feather-crested soldiers fought past the walls of Korsapan.

The Racs surveyed Ergan with regret. "Now we must go, and still you will not submit to us."

"I am Ervard," croaked that which lay on the table. "Ervard the trader."

A splintering crash sounded overhead.

"We must go," said the Racs. "Your people have stormed the city. If you tell the truth, you may live. If you lie, we kill you. So there is your choice. Your life for the truth."

"The truth?" muttered Ergan. "It is a trick—" And then he caught the victory chant of the Belaclaw soldiery. "The truth? Why not?...Very well." And he said, "I am Ervard," for now he believed this to be the truth.

Galactic Prime was a lean man with reddish-brown hair sparse across a fine arch of skull. His face, undistinguished otherwise, was given power by great dark eyes flickering with a light like fire behind smoke. Physically he had passed the peak of his youth; his arms and legs were thin and loose-jointed; his head inclined forward as if weighted by the intricate machinery of his brain.

Arising from the couch, smiling faintly, he looked across the arcade to the eleven Elders. They sat at a table of polished wood, backs to a wall festooned with vines. They were grave men, slow in their motions, and their faces were lined with wisdom and insight. By the ordained system, Prime was the executive of the universe, the Elders the deliberative body, invested with certain restrictive powers.

"Well?"

The Chief Elder without haste raised his eyes from the computer. "You are the first to arise from the couch."

Prime turned a glance up the arcade, still smiling faintly. The others lay variously: some with arms clenched, rigid as bars; others huddled in foetal postures. One had slumped from the couch half to the floor; his eyes were open, staring at remoteness.

Prime returned to the Chief Elder, who watched him with detached curiosity. "Has the optimum been established?"

The Chief Elder consulted the computer. "Twenty-six thirty-seven is the optimum score."

Prime waited, but the Chief Elder said no more. Prime stepped to the alabaster balustrade beyond the couches. He leaned forward, looked out across the vista — miles and miles of sunny haze, with a twinkling sea in the distance. A breeze blew past his face, ruffling the scant russet strands of his hair. He took a deep breath, flexed his fingers and hands, for the memory of the Rac torturers was still heavy on his mind. After a moment he swung around, leaned back, resting his elbows upon the balustrade. He glanced once more down the line of couches; there were still no signs of vitality from the candidates.

"Twenty-six thirty-seven," he muttered. "I venture to estimate my own score at twenty-five ninety. In the last episode I recall an incomplete retention of personality."

"Twenty-five seventy-four," said the Chief Elder. "The computer judged Bearwald the Halforn's final defiance of the Brand warriors unprofitable."

Prime considered. "The point is well made. Obstinacy serves no purpose unless it advances a predetermined end. It is a flaw I must seek to temper." He looked along the line of Elders, from face to face. "You make no enunciations, you are curiously mute."

He waited; the Chief Elder made no response.

"May I enquire the high score?"

"Twenty-five seventy-four."

Prime nodded. "Mine."

"Yours is the high score," said the Chief Elder.

Prime's smile disappeared; a puzzled line appeared across his brow. "In spite of this, you are still reluctant to confirm my second span of authority; there are still doubts among you."

"Doubts and misgivings," replied the Chief Elder.

Prime's mouth pulled in at the corners, although his brows were still raised in polite inquiry. "Your attitude puzzles me. My record is one of selfless service. My intelligence is phenomenal, and in this final test, which I designed to dispel your last doubts, I attained the highest score. I have proved my social intuition and flexibility, my leadership, devotion to duty, imagination and resolution. In every commensurable aspect, I fulfill best the qualifications for the office I hold."

The Chief Elder looked up and down the line of his fellows. There were none who wished to speak. The Chief Elder squared himself in his chair, sat back.

"Our attitude is difficult to represent. Everything is as you say. Your intelligence is beyond dispute, your character is exemplary, you have served your term with honor and devotion. You have earned our respect, admiration and gratitude. We realize also that you seek this second term from praiseworthy motives: you regard yourself as the man best able to coordinate the complex business of the galaxy."

Prime nodded grimly. "But you think otherwise."

"Our position is perhaps not quite so blunt."

"Precisely what is your position?" Prime gestured along the couches. "Look at these men. They are the finest of the galaxy. One man is dead. That one stirring on the third couch has lost his mind; he is a lunatic. The others are sorely shaken. And never forget that this test has been expressly designed to measure the qualities essential to the Galactic Prime."

"This test has been of great interest to us," said the Chief Elder mildly. "It has considerably affected our thinking."

Prime hesitated, plumbing the unspoken overtones of the words. He came forward, seated himself across from the line of Elders. With a narrow glance he searched the faces of the eleven men, tapped once, twice, three times with his fingertips on the polished wood, leaned back in the chair.

"As I have pointed out, the test has gauged each candidate for the exact qualities essential to the optimum conduct of office, in this fashion: Earth of the twentieth century is a planet of intricate conventions; on Earth the candidate, as Arthur Caversham, is required to use his social intuition — a quality highly important in this galaxy of two billion suns. On Belotsi, Bearwald the Halforn is tested for courage and the ability to conduct positive action. At the dead city Therlatch on Praesepe Three, the candidate, as Ceistan, is rated for devotion to duty, and as Dobnor Daksat at the Imagicon on Staff, his creative conceptions are rated against the most fertile imaginations alive. Finally as Ergan, on Chankozar, his will, persistence and ultimate fiber are explored to their extreme limits.

"Each candidate is placed in the identical set of circumstances by a trick of temporal, dimensional and cerebro-neural meshing, which is rather complicated for the present discussion. Sufficient that each candidate is objectively rated by his achievements, and that the results are commensurable."

He paused, looked shrewdly along the line of grave faces. "I must emphasize that although I myself designed and arranged the test, I thereby gained no advantage. The mnemonic synapses are entirely disengaged from incident to incident, and only the candidate's basic personality acts. All were tested under precisely the same conditions. In my opinion the scores registered by the computer indicate an objective and reliable index of the candidate's ability for the highly responsible office of Galactic Executive."

The Chief Elder said, "The scores are indeed significant."

"Then — you approve my candidacy?"

The Chief Elder smiled. "Not so fast. Admittedly you are intelligent, admittedly you have accomplished much during your term as Prime. But much remains to be done."

"Do you suggest that another man would have achieved more?"

The Chief Elder shrugged. "I have no conceivable way of knowing. I point out your achievements, such as the Glenart civilization, the Dawn Time on Masilis, the reign of King Karal on Aevir, the suppression of the Arkid Revolt. There are many such examples. But there are also shortcomings: the totalitarian governments on Earth, the savagery on Belotsi and Chankozar, so pointedly emphasized in your test. Then there is the decadence of the planets in the Eleven Hundred Ninth Cluster, the rise of the Priest-kings on Fiir, and much else."

Prime clenched his mouth and the fires behind his eyes burnt more brightly.

The Chief Elder continued. "One of the most remarkable phenomena of the galaxy is the tendency of humanity to absorb and manifest the personality of the Prime. There seems to be a tremendous resonance which vibrates from the brain of the Prime through the minds of man from Center to the outer fringes. It is a matter which should be studied, analyzed and subjected to control. The effect is as if every thought of the Prime is magnified a billion-fold, as if every mood sets the tone for a thousand civilizations, every facet of his personality reflects in the ethics of a thousand cultures."

Prime said tonelessly, "I have remarked this phenomenon and have thought much on it. Prime's commands are promulgated in such a way as to exert subtle rather than overt influence; perhaps here is the background of the matter. In any event, the fact of this influence is even more reason to select for the office a man of demonstrated virtue."

"Well put," said the Chief Elder. "Your character is indeed beyond reproach. However, we of the Elders are concerned by the rising tide of authoritarianism among the planets of the galaxy. We suspect that this principle of resonance is at work. You are a man of intense and indomitable will, and we feel that your influence has unwittingly prompted an irruption of autarchies."

Prime was silent a moment. He looked down the line of couches where the other candidates were recovering awareness. They were men of various races: a pale Northkin of Palast, a stocky red Hawolo, a grey-haired grey-eyed Islander from the Sea Planet — each the outstanding man of the planet of his birth. Those who had returned to consciousness sat quietly, collecting their wits, or lay back on the couch, trying to expunge the test from their minds. There had been a toll taken: one lay dead, another bereft of his wits crouched whimpering beside his couch.

The Chief Elder said, "The objectionable aspects of your character are perhaps best exemplified by the test itself."

Prime opened his mouth; the Chief Elder held up his hand. "Let me speak; I will try to deal fairly with you. When I am done, you may say your say.

"I repeat that your basic direction is displayed by the details of the test that you devised. The qualities you measured were those which you considered the most important: that is, those ideals by which you guide your own life. This arrangement I am sure was completely unconscious, and hence completely revealing. You conceive the essential characteristics of the Prime to be social intuition, aggressiveness, loyalty, imagination and dogged persistence. As a man of strong character you seek to exemplify these ideals in your own conduct; therefore it is not at all surprising that in this test, designed by you, with a scoring system calibrated by you, your score should be highest.

"Let me clarify the idea by an analogy. If the Eagle were conducting a test to determine the King of Beasts, he would rate all the candidates on their ability to fly; necessarily he would win. In this fashion the Mole would consider ability to dig important; by his system of testing *he* would inevitably emerge King of Beasts."

Prime laughed sharply, ran a hand through his sparse red-brown locks. "I am neither Eagle nor Mole."

The Chief Elder shook his head. "No. You are zealous, dutiful, imaginative, indefatigable — so you have demonstrated, as much by specifying tests for these characteristics as by scoring high in these same tests. But conversely, by the very absence of other tests you demonstrate deficiencies in your character."

"And these are?"

"Sympathy. Compassion. Kindness." The Chief Elder settled back in his chair. "Strange. Your predecessor two times removed was rich in these qualities. During his term, the great humanitarian systems based on the idea of human brotherhood sprang up across the universe. Another example of resonance — but I digress."

Prime said with a sardonic twitch of his mouth, "May I ask this: have you selected the next Galactic Prime?"

The Chief Elder nodded. "A definite choice has been made."

"What was his score in the test?"

"By your scoring system — seventeen eighty. He did poorly as Arthur Caversham; he tried to explain the advantages of nudity to the policeman. He lacked the ability to concoct an instant subterfuge; he has little of your quick craft. As Arthur Caversham he found himself naked. He is sincere and straightforward, hence tried to expound the positive motivations for his state, rather than discover the means to evade the penalties."

"Tell me more about this man," said Prime shortly.

"As Bearwald the Halforn, he led his band to the hive of the Brands on Mount Medallion, but instead of burning the hive, he called forth to the queen, begging her to end the useless slaughter. She reached out from the doorway, drew him within and killed him. He failed — but the computer still rated him highly on his forthright approach.

"At Therlatch, his conduct was as irreproachable as yours, and at the Imagicon his performance was adequate. Yours approached the brilliance of the Master Imagists, which is high achievement indeed.

"The Rac tortures are the most trying element of the test. You knew well you could resist limitless pain; therefore you ordained that all other candidates must likewise possess this attribute. The new Prime is sadly deficient here. He is sensitive, and the idea of one man intentionally inflicting pain upon another sickens him. I may add that none of the candidates achieved a perfect count in the last episode. Two others equaled your score —"

Prime evinced interest. "Which are they?"

The Chief Elder pointed them out — a tall hard-muscled man with rock-hewn face standing by the alabaster balustrade gazing moodily out across the sunny distance, and a man of middle age who sat with his legs folded under him, watching a point three feet before him with an expression of imperturbable placidity.

"One is utterly obstinate and hard," said the Chief Elder. "He refused to say a single word. The other assumes an outer objectivity when unpleasantness overtakes him. Others among the candidates fared not so well; mental readjustment and therapy will be necessary in almost all cases."

Their eyes went to the witless creature with vacant eyes who padded up and down the aisle, muttering quietly to himself.

"The tests were by no means valueless," said the Chief Elder. "We learned a great deal. By your system of scoring, the competition rated you most high. By other standards which we Elders postulated, your place was lower."

With a tight mouth Prime inquired, "Who is this paragon of altruism, kindliness, sympathy and generosity?"

The lunatic wandered close, fell on his hands and knees, crawled whimpering to the wall. He pressed his face to the cool stone, stared blankly up at Prime. His mouth hung loose, his chin was wet, his eyes rolled apparently free of each other.

The Chief Elder smiled in great compassion; he stroked the mad creature's head. "This is he. Here is the man we select."

The old Galactic Prime sat silent, mouth compressed, eyes burning like far volcanoes.

At his feet the new Prime, Lord of Two Billion Suns, found a dead leaf, put it into his mouth, and began to chew.

THE MEN RETURN

THE RELICT CAME FURTIVELY down the crag, a shambling gaunt creature with tortured eyes. He moved in a series of quick dashes using panels of dark air for concealment, running behind each passing shadow, at times crawling on all fours, head low to the ground. Arriving at the final low outcrop of rock, he halted and peered across the plain.

Far away rose low hills, blurring into the sky, which was mottled and sallow like poor milk-glass. The intervening plain spread like rotten velvet, black-green and wrinkled, streaked with ocher and rust. A fountain of liquid rock jetted high in the air, branched out into black coral. In the middle distance a family of gray objects evolved with a sense of purposeful destiny: spheres melted into pyramids, became domes, tufts of white spires, sky-piercing poles; then, as a final tour de force, tesseracts.

The Relict cared nothing for this; he needed food and out on the plain were plants. They would suffice in lieu of anything better. They grew in the ground, or sometimes on a floating lump of water, or surrounding a core of hard black gas. There were dank black flaps of leaf, clumps of haggard thorn, pale green bulbs, stalks with leaves and contorted flowers. There were no recognizable species, and the Relict had no means of knowing if the leaves and tendrils he had eaten yesterday would poison him today.

He tested the surface of the plain with his foot. The glassy surface (though it likewise seemed a construction of red and gray-green pyramids) accepted his weight, then suddenly sucked at his leg. In a frenzy he tore himself free, jumped back, squatted on the temporarily solid rock.

Hunger rasped at his stomach. He must eat. He contemplated the plain. Not too far away a pair of Organisms played — sliding, diving, dancing, striking flamboyant poses. Should they approach he would try to kill one of them. They resembled men, and so should make a good meal.

He waited. A long time? A short time? It might have been either; duration had neither quantitative nor qualitative reality. The sun had vanished, and there was no standard cycle or recurrence. 'Time' was a word blank of meaning.

Matters had not always been so. The Relict retained a few tattered recollections of the old days, before system and logic had been rendered obsolete. Man had dominated Earth by virtue of a single assumption: that an effect could be traced to a cause, itself the effect of a previous cause.

Manipulation of this basic law yielded rich results; there seemed no need for any other tool or instrumentality. Man congratulated himself on his generalized structure. He could live on desert, on plain or ice, in forest or in city; Nature had not shaped him to a special environment.

He was unaware of his vulnerability. Logic was the special environment; the brain was the special tool.

Then came the terrible hour when Earth swam into a pocket of non-causality, and all the ordered tensions of cause–effect dissolved. The special tool was useless; it had no purchase on reality. From the two billions of men, only a few survived — the mad. They were now the Organisms, lords of the era, their discords so exactly equivalent to the vagaries of the land as to constitute a peculiar wild wisdom. Or perhaps the disorganized matter of the world, loose from the old organization, was peculiarly sensitive to psycho-kinesis.

A handful of others, the Relicts, managed to exist, but only through a delicate set of circumstances. They were the ones most strongly charged with the old causal dynamic. It persisted sufficiently to control the metabolism of their bodies, but could extend no further. They were fast dying out, for sanity provided no leverage against the environment. Sometimes their own minds sputtered and jangled, and they would go raving and leaping out across the plain.

The Organisms observed with neither surprise nor curiosity; how could surprise exist? The mad Relict might pause by an Organism, and try to duplicate the creature's existence. The Organism ate a mouthful of plant; so did the Relict. The Organism rubbed his feet with crushed water; so did the Relict. Presently the Relict would die of poison or rent bowels or skin lesions, while the Organism relaxed in the dank black grass. Or the Organism might seek to eat the Relict; and the Relict would run off in terror, unable to abide any part of the world — running, bounding, breasting the thick air; eyes wide, mouth open, calling and gasping until finally he foundered in a pool of black iron or blundered into a vacuum pocket, to bat around like a fly in a bottle.

The Relicts now numbered very few. Finn, he who crouched on the rock overlooking the plain, lived with four others. Two of these were old men and soon would die. Finn likewise would die unless he found food.

Out on the plain one of the Organisms, Alpha, sat down, caught a handful of air, a globe of blue liquid, a rock, kneaded them together, pulled the mixture like taffy, gave it a great heave. It uncoiled from his hand like rope. The Relict crouched low. No telling what deviltry would occur to the creature. He and all the rest of them — unpredictable! The Relict valued their flesh as food; but the Organisms would eat him if opportunity offered. In the competition he was at a great disadvantage. Their random acts baffled him. If, seeking to escape, he ran, the worst terror would begin. The direction he set his face was seldom the direction the varying frictions of the ground let him move. But the Organisms were as random and uncommitted as the environment, and the double set of disorders sometimes compounded, sometimes canceled each other. In the latter case the Organism might catch him... It was inexplicable. But then, what was not? The word 'explanation' had no meaning.

They were moving toward him; had they seen him? He flattened himself against the sullen yellow rock.

The two Organisms paused not far away. He could hear their sounds, and crouched, sick from conflicting pangs of hunger and fear.

Alpha sank to his knees, lay flat on his back, arms and legs flung out at random, addressing the sky in a series of musical cries, sibilants, guttural groans. It was a personal language he had only now improvised, but Beta understood him well.

"A vision," cried Alpha. "I see past the sky. I see knots, spinning circles. They tighten into hard points; they will never come undone."

Beta perched on a pyramid, glanced over his shoulder at the mottled sky.

"An intuition," chanted Alpha, "a picture out of the other time. It is hard, merciless, inflexible."

Beta poised on the pyramid, dove through the glassy surface, swam under Alpha, emerged, lay flat beside him.

"Observe the Relict on the hillside. In his blood is the whole of the old race — the narrow men with minds like cracks. He has exuded the intuition. Clumsy thing — a blunderer," said Alpha.

"They are all dead, all of them," said Beta. "Although three or four remain." (When *past, present* and *future* are no more than ideas left over from another era, like boats on a dry lake — then the completion of a process can never be defined.)

Alpha said, "This is the vision. I see the Relicts swarming the Earth; then whisking off to nowhere, like gnats in the wind. This is behind us."

The Organisms lay quiet, considering the vision.

A rock, or perhaps a meteor, fell from the sky, struck into the surface of the pond. It left a circular hole which slowly closed. From another part of the pool a gout of fluid splashed into the air, floated away.

Alpha spoke: "Again — the intuition comes strong! There will be lights in the sky."

The fever died in him. He hooked a finger into the air, hoisted himself to his feet.

Beta lay quiet. Slugs, ants, flies, beetles were crawling on him, boring, breeding. Alpha knew that Beta could arise, shake off the insects, stride off. But Beta seemed to prefer passivity. That was well enough. He could produce another Beta should he choose, or a dozen of him. Sometimes the world swarmed with Organisms, all sorts, all colors, tall as steeples, short and squat as flower-pots. Sometimes they hid quietly in deep caves, and sometimes the tentative substance of Earth would shift, and perhaps one, or perhaps thirty, would be shut in the subterranean cocoon, and all would sit gravely waiting, until such time as the ground would open and they could peer blinking and pallid out into the light.

"I feel a lack," said Alpha. "I will eat the Relict." He set forth, and sheer chance brought him near to the ledge of yellow rock. Finn the Relict sprang to his feet in panic.

Alpha tried to communicate so that Finn might pause while Alpha ate. But Finn had no grasp for the many-valued overtones of Alpha's voice. He seized a rock, hurled it at Alpha. The rock puffed into a cloud of dust, blew back into the Relict's face.

Alpha moved closer, extended his long arms. The Relict kicked. His feet went out from under him and he slid out on the plain. Alpha ambled complacently behind him. Finn began to crawl away. Alpha moved off to the right — one direction was as good as another. He collided with Beta, and began to eat Beta instead of the Relict. The Relict hesitated; then approached, and joining Alpha, pushed chunks of pink flesh into his mouth.

Alpha said to the Relict, "I was about to communicate an intuition to him whom we dine upon. I will speak to you."

Finn could not understand Alpha's personal language. He ate as rapidly as possible.

Alpha spoke on. "There will be lights in the sky. The great lights."

Finn rose to his feet and warily watching Alpha, seized Beta's legs, began to pull him toward the hill. Alpha watched with quizzical unconcern.

It was hard work for the spindly Relict. Sometimes Beta floated; sometimes he wafted off on the air; sometimes he adhered to the terrain. At last he sank into a knob of granite which froze around him. Finn tried to jerk Beta loose, and then to pry him up with a stick, without success.

He ran back and forth in an agony of indecision. Beta began to collapse, wither, like a jellyfish on hot sand. The Relict abandoned the hulk. Too late, too late! Food going to waste! The world was a hideous place of frustration!

Temporarily his belly was full. He started back up the crag, and presently found the camp, where the four other Relicts waited — two ancient males, two females. The females, Gisa and Reak, like Finn, had been out foraging. Gisa had brought in a slab of lichen; Reak a bit of nameless carrion.

The old men, Boad and Tagart, sat quietly waiting either for food or for death.

The women greeted Finn sullenly. "Where is the food you went forth to find?"

"I had a whole carcass," said Finn. "I could not carry it."

Boad had slyly stolen the slab of lichen and was cramming it into his mouth. It came alive, quivered and exuded a red ichor which was poison, and the old man died.

"Now there is food," said Finn. "Let us eat."

But the poison created a putrescence; the body seethed with blue foam, flowed away of its own energy.

The women turned to look at the other old man, who said in a quavering voice, "Eat me if you must — but why not choose Reak, who is younger than I?"

Reak, the younger of the women, gnawing on the bit of carrion, made no reply.

Finn said hollowly, "Why do we worry ourselves? Food is ever more difficult, and we are the last of all men."

"No, no," spoke Reak, "not the last. We saw others on the green mound."

"That was long ago," said Gisa. "Now they are surely dead."

"Perhaps they have found a source of food," suggested Reak.

Finn rose to his feet, looked across the plain. "Who knows? Perhaps there is a more pleasant land beyond the horizon."

"There is nothing anywhere but waste and evil creatures," snapped Gisa.

"What could be worse than here?" Finn argued calmly.

No one could find grounds for disagreement.

"Here is what I propose," said Finn. "Notice this tall peak. Notice the layers of hard air. They bump into the peak, they bounce off, they float in and out and disappear past the edge of sight. Let us all climb this peak, and when a sufficiently large bank of air passes, we will throw ourselves on top, and allow it to carry us to the beautiful regions which may exist just out of sight."

There was argument. The old man Tagart protested his feebleness; the women derided the possibility of the bountiful regions Finn envisioned, but presently, grumbling and arguing, they began to clamber up the pinnacle.

It took a long time; the obsidian was soft as jelly and Tagart several times professed himself at the limit of his endurance. But still they climbed, and at last reached the pinnacle. There was barely room to stand. They could see in all directions, far out over the landscape, till vision was lost in the watery gray.

The women bickered and pointed in various directions, but there was small sign of happier territory. In one direction blue-green hills shivered like bladders full of oil. In another direction lay a streak of black—a gorge or a lake of clay. In another direction were blue-green hills—the same they had seen in the first direction; somehow there had been a shift. Below was the plain, gleaming like an iridescent beetle, here and there pocked with black velvet spots, overgrown with questionable vegetation.

They saw Organisms, a dozen shapes loitering by ponds, munching vegetable pods or small rocks or insects. There came Alpha. He moved slowly, still awed by his vision, ignoring the other Organisms. Their play went on, but presently they stood quiet, sharing the oppression.

On the obsidian peak, Finn caught hold of a passing filament of air, drew it in. "Now—all on, and we sail away to the Land of Plenty."

"No," protested Gisa, "there is no room, and who knows if it will fly in the right direction?"

"Where is the right direction?" asked Finn. "Does anyone know?"

No one knew, but the women still refused to climb aboard the filament. Finn turned to Tagart. "Here, old one, show these women how it is; climb on!"

"No, no," he cried. "I fear the air; this is not for me."

"Climb on, old man, then we follow."

Wheezing and fearful, clenching his hands deep into the spongy mass, Tagart pulled himself out onto the air, spindly shanks hanging over into nothing. "Now," spoke Finn, "who next?"

The women still refused. "You go then, yourself," cried Gisa.

"And leave you, my last guarantee against hunger? Aboard now!"

"No, the air is too small; let the old one go and we will follow on a larger."

"Very well." Finn released his grip. The air floated off over the plain, Tagart straddling and clutching for dear life.

They watched him curiously. "Observe," said Finn, "how fast and easily moves the air. Above the Organisms, over all the slime and uncertainty."

But the air itself was uncertain, and the old man's raft dissolved. Clutching at the departing wisps, Tagart sought to hold his cushion together. It fled from under him, and he fell.

On the peak the three watched the spindly shape flap and twist on its way to earth far below.

"Now," Reak exclaimed in vexation, "we even have no more meat."

"None," said Gisa, "except the visionary Finn himself."

They surveyed Finn. Together they would more than outmatch him.

"Careful," cried Finn. "I am the last of the Men. You are my women, subject to my orders."

They ignored him, muttering to each other, looking at him from the side of their faces.

"Careful!" cried Finn. "I will throw you both from this peak."

"That is what we plan for you," said Gisa. They advanced with sinister caution.

"Stop! I am the last man!"

"We are better off without you."

"One moment! Look at the Organisms!"

The women looked. The Organisms stood in a knot, staring at the sky.

"Look at the sky!"

The women looked; the frosted glass was cracking, breaking, curling aside.

"The blue! The blue sky of old times!"

A terribly bright light burnt down, seared their eyes. The rays warmed their naked backs.

"The sun," they said in awed voices. "The sun has come back to Earth."

The shrouded sky was gone; the sun rode proud and bright in a sea of blue. The ground below churned, cracked, heaved, solidified. They felt the obsidian harden under their feet; its color shifted to glossy black. The Earth, the sun, the galaxy, had departed the region of freedom; the other time with its restrictions and logic was once more with them.

"This is Old Earth," cried Finn. "We are Men of Old Earth! The land is once again ours!"

"And what of the Organisms?"

"If this is the Earth of old, then let the Organisms beware!"

✳

The Organisms stood on a low rise of ground beside a runnel of water that was rapidly becoming a river flowing out onto the plain.

Alpha cried, "Here is my intuition! It is exactly as I knew. The freedom is gone; the tightness, the constriction are back!"

"How will we defeat it?" asked another Organism.

"Easily," said a third. "Each must fight a part of the battle. I plan to hurl myself at the sun, and blot it from existence." And he crouched, threw himself into the air. He fell on his back and broke his neck.

"The fault," said Alpha, "is in the air; because the air surrounds all things."

Six Organisms ran off in search of air, and stumbling into the river, drowned.

"In any event," said Alpha, "I am hungry." He looked around for suitable food. He seized an insect which stung him. He dropped it. "My hunger remains."

He spied Finn and the two women descending from the crag. "I will eat one of the Relicts," he said. "Come, let us all eat."

Three of them started off — as usual in random directions. By chance Alpha came face to face with Finn. He prepared to eat, but Finn picked up a rock. The rock remained a rock: hard, sharp, heavy. Finn swung it down, taking joy in the inertia. Alpha died with a crushed skull. One of the other Organisms attempted to step across a crevasse twenty feet wide and was engulfed; the other sat down, swallowed rocks to assuage his hunger, and presently went into convulsions.

Finn pointed here and there around the fresh new land. "In that quarter, the new city, like that of the legends. Over here the farms, the cattle."

"We have none of these," protested Gisa.

"No," said Finn. "Not now. But once more the sun rises and sets, once more rock has weight and air has none. Once more water falls as rain and flows to the sea." He stepped forward over the fallen Organism. "Let us make plans."

ULLWARD'S RETREAT

BRUHAM ULLWARD HAD INVITED three friends to lunch at his ranch: Ted and Ravelin Seehoe, and their adolescent daughter Iugenae. After an eye-bulging feast, Ullward offered around a tray of the digestive pastilles which had won him his wealth.

"A wonderful meal," said Ted Seehoe reverently. "Too much, really. I'll need one of these. The algae was absolutely marvelous."

Ullward made a smiling, easy gesture. "It's the genuine stuff."

Ravelin Seehoe, a fresh-faced, rather positive young woman of eighty or ninety, reached for a pastille. "A shame there's not more of it. The synthetic we get is hardly recognizable as algae."

"It's a problem," Ullward admitted. "I clubbed up with some friends; we bought a little mat in the Ross Sea and grow all our own."

"Think of that," exclaimed Ravelin. "Isn't it frightfully expensive?"

Ullward pursed his lips whimsically. "The good things in life come high. Luckily, I'm able to afford a bit extra."

"What I keep telling Ted—" began Ravelin, then stopped as Ted turned her a keen warning glance.

Ullward bridged the rift. "Money isn't everything. I have a flat of algae, my ranch; you have your daughter — and I'm sure you wouldn't trade."

Ravelin regarded Iugenae critically. "I'm not so sure."

Ted patted Iugenae's hand. "When do you have your own child, Lamster* Ullward?"

"Still some time yet. I'm thirty-seven billion down the list."

---

* Lamster: contraction of Landmaster — the polite form of address in current use.

"A pity," said Ravelin Seehoe brightly, "when you could give a child so many advantages."

"Some day, some day, before I'm too old."

"A shame," said Ravelin, "but it has to be. Another fifty billion people and we'd have no privacy whatever!" She looked admiringly around the room, which was used for the sole purpose of preparing food and dining.

Ullward put his hands on the arms of his chair, hitched forward a little. "Perhaps you'd like to look around the ranch?" He spoke in a casual voice, glancing from one to the other.

Iugenae clapped her hands; Ravelin beamed. "If it wouldn't be too much trouble!"

"Oh, we'd love to, Lamster Ullward!" cried Iugenae.

"I've always wanted to see your ranch," said Ted. "I've heard so much about it."

"It's an opportunity for Iugenae I wouldn't want her to miss," said Ravelin. She shook her finger at Iugenae. "Remember, Miss Puss, notice everything very carefully — and don't touch!"

"May I take pictures, Mother?"

"You'll have to ask Lamster Ullward."

"Of course, of course," said Ullward. "Why in the world not?" He rose to his feet — a man of more than middle stature, more than middle pudginess, with straight sandy hair, round blue eyes, a prominent beak of a nose. Almost three hundred years old, he guarded his health with great zeal, and looked little more than two hundred.

He stepped to the door, checked the time, touched a dial on the wall. "Are you ready?"

"Yes, we're quite ready," said Ravelin.

Ullward snapped back the wall, to reveal a view over a sylvan glade. A fine oak tree shaded a pond growing with rushes. A path led through a field toward a wooded valley a mile in the distance.

"Magnificent," said Ted. "Simply magnificent!"

They stepped outdoors into the sunlight. Iugenae flung her arms out, twirled, danced in a circle. "Look! I'm all alone! I'm out here all by myself!"

"Iugenae!" called Ravelin sharply. "Be careful! Stay on the path! That's real grass and you mustn't damage it."

Iugenae ran ahead to the pond. "Mother!" she called back. "Look at these funny little jumpy things! And look at the flowers!"

"The animals are frogs," said Ullward. "They have a very interesting life-history. You see the little fishlike things in the water?"

"Aren't they funny! Mother, do come here!"

"Those are called tadpoles and they will presently become frogs, indistinguishable from the ones you see."

Ravelin and Ted advanced with more dignity, but were as interested as Iugenae in the frogs.

"Smell the fresh air," Ted told Ravelin. "You'd think you were back in the early times."

"It's absolutely exquisite," said Ravelin. She looked around her. "One has the feeling of being able to wander on and on and on."

"Come around over here," called Ullward from beyond the pool. "This is the rock garden."

In awe, the guests stared at the ledge of rock, stained with red and yellow lichen, tufted with green moss. Ferns grew from a crevice; there were several fragile clusters of white flowers.

"Smell the flowers, if you wish," Ullward told Iugenae. "But please don't touch them; they stain rather easily."

Iugenae sniffed. "Mmmm!"

"Are they real?" asked Ted.

"The moss, yes. That clump of ferns and these little succulents are real. The flowers were designed for me by a horticulturist and are exact replicas of certain ancient species. We've actually improved on the odor."

"Wonderful, wonderful," said Ted.

"Now come this way — no, don't look back; I want you to get the total effect…" An expression of vexation crossed his face.

"What's the trouble?" asked Ted.

"It's a damned nuisance," said Ullward. "Hear that sound?"

Ted became aware of a faint rolling rumble, deep and almost unheard. "Yes. Sounds like some sort of factory."

"It is. On the floor below. A rug-works. One of the looms creates this terrible row. I've complained, but they pay no attention…Oh, well, ignore it. Now stand over here — and look around!"

His friends gasped in rapture. The view from this angle was of a rustic bungalow in an Alpine valley, the door being the opening into Ullward's dining room.

"What an illusion of distance!" exclaimed Ravelin. "A person would almost think he was alone."

"A beautiful piece of work," said Ted. "I'd swear I was looking into ten miles — at least five miles — of distance."

"I've got a lot of space here," said Ullward proudly. "Almost three-quarters of an acre. Would you like to see it by moonlight?"

"Oh, could we?"

Ullward went to a concealed switch-panel; the sun seemed to race across the sky. A fervent glow of sunset lit the valley; the sky burned peacock blue, gold, green, then came twilight — and the rising full moon came up behind the hill.

"This is absolutely marvelous," said Ravelin softly. "How can you bring yourself to leave it?"

"It's hard," admitted Ullward. "But I've got to look after business too. More money, more space."

He turned a knob; the moon floated across the sky, sank. Stars appeared, forming the age-old patterns. Ullward pointed out the constellations and the first-magnitude stars by name, using a pencil-torch for a pointer. Then the sky flushed with lavender and lemon yellow and the sun appeared once more. Unseen ducts sent a current of cool air through the glade.

"Right now I'm negotiating for an area behind this wall here." He tapped at the depicted mountainside, an illusion given reality and three-dimensionality by laminations inside the pane. "It's quite a large area — over a hundred square feet. The owner wants a fortune, naturally."

"I'm surprised he wants to sell," said Ted. "A hundred square feet means real privacy."

"There's been a death in the family," explained Ullward. "The owner's four-great-grandfather passed on and the space is temporarily surplus."

Ted nodded. "I hope you're able to get it."

"I hope so too. I've got rather flamboyant ambitions — eventually I hope to own the entire quarterblock — but it takes time. People don't like to sell their space and everyone is anxious to buy."

"Not we," said Ravelin cheerfully. "We have our little home. We're snug and cozy and we're putting money aside for investment."

"Wise," agreed Ullward. "A great many people are space-poor. Then when a chance to make real money comes up, they're undercapitalized. Until I scored with the digestive pastilles, I lived in a single rented locker. I was cramped — but I don't regret it today."

They returned through the glade toward Ullward's house, stopping at the oak tree. "This is my special pride," said Ullward. "A genuine oak tree!"

"Genuine?" asked Ted in astonishment. "I assumed it was simulation."

"So many people do," said Ullward. "No, it's genuine."

"Take a picture of the tree, Iugenae, please. But don't touch it. You might damage the bark."

"Perfectly all right to touch the bark," assured Ullward. He looked up into the branches, then scanned the ground. He stooped, picked up a fallen leaf. "This grew on the tree," he said. "Now, Iugenae, I want you to come with me." He went to the rock garden, pulled a simulated rock aside, to reveal a cabinet with washbasin. "Watch carefully." He showed her the leaf. "Notice? It's dry and brittle and brown."

"Yes, Lamster Ullward." Iugenae craned her neck.

"First I dip it in this solution." He took a beaker full of dark liquid from a shelf. "So. That restores the green color. We wash off the excess, then dry it. Now we rub this next fluid carefully into the surface. Notice, it's flexible and strong now. One more solution — a plastic coating — and there we are, a true oak leaf, perfectly genuine. It's yours."

"Oh, Lamster Ullward! Thank you ever so much!" She ran off to show her father and mother, who were standing by the pool, luxuriating in the feeling of space, watching the frogs. "See what Lamster Ullward gave me!"

"You be very careful with it," said Ravelin. "When we get home, we'll find a nice little frame and you can hang it in your locker."

The simulated sun hung in the western sky. Ullward led the group to a sundial. "An antique, countless years old. Pure marble, carved by hand. It works too — entirely functional. Notice. Three-fifteen by the shadow on the dial..." He peered at his beltwatch, squinted at the sun.

"Excuse me one moment." He ran to the control board, made an adjustment. The sun lurched ten degrees across the sky. Ullward returned, checked the sundial. "That's better. Notice. Three-fifty by the sundial, three-fifty by my watch. Isn't that something now?"

"It's wonderful," said Ravelin earnestly.

"It's the loveliest thing I've ever seen," chirped Iugenae.

Ravelin looked around the ranch, sighed wistfully. "We hate to leave, but I think we must be returning home."

"It's been a wonderful day, Lamster Ullward," said Ted. "A wonderful lunch, and we enjoyed seeing your ranch."

"You'll have to come out again," invited Ullward. "I always enjoy company."

He led them into the dining room, through the living room-bedroom to the door. The Seehoe family took a last look across the spacious interior, pulled on their mantles, stepped into their run-shoes, made their farewells. Ullward slid back the door. The Seehoes looked out, waited till a gap appeared in the traffic. They waved good-bye, pulled the hoods over their heads, stepped out into the corridor.

The run-shoes spun them toward their home, selecting the appropriate turnings, sliding automatically into the correct lift- and drop-pits. Deflection fields twisted them through the throngs. Like the Seehoes, everyone wore mantle and hood of filmy reflective stuff to safeguard privacy. The illusion-pane along the ceiling of the corridor presented a view of towers dwindling up into a cheerful blue sky, as if the pedestrian were moving along one of the windy upper passages.

The Seehoes approached their home. Two hundred yards away, they angled over to the wall. If the flow of traffic carried them past, they would be forced to circle the block and make another attempt to enter. Their door slid open as they spun near; they ducked into the opening, swinging around on a metal grab-bar.

They removed their mantles and run-shoes, sliding skillfully past each other. Iugenae pivoted into the bathroom and there was room for both Ted and Ravelin to sit down. The house was rather small for the three of them; they could well have used another twelve square feet, but rather than pay exorbitant rent, they preferred to save the money with an eye toward Iugenae's future.

Ted sighed in satisfaction, stretching his legs luxuriously under Ravelin's chair. "Ullward's ranch notwithstanding, it's nice to be home."

Iugenae backed out of the bathroom.

Ravelin looked up. "It's time for your pill, dear."

Iugenae screwed up her face. "Oh, Mama! Why do I have to take pills? I feel perfectly well."

"They're good for you, dear."

Iugenae sullenly took a pill from the dispenser. "Runy says you make us take pills to keep us from growing up."

Ted and Ravelin exchanged glances.

"Just take your pill," said Ravelin, "and never mind what Runy says."

"But how is it that I'm 38 and Ermara Burk's only 32 and she's got a figure and I'm like a slat?"

"No arguments, dear. Take your pill."

Ted jumped to his feet. "Here, Babykin, sit down."

Iugenae protested, but Ted held up his hand. "I'll sit in the niche. I've got a few calls that I have to make."

He sidled past Ravelin, seated himself in the niche in front of the communication screen. The illusion-pane behind him was custom-built — Ravelin, in fact, had designed it herself. It simulated a merry little bandit's den, the walls draped in red and yellow silk, a bowl of fruit on the rustic table, a guitar on the bench, a copper teakettle simmering on the countertop stove. The pane had been rather expensive, but when anyone communicated with the Seehoes, it was the first thing they saw, and here the house-proud Ravelin had refused to stint.

Before Ted could make his call, the signal light flashed. He answered; the screen opened to display his friend Loren Aigle, apparently sitting in an airy arched rotunda, against a background of fleecy clouds — an illusion which Ravelin had instantly recognized as an inexpensive stock effect.

Loren and Elme, his wife, were anxious to hear of the Seehoes' visit to the Ullward ranch. Ted described the afternoon in detail. "Space, space and more space! Isolation pure and simple! Absolute privacy! You can hardly imagine it! A fortune in illusion-panes."

"Nice," said Loren Aigle. "I'll tell you one you'll find hard to believe. Today I registered a whole planet to a man." Loren worked in the Certification Bureau of the Extraterrestrial Properties Agency.

Ted was puzzled and uncomprehending. "A whole planet? How so?"

Loren explained. "He's a free-lance spaceman. Still a few left."

"But what's he planning to do with an entire planet?"

"Live there, he claims."

"Alone?"

Loren nodded. "I had quite a chat with him. Earth is all very well, he says, but he prefers the privacy of his own planet. Can you imagine that?"

"Frankly, no! I can't imagine the fourth dimension either. What a marvel, though!"

The conversation ended and the screen faded. Ted swung around to his wife. "Did you hear that?"

Ravelin nodded; she had heard but not heeded. She was reading the menu supplied by the catering firm to which they subscribed. "We won't want anything heavy after that lunch. They've got simulated synthetic algae again."

Ted grunted. "It's never as good as the genuine synthetic."

"But it's cheaper and we've all had an enormous lunch."

"Don't worry about me, Mom!" sang Iugenae. "I'm going out with Runy."

"Oh, you are, are you? And where are you going, may I ask?"

"A ride around the world. We're catching the seven o'clock shuttle, so I've got to hurry."

"Come right home afterward," said Ravelin severely. "Don't go anywhere else."

"For heaven's sake, Mother, you'd think I was going to elope or something."

"Mind what I say, Miss Puss. I was a girl once myself. Have you taken your medicine?"

"Yes, I've taken my medicine."

Iugenae departed; Ted slipped back into the niche. "Who are you calling now?" asked Ravelin.

"Lamster Ullward. I want to thank him for going to so much trouble for us."

Ravelin agreed that an algae-and-margarine call was no more than polite.

Ted called, expressed his thanks, then — almost as an afterthought — chanced to mention the man who owned a planet.

"An entire planet?" inquired Ullward. "It must be inhabited."

"No, I understand not, Lamster Ullward. Think of it! Think of the privacy!"

"Privacy!" exclaimed Ullward bluffly. "My dear fellow, what do you call this?"

"Oh, naturally, Lamster Ullward — you have a real showplace."

"The planet must be very primitive," Ullward reflected. "An engaging idea, of course — if you like that kind of thing. Who is this man?"

"I don't know, Lamster Ullward. I could find out, if you like."

"No, no, don't bother. I'm not particularly interested. Just an idle thought." Ullward laughed his hearty laugh. "Poor man. Probably lives in a dome."

"That's possible, of course, Lamster Ullward. Well, thanks again, and good night."

The spaceman's name was Kennes Mail. He was short and thin, tough as synthetic herring, brown as toasted yeast. He had a close-cropped pad of gray hair, a keen, if ingenuous, blue gaze. He showed a courteous interest in Ullward's ranch, but Ullward thought his recurrent use of the word 'clever' rather tactless.

As they returned to the house, Ullward paused to admire his oak tree.

"It's absolutely genuine, Lamster Mail! A living tree, survival of past ages! Do you have trees as fine as that on your planet?"

Kennes Mail smiled. "Lamster Ullward, that's just a shrub. Let's sit somewhere and I'll show you photographs."

Ullward had already mentioned his interest in acquiring extraterrestrial property; Mail, admitting that he needed money, had given him to understand that some sort of deal might be arranged. They sat at a table; Mail opened his case. Ullward switched on the wall-screen.

"First I'll show you a map," said Mail. He selected a rod, dropped it into the table socket. On the wall appeared a world projection: oceans; an enormous equatorial landmass named Gaea; the smaller subcontinents Atalanta, Persephone, Alcyone. A box of descriptive information read:

MAIL'S PLANET

Claim registered and endorsed at
Extraterrestrial Properties Agency

Surface area:	.87 Earth normal
Gravity:	.93 Earth normal
Diurnal rotation:	22.15 Earth hours
Annual revolution:	2.97 Earth years
Atmosphere:	Invigorating
Climate:	Salubrious
Noxious conditions and influences:	None
Population:	1

Mail pointed to a spot on the eastern shore of Gaea. "I live here. Just got a rough camp at present. I need money to do a bit better for myself. I'm willing to lease off one of the smaller continents, or, if you prefer, a section of Gaea, say from Murky Mountains west to the ocean."

Ullward, with a cheerful smile, shook his head. "No sections for me, Lamster Mail. I want to buy the world outright. You set your price; if it's within reason, I'll write a check."

Mail glanced at him sidewise. "You haven't even seen the photographs."

"True." In a businesslike voice, Ullward said, "By all means, the photographs."

Mail touched the projection button. Landscapes of an unfamiliar wild beauty appeared on the screen. There were mountain crags and roaring rivers, snow-powdered forests, ocean dawns and prairie sunsets, green hillsides, meadows spattered with blossoms, beaches white as milk.

"Very pleasant," said Ullward. "Quite nice." He pulled out his checkbook. "What's your price?"

Mail chuckled and shook his head. "I won't sell. I'm willing to lease off a section — providing my price is met and my rules are agreed to."

Ullward sat with compressed lips. He gave his head a quick little jerk. Mail started to rise to his feet.

"No, no," said Ullward hastily. "I was merely thinking...Let's look at the map again."

Mail returned the map to the screen. Ullward made careful inspection of the various continents, inquired as to physiography, climate, flora and fauna.

Finally he made his decision. "I'll lease Gaea."

"No, Lamster Ullward!" declared Mail. "I'm reserving this entire area — from Murky Mountains and the Calliope River east. This western section is open. It's maybe a little smaller than Atalanta or Persephone, but the climate is warmer."

"There aren't any mountains on the western section," Ullward protested. "Only these insignificant Rock Castle Crags."

"They're not so insignificant," said Mail. "You've also got the Purple Bird Hills, and down here in the south is Mount Cairasco — a live volcano. What more do you need?"

Ullward glanced across his ranch. "I'm in the habit of thinking big."

"West Gaea is a pretty big chunk of property."

"Very well," said Ullward. "What are your terms?"

"So far as money goes, I'm not greedy," Mail said. "For a twenty-year lease: two hundred thousand a year, the first five years in advance."

Ullward made a startled protest. "Great guns, Lamster Mail! That's almost half my income!"

Mail shrugged. "I'm not trying to get rich. I want to build a lodge for myself. It costs money. If you can't afford it, I'll have to speak to someone who can."

Ullward said in a nettled voice, "I can afford it, certainly — but my entire ranch here cost less than a million."

"Well, either you want it or you don't," said Mail. "I'll tell you my rules, then you can make up your mind."

"What rules?" demanded Ullward, his face growing red.

"They're simple and their only purpose is to maintain privacy for both of us. First, you have to stay on your own property. No excursions hither and yon on my property. Second, no subleasing. Third, no residents except yourself, your family and your servants. I don't want any artists' colony springing up, nor any wild noisy resort atmosphere.

Naturally you're entitled to bring out your guests, but they've got to keep to your property just like yourself."

He looked sidewise at Ullward's glum face. "I'm not trying to be tough, Lamster Ullward. Good fences make good neighbors, and it's better that we have the understanding now than hard words and beam-gun evictions later."

"Let me see the photographs again," said Ullward. "Show me West Gaea."

He looked, heaved a deep sigh. "Very well. I agree."

The construction crew had departed. Ullward was alone on West Gaea. He walked around the new lodge, taking deep breaths of pure quiet air, thrilling to the absolute solitude and privacy. The lodge had cost a fortune, but how many other people of Earth owned — leased, rather — anything to compare with this?

He walked out on the front terrace, gazed proudly across miles — genuine unsimulated miles — of landscape. For his home site, he had selected a shelf in the foothills of the Ullward Range (as he had renamed the Purple Bird Hills). In front spread a great golden savannah dotted with blue-green trees; behind rose a tall gray cliff.

A stream rushed down a cleft in the rock, leaping, splashing, cooling the air, finally flowing into a beautiful clear pool, beside which Ullward had erected a cabana of red, green and brown plastic. At the base of the cliff and in crevices grew clumps of spiky blue cactus, lush green bushes covered with red trumpet-flowers, a thick-leafed white plant holding up a stalk clustered with white bubbles.

Solitude! The real thing! No thumping of factories, no roar of traffic two feet from one's bed. One arm outstretched, the other pressed to his chest, Ullward performed a stately little jig of triumph on the terrace. Had he been able, he might have turned a cartwheel. When a person has complete privacy, absolutely nothing is forbidden!

Ullward took a final turn up and down the terrace, made a last appreciative survey of the horizon. The sun was sinking through banks of fire-fringed clouds. Marvelous depth of color, a tonal brilliance to be matched only in the very best illusion-panes!

He entered the lodge, made a selection from the nutrition locker.

After a leisurely meal, he returned to the lounge. He stood thinking for a moment, then went out upon the terrace, strolled up and down. Wonderful! The night was full of stars, hanging like blurred white lamps, almost as he had always imagined them.

After ten minutes of admiring the stars, he returned into the lodge. Now what? The wall-screen, with its assortment of recorded programs. Snug and comfortable, Ullward watched the performance of a recent musical comedy.

Real luxury, he told himself. Pity he couldn't invite his friends out to spend the evening. Unfortunately impossible, considering the inconvenient duration of the trip between Mail's Planet and Earth. However — only three days until the arrival of his first guest. She was Elf Intry, a young woman who had been more than friendly with Ullward on Earth. When Elf arrived, Ullward would broach a subject which he had been mulling over for several months — indeed, ever since he had first learned of Mail's Planet.

Elf Intry arrived early in the afternoon, coming down to Mail's Planet in a capsule discharged from the weekly Outer Ring Express packet. A woman of normally good disposition, she greeted Ullward in a seethe of indignation. "Just who is that brute around the other side of the planet? I thought you had absolute privacy here!"

"That's just old Mail," said Ullward evasively. "What's wrong?"

"The fool on the packet set me the wrong coordinates and the capsule came down on a beach. I noticed a house and then I saw a naked man jumping rope behind some bushes. I thought it was you, of course. I went over and said 'Boo!' You should have heard the language he used!" She shook her head. "I don't see why you allow such a boor on your planet."

The buzzer on the communication screen sounded. "That's Mail now," said Ullward. "You wait here. I'll tell him how to speak to my guests!"

He presently returned to the terrace. Elf came over to him, kissed his nose. "Ully, you're pale with rage! I hope you didn't lose your temper."

"No," said Ullward. "We merely — well, we had an understanding. Come along, look over the property."

He took Elf around to the back, pointing out the swimming pool, the waterfall, the mass of rock above. "You won't see that effect on any illusion-pane! That's genuine rock!"

"Lovely, Ully. Very nice. The color might be just a trifle darker, though. Rock doesn't look like that."

"No?" Ullward inspected the cliff more critically. "Well, I can't do anything about it. How about the privacy?"

"Wonderful! It's so quiet, it's almost eerie!"

"Eerie?" Ullward looked around the landscape. "It hadn't occurred to me."

"You're not sensitive to these things, Ully. Still, it's very nice, if you can tolerate that unpleasant creature Mail so close."

"Close?" protested Ullward. "He's on the other side of the continent!"

"True," said Elf. "It's all relative, I suppose. How long do you expect to stay out here?"

"That depends. Come along inside. I want to talk with you."

He seated her in a comfortable chair, brought her a globe of Gluco-Fructoid Nectar. For himself, he mixed ethyl alcohol, water, a few drops of Haig's Oldtime Esters.

"Elf, where do you stand in the reproduction list?"

She raised her fine eyebrows, shook her head. "So far down, I've lost count. Fifty or sixty billion."

"I'm down thirty-seven billion. It's one reason I bought this place. Waiting list, piffle! Nobody stops Bruham Ullward's breeding on his own planet!"

Elf pursed her lips, shook her head sadly. "It won't work, Ully."

"And why not?"

"You can't take the children back to Earth. The list would keep them out."

"True, but think of living here, surrounded by children. All the children you wanted! And utter privacy to boot! What more could you ask for?"

Elf sighed. "You fabricate a beautiful illusion-pane, Ully. But I think not. I love the privacy and solitude — but I thought there'd be more people to be private from."

✳

The Outer Ring Express packet came past four days later. Elf kissed Ullward good-bye. "It's simply exquisite here, Ully. The solitude is so magnificent, it gives me gooseflesh. I've had a wonderful visit." She climbed into the capsule. "See you on Earth."

"Just a minute," said Ullward suddenly. "I want you to post a letter or two for me."

"Hurry. I've only got twenty minutes."

Ullward was back in ten minutes. "Invitations," he told her breath-lessly. "Friends."

"Right." She kissed his nose. "Good-bye, Ully." She slammed the port; the capsule rushed away, whirling up to meet the packet.

The new guests arrived three weeks later: Frobisher Worbeck, Liornetta Stobart, Harris and Hyla Cabe, Ted and Ravelin and Iugenae Seehoe, Juvenal Aquister and his son Runy.

Ullward, brown from long days of lazing in the sun, greeted them with great enthusiasm. "Welcome to my little retreat! Wonderful to see you all! Frobisher, you pink-cheeked rascal! And Iugenae! Prettier than ever! Be careful, Ravelin — I've got my eye on your daughter! But Runy's here, guess I'm out of the picture! Liornetta, damned glad you could make it! And Ted! Great to see you, old chap! This is all your doing, you know! Harris, Hyla, Juvenal — come on up! We'll have a drink, a drink, a drink!"

Running from one to the other, patting arms, herding the slow-moving Frobisher Worbeck, he conducted his guests up the slope to the terrace. Here they turned to survey the panorama. Ullward listened to their remarks, mouth pursed against a grin of gratification.

"Magnificent!"

"Grand!"

"Absolutely genuine!"

"The sky is so far away, it frightens me!"

"The sunlight's so pure!"

"The genuine thing's always best, isn't it?"

Runy said a trifle wistfully, "I thought you were on a beach, Lamster Ullward."

"Beach? This is mountain country, Runy. Land of the wide open spaces! Look out over that plain!"

Liornetta Stobart patted Runy's shoulder. "Not every planet has beaches, Runy. The secret of happiness is to be content with what one has."

Ullward laughed gaily. "Oh, I've got beaches, never fear for that! There's a fine beach — ha, ha — five hundred miles due west. Every step Ullward domain!"

"Can we go?" asked Iugenae excitedly. "Can we go, Lamster Ullward?"

"We certainly can! That shed down the slope is headquarters for the Ullward Airlines. We'll fly to the beach, swim in Ullward Ocean! But now refreshment! After that crowded capsule, your throats must be like paper!"

"It wasn't too crowded," said Ravelin Seehoe. "There were only nine of us." She looked critically up at the cliff. "If that were an illusion-pane, I'd consider it grotesque."

"My dear Ravelin!" cried Ullward. "It's impressive! Magnificent!"

"All of that," agreed Frobisher Worbeck, a tall sturdy man, white-haired, red-jowled, with a blue benevolent gaze. "And now, Bruham, what about those drinks?"

"Of course! Ted, I know you of old. Will you tend bar? Here's the alcohol, here's water, here are the esters. Now, you two," Ullward called to Runy and Iugenae. "How about some nice cold soda pop?"

"What kind is there?" asked Runy.

"All kinds, all flavors. This is Ullward's Retreat! We've got methylamyl glutamine, cycloprodacterol phosphate, metathiobromine-4-glyco-citrose…"

Runy and Iugenae expressed their preferences; Ullward brought the globes, then hurried to arrange tables and chairs for the adults. Presently everyone was comfortable and relaxed.

Iugenae whispered to Ravelin, who smiled and nodded indulgently. "Lamster Ullward, you remember the beautiful oak leaf you gave Iugenae?"

"Of course I do."

"It's still as fresh and green as ever. I wonder if Iugenae might have a leaf or two from some of these other trees?"

"My dear Ravelin!" Ullward roared with laughter. "She can have an entire tree!"

"Oh Mother! Can—"

"Iugenae, don't be ridiculous!" snapped Ted. "How could we get it home? Where would we plant the thing? In the bathroom?"

Ravelin said, "You and Runy find some nice leaves, but don't wander too far."

"No, Mother." She beckoned to Runy. "Come along, dope. Bring a basket."

The others of the party gazed out over the plain. "A beautiful view, Ullward," said Frobisher Worbeck. "How far does your property extend?"

"Five hundred miles west to the ocean, six hundred miles east to the mountains, eleven hundred miles north and two hundred miles south."

Worbeck shook his head solemnly. "Nice. A pity you couldn't get the whole planet. Then you'd have real privacy!"

"I tried, of course," said Ullward. "The owner refused to consider the idea."

"A pity."

Ullward brought out a map. "However, as you see, I have a fine volcano, a number of excellent rivers, a mountain range, and down here on the delta of Cinnamon River an absolutely miasmic swamp."

Ravelin pointed to the ocean. "Why, it's Lonesome Ocean! I thought the name was Ullward Ocean."

Ullward laughed uncomfortably. "Just a figure of speech — so to speak. My rights extend ten miles. More than enough for swimming purposes."

"No freedom of the seas here, eh, Lamster Ullward?" laughed Harris Cabe.

"Not exactly," confessed Ullward.

"A pity," said Frobisher Worbeck.

Hyla Cabe pointed to the map. "Look at these wonderful mountain ranges! The Magnificent Mountains! And over here — the Elysian Gardens! I'd love to see them, Lamster Ullward."

Ullward shook his head in embarrassment. "Impossible, I'm afraid. They're not on my property. I haven't even seen them myself."

His guests stared at him in astonishment. "But surely—"

"It's an atom-welded contract with Lamster Mail," Ullward explained. "He stays on his property, I stay on mine. In this way, our privacy is secure."

"Look," Hyla Cabe said aside to Ravelin. "The Unimaginable Caverns! Doesn't it make you simply wild not to be able to see them?"

Aquister said hurriedly, "It's a pleasure to sit here and just breathe this wonderful fresh air. No noise, no crowds, no bustle or hurry…"

The party drank and chatted and basked in the sunshine until late afternoon. Enlisting the aid of Ravelin Seehoe and Hyla Cabe, Ullward set out a simple meal of yeast pellets, processed protein, thick slices of algae crunch.

"No animal flesh, cooked vegetation?" questioned Worbeck curiously.

"Tried them the first day," said Ullward. "Revolting. Sick for a week."

After dinner, the guests watched a comic melodrama on the wall-screen. Then Ullward showed them to their various cubicles, and after a few minutes of badinage and calling back and forth, the lodge became quiet.

Next day, Ullward ordered his guests into their bathing suits. "We're off to the beach, we'll gambol on the sand, we'll frolic in the surf of Lonesome Ullward Ocean!"

The guests piled happily into the air-car. Ullward counted heads. "All aboard! We're off!"

They rose and flew west, first low over the plain, then high into the air, to obtain a panoramic view of the Rock Castle Crags.

"The tallest peak — there to the north — is almost ten thousand feet high. Notice how it juts up, just imagine the mass! Solid rock! How'd you like that dropped on your toe, Runy? Not so good, eh? In a moment, we'll see a precipice over a thousand feet straight up and down. There — now! Isn't that remarkable?"

"Certainly impressive," agreed Ted.

"What those Magnificent Mountains must be like!" said Harris Cabe with a wry laugh.

"How tall are they, Lamster Ullward?" inquired Liornetta Stobart.

"What? Which?"

"The Magnificent Mountains."

"I don't know for sure. Thirty or forty thousand feet, I suppose."

"What a marvelous sight they must be!" said Frobisher Worbeck. "Probably make these look like foothills."

"These are beautiful too," Hyla Cabe put in hastily.

"Oh, naturally," said Frobisher Worbeck. "A damned fine sight! You're a lucky man, Bruham!"

Ullward laughed shortly, turned the air-car west. They flew across a rolling forested plain and presently Lonesome Ocean gleamed in the distance. Ullward slanted down, landed the air-car on the beach, and the party alighted.

The day was warm, the sun hot. A fresh wind blew in from the ocean. The surf broke upon the sand in massive roaring billows.

The party stood appraising the scene. Ullward swung his arms. "Well, who's for it? Don't wait to be invited! We've got the whole ocean to ourselves!"

Ravelin said, "It's so rough! Look how that water crashes down!"

Liornetta Stobart turned away with a shake of her head. "Illusion-pane surf is always so gentle. This could lift you right up and give you a good shaking!"

"I expected nothing quite so vehement," Harris Cabe admitted.

Ravelin beckoned to Iugenae. "You keep well away, Miss Puss. I don't want you swept out to sea. You'd find it Lonesome Ocean indeed!"

Runy approached the water, waded gingerly into a sheet of retreating foam. A comber thrashed down at him and he danced quickly back up the shore.

"The water's cold," he reported.

Ullward poised himself. "Well, here goes! I'll show you how it's done!" He trotted forward, stopped short, then flung himself into the face of a great white comber.

The party on the beach watched.

"Where is he?" asked Hyla Cabe.

Iugenae pointed. "I saw part of him out there. A leg, or an arm."

"There he is!" cried Ted. "Woof! Another one's caught him. I suppose some people might consider it sport…"

Ullward staggered to his feet, lurched through the retreating wash to shore. "Hah! Great! Invigorating! Ted! Harris! Juvenal! Take a go at it!"

Harris shook his head. "I don't think I'll try it today, Bruham."

"The next time for me too," said Juvenal Aquister. "Perhaps it won't be so rough."

"But don't let us stop you!" urged Ted. "You swim as long as you like. We'll wait here for you."

"Oh, I've had enough for now," said Ullward. "Excuse me while I change."

When Ullward returned, he found his guests seated in the air-car. "Hello! Everyone ready to go?"

"It's hot in the sun," explained Liornetta, "and we thought we'd enjoy the view better from inside."

"When you look through the glass, it's almost like an illusion-pane," said Iugenae.

"Oh, I see. Well, perhaps you're ready to visit other parts of the Ullward domain?"

The proposal met with approval; Ullward took the air-car into the air. "We can fly north over the pine woods, south over Mount Cairasco, which unfortunately isn't erupting just now."

"Anywhere you like, Lamster Ullward," said Frobisher Worbeck. "No doubt it's all beautiful."

Ullward considered the varied attractions of his leasehold. "Well, first to the Cinnamon Swamp."

For two hours they flew, over the swamp, across the smoking crater of Mount Cairasco, east to the edge of Murky Mountains, along Calliope River to its source in Goldenleaf Lake. Ullward pointed out noteworthy views, interesting aspects. Behind him, the murmurs of admiration dwindled and finally died.

"Had enough?" Ullward called back gaily. "Can't see half a continent in one day! Shall we save some for tomorrow?"

There was a moment's stillness. Then Liornetta Stobart said, "Lamster Ullward, we're simply dying for a peek at the Magnificent Mountains. I wonder — do you think we could slip over for a quick look? I'm sure Lamster Mail wouldn't really mind."

Ullward shook his head with a rather stiff smile. "He's made me agree to a very definite set of rules. I've already had one brush with him."

"How could he possibly find out?" asked Juvenal Aquister.

"He probably wouldn't find out," said Ullward, "but —"

"It's a damned shame for him to lock you off into this drab little peninsula!" Frobisher Worbeck said indignantly.

"Please, Lamster Ullward," Iugenae wheedled.

"Oh, very well," Ullward said recklessly.

He turned the air-car east. The Murky Mountains passed below. The party peered from the windows, exclaiming at the marvels of the forbidden landscape.

"How far are the Magnificent Mountains?" asked Ted.

"Not far. Another thousand miles."

"Why are you hugging the ground?" asked Frobisher Worbeck. "Up in the air, man! Let's see the countryside!"

Ullward hesitated. Mail was probably asleep. And, in the last analysis, he really had no right to forbid an innocent little —

"Lamster Ullward," called Runy, "there's an air-car right behind us."

The air-car drew up level. Kennes Mail's blue eyes met Ullward's across the gap. He motioned Ullward down.

Ullward compressed his mouth, swung the air-car down. From behind him came murmurs of sympathy and outrage.

Below was a dark pine forest; Ullward set down in a pretty little glade. Mail landed nearby, jumped to the ground, signaled to Ullward. The two men walked to the side. The guests murmured together and shook their heads.

Ullward presently returned to the air-car. "Everybody please get in," he said crisply.

They rose into the air and flew west. "What did the chap have to say for himself?" queried Worbeck.

Ullward chewed at his lips. "Not too much. Wanted to know if I'd lost the way. I told him one or two things. Reached an understanding…" His voice dwindled, then rose in a burst of cheerfulness. "We'll have a party back at the lodge. What do we care for Mail and his confounded mountains?"

"That's the spirit, Bruham!" cried Frobisher Worbeck.

Both Ted and Ullward tended bar during the evening. Either one or the other mingled rather more alcohol to rather less esters into the drinks than standard practice recommended. As a result, the party became quite loud and gay. Ullward damned Mail's interfering habits; Worbeck explored six thousand years of common law in an effort to prove Mail a domineering tyrant; the women giggled; Iugenae and Runy watched cynically, then presently went off to attend to their own affairs.

In the morning, the group slept late. Ullward finally tottered out on the terrace, to be joined one at a time by the others. Runy and Iugenae were missing.

"Young rascals," groaned Worbeck. "If they're lost, they'll have to find their own way back. No search parties for me."

At noon, Runy and Iugenae returned in Ullward's air-car.

"Good heavens," shrieked Ravelin. "Iugenae, come here this instant! Where have you been?"

Juvenal Aquister surveyed Runy sternly. "Have you lost your mind, taking Lamster Ullward's air-car without his permission?"

"I asked him last night," Runy declared indignantly. "He said yes, take anything except the volcano because that's where he slept when his feet got cold, and the swamp because that's where he dropped his empty containers."

"Regardless," said Juvenal in disgust, "you should have had better sense. Where have you been?"

Runy fidgeted. Iugenae said, "Well, we went south for a while, then turned and went east — I think it was east. We thought if we flew low, Lamster Mail wouldn't see us. So we flew low, through the mountains, and pretty soon we came to an ocean. We went along the beach and came to a house. We landed to see who lived there, but nobody was home."

Ullward stifled a groan.

"What would anyone want with a pen of birds?" asked Runy.

"Birds? What birds? Where?"

"At the house. There was a pen with a lot of big birds, but they kind of got loose while we were looking at them and all flew away."

"Anyway," Iugenae continued briskly, "we decided it was Lamster Mail's house, so we wrote a note, telling what everybody thinks of him and pinned it to his door."

Ullward rubbed his forehead. "Is that all?"

"Well, practically all." Iugenae became diffident. She looked at Runy and the two of them giggled nervously.

"There's more?" yelled Ullward. "What, in heaven's name?"

"Nothing very much," said Iugenae, following a crack in the terrace with her toe. "We put a booby-trap over the door — just a bucket of water. Then we came home."

The screen buzzer sounded from inside the lodge. Everybody looked at Ullward. Ullward heaved a deep sigh, rose to his feet, went inside.

That very afternoon, the Outer Ring Express packet was due to pass the junction point. Frobisher Worbeck felt sudden and acute qualms of conscience for the neglect his business suffered while he dawdled away hours in idle enjoyment.

"But my dear old chap!" exclaimed Ullward. "Relaxation is good for you!"

True, agreed Frobisher Worbeck, if one could make himself oblivious to the possibility of fiasco through the carelessness of underlings. Much as he deplored the necessity, in spite of his inclination to loiter for weeks, he felt impelled to leave — and not a minute later than that very afternoon.

Others of the group likewise remembered important business which they had to see to, and those remaining felt it would be a shame and an imposition to send up the capsule half-empty and likewise decided to return.

Ullward's arguments met unyielding walls of obstinacy. Rather glumly, he went down to the capsule to bid his guests farewell. As they climbed through the port, they expressed their parting thanks:

"Bruham, it's been absolutely marvelous!"

"You'll never know how we've enjoyed this outing, Lamster Ullward!"

"The air, the space, the privacy — I'll never forget!"

"It was the most, to say the least."

The port thumped into its socket. Ullward stood back, waving rather uncertainly.

Ted Seehoe reached to press the Active button. Ullward sprang forward, pounded on the port.

"Wait!" he bellowed. "A few things I've got to attend to! I'm coming with you!"

*

"Come in, come in," said Ullward heartily, opening the door to three of his friends: Coble and his wife Heulia Sansom, and Coble's young, pretty cousin Landine. "Glad to see you!"

"And we're glad to come! We've heard so much of your wonderful ranch, we've been on pins and needles all day!"

"Oh, come now! It's not so marvelous as all that!"

"Not to you, perhaps — you live here!"

Ullward smiled. "Well, I must say I live here and still like it. Would you like to have lunch, or perhaps you'd prefer to walk around for a few minutes? I've just finished making a few changes, but I'm happy to say everything is in order."

"Can we just take a look?"

"Of course. Come over here. Stand just so. Now — are you ready?"

"Ready."

Ullward snapped the wall back.

"Ooh!" breathed Landine. "Isn't it beautiful!"

"The space, the open feeling!"

"Look, a tree! What a wonderful simulation!"

"That's no simulation," said Ullward. "That's a genuine tree!"

"Lamster Ullward, are you telling the truth?"

"I certainly am. I never tell lies to a lovely young lady. Come along, over this way."

"Lamster Ullward, that cliff is so convincing, it frightens me."

Ullward grinned. "It's a good job." He signaled a halt. "Now — turn around."

The group turned. They looked out across a great golden savannah, dotted with groves of blue-green trees. A rustic lodge commanded the view, the door being the opening into Ullward's living room.

The group stood in silent admiration. Then Heulia sighed. "Space. Pure space."

"I'd swear I was looking miles," said Coble.

Ullward smiled, a trifle wistfully. "Glad you like my little retreat. Now what about lunch? Genuine algae!"

DODKIN'S JOB

THE THEORY OF ORGANIZED SOCIETY — as developed by Kinch, Kolbig, Penton and others — yields such a wealth of significant information, such manifold intricacies and portentous projections, that occasionally it is well to consider the deceptively simple premise — here stated by Kolbig:

> When self-willed micro-units combine to form and sustain a durable macro-unit, certain freedoms of action are curtailed.
> This is the basic process of Organization.
> The more numerous and erratic the micro-units, the more complex must be the structure and function of the macro-unit — hence the more pervasive and restricting the details of Organization.

> — from Leslie Penton, *First Principles of Organization*

In general the population of the City had become forgetful of curtailed freedoms, as a snake no longer remembers the legs of his forebears. Somewhere someone has stated, "When the discrepancy between the theory and practice of a culture is very great, this indicates that the culture is undergoing rapid change." By such a test the culture of the City was stable, if not static. The population ordered their lives by schedule, classification and precedent, satisfied with the bland rewards of Organization.

But in the healthiest tissue bacteria exist, and the most negligible impurity flaws a critical crystallization. Luke Grogatch was forty, thin and angular, dour of forehead, sardonic of mouth and eyebrow, with a sidewise twist to his head as if he suffered from earache. He was too astute to profess Nonconformity, too perverse to strive for improved status, too pessimistic, captious, sarcastic and outspoken to keep the jobs to which he found himself assigned. Each new reclassification depressed his status, each new job he disliked with increasing fervor.

Finally, rated as *Flunky/Class D/Unskilled,* Luke was dispatched to the District 8892 Sewer Maintenance Department and from there ordered out as night-shift swamper on Tunnel Gang No. 3's rotary drilling machine.

Reporting for work, Luke presented himself to the gang foreman, Fedor Miskitman, a big buffalo-faced man with flaxen hair and placid blue eyes. Miskitman produced a shovel and took Luke to a position close up behind the drilling machine's cutting head. Here, said Miskitman, was Luke's station. Luke would be required to keep the tunnel floor clean of loose rock and gravel. When the tunnel broke through into an old sewer, there would be scale and that detritus known as 'wet waste' to remove. Luke must keep the dust trap clean and in optimum adjustment. During the breaks he must lubricate those bearings isolated from the automatic lubrication system, and replace broken teeth on the cutting head as necessary.

Luke inquired if this was the extent of his duties, his voice strong with an irony the guileless Fedor Miskitman failed to notice.

"That is all," said Miskitman. He handed Luke the shovel. "Mostly it is the trash. The floor must be clean."

Luke suggested a modification of the hopper jaws which would tend to eliminate the spill of broken rock; in fact, argued Luke, why bother at all? Let the rock lay where it fell. The concrete lining of the tunnel would mask so trivial a scatter of gravel. Miskitman dismissed the suggestion out of hand: the rock must be removed. Luke asked why, and Miskitman told him, "That is the way the job is done."

Luke made a rude noise under his breath. He tested the shovel, and shook his head in dissatisfaction. The handle was too long, the blade too short. He reported this fact to Miskitman, who merely glanced at his watch and signaled the drill operator. The machine whined into revolution, and with an ear-splitting roar made contact with the rock. Miskitman departed, and Luke went to work.

During the shift he found that if he worked in a half-crouch most of the hot dust-laden exhaust would pass over his head. Changing a cutting tooth during the first rest period he burned a blister on his left thumb. At the end of the shift a single consideration deterred Luke from declaring himself unqualified: he would be declassified from *Flunky/Class D/Unskilled* to *Junior Executive*, with a corresponding cut in expense account. Such a declassification would take him to the very bottom of the Status List, and could not be countenanced; his present expense account was barely adequate, comprising nutrition at a Type RP Victualing Service, sleeping space in a Sublevel 22 dormitory, and sixteen Special Coupons per month. He took Class 14 Erotic Processing, and was allowed twelve hours per month at his Recreation Club, with optional use of barbells, table-tennis equipment, two miniature bowling alleys, and any of the six telescreens tuned permanently to Band H.

Luke often daydreamed of a more sumptuous life: AAA nutrition, a suite of rooms for his exclusive use, Special Coupons by the bale, Class 7 Erotic Processing, or even Class 6, or 5: despite Luke's contempt for the High Echelon he had no quarrel with High Echelon perquisites. And always as a bitter coda to the daydreams came the conviction that he might have enjoyed these good things in all reality. He had watched his fellows jockeying; he knew all the tricks and techniques: the beavering, the gregarization, the smutting, knuckling and subuculation...

"I'd rather be Class D Flunky," sneered Luke to himself.

Occasionally a measure of doubt would seep into Luke's mind. Perhaps he merely lacked the courage to compete, to come to grips with the world! And the seep of doubt would become a trickle of self-contempt. A Nonconformist, that's what he was — and lacked the courage to admit it!

Then Luke's obstinacy would reassert itself. Why admit to Nonconformity when it meant a trip to the Disorganized House? A fool's trick — and Luke was no fool. Perhaps he was a Nonconformist in all reality; again perhaps not — he had never really made up his mind. He presumed that he was suspected; occasionally he intercepted queer side-glances and significant jerks of the head among his fellow workers. Let them leer. They could prove nothing.

But now... he was Luke Grogatch, Class D Flunky, separated by a single status from the nonclassified sediment of criminals, idiots, children and proved Nonconformists. Luke Grogatch, who had dreamed such dreams of the High Echelon, of pride and independence! Instead — Luke Grogatch, Class D Flunky. Taking orders from a hay-headed lunk, working with semiskilled laborers with status almost as low as his own: Luke Grogatch, flunky.

Seven weeks passed. Luke's dislike for his job became a mordant passion. The work was arduous, hot, repellent. Fedor Miskitman turned an uncomprehending gaze on Luke's most rancorous grimaces, grunted and shrugged at Luke's suggestions and arguments. This was the way things were done — his manner implied — always had been done, and always would be done.

Fedor Miskitman received a daily policy directive from the works superintendent which he read to the crew during the first rest break of the shift. These directives generally dealt with such matters as work norms, team spirit and cooperation; pleas for a finer polish on the concrete; warnings against off-shift indulgence which might dull enthusiasm and decrease work efficiency. Luke usually paid small heed, until one day Fedor Miskitman, pulling out the familiar yellow sheet, read in his stolid voice:

PUBLIC WORKS DEPARTMENT, PUBLIC UTILITIES DIVISION

AGENCY OF SANITARY WORKS, DISTRICT 8892

SEWAGE DISPOSAL SECTION

. . . .

Bureau of Sewer Construction and Maintenance

Office of Procurement

Policy Directive:	6511 Series BV96
Order Code:	GZP — AAR — REG
Reference:	G98 — 7542
Date Code:	BT — EQ — LLT
Authorized:	LL8 — P-SC 8892
Checked:	48
Counterchecked:	92C

From: Lavester Limon, Manager, Office of Procurement
Through: All construction and maintenance offices
To: All construction and maintenance superintendents
Attention: All job foremen

Subject: Tool longevity, the promotion thereof
Instant of Application: Immediate
Duration of Relevance: Permanent
Substance: At beginning of each shift all hand-tools shall be checked out of District 8892 Sewer Maintenance Warehouse. At close of each shift all hand-tools shall be carefully cleaned and returned to District 8892 Sewer Maintenance Warehouse.

Directive reviewed
and transmitted: Butry Keghorn, General Superintendent of Construction, Bureau of Sewer Construction
Clyde Kaddo, Superintendent of Sewer Maintenance

As Fedor Miskitman read the 'Substance' section, Luke expelled his breath in an incredulous snort. Miskitman finished, folded the sheet with careful movements of his thick fingers, looked at his watch. "That is the directive. We are twenty-five seconds over time; we must get back to work."

"Just a minute," said Luke. "One or two things about that directive I want explained."

Miskitman turned his mild gaze upon Luke. "You did not understand it?"

"Not altogether. Who does it apply to?"

"It is an order for the entire gang."

"What do they mean 'hand-tools'?"

"These are tools which are held in the hands."

"Does that mean a shovel?"

"A shovel?" Miskitman shrugged his burly shoulders. "A shovel is a hand-tool."

Luke asked in a voice of hushed wonder: "They want me to polish my shovel, carry it four miles to the warehouse, then pick it up tomorrow and carry it back here?"

Miskitman unfolded the directive, held it at arm's length, read with moving lips. "That is the order." He refolded the paper, returned it to his pocket.

Luke again feigned astonishment. "Certainly there's a mistake."

"A mistake?" Miskitman was puzzled. "Why should there be a mistake?"

"They can't be serious," said Luke. "It's not only ridiculous, it's peculiar."

"I do not know," said Miskitman incuriously. "To work. We are late one minute and a half."

"I assume that all this cleaning and transportation is done on Organization time," Luke suggested.

Miskitman unfolded the directive, held it at arm's length, read. "It does not say so. Our quota is not different." He folded the directive, put it in his pocket.

Luke spat on the rock floor. "I'll bring my own shovel. Let 'em carry around their own precious hand-tools."

Miskitman scratched his chin, once more re-read the directive. He shook his head dubiously. "The order says that all hand-tools must be cleaned and taken to the warehouse. It does not say who owns the tools."

Luke could hardly speak for exasperation. "You know what I think of that directive?"

Fedor Miskitman paid him no heed. "To work. We are over time."

"If I was general superintendent —" Luke began, but Miskitman rumbled roughly. "We do not earn perquisites by talking. To work. We are late."

The rotary cutter started up; seventy-two teeth snarled into gray-brown sandstone. Hopper jaws swallowed the chunks, passing them down an epiglottis into a feeder gut which evacuated far down the tunnel into lift-buckets. Stray chips rained upon the tunnel floor, which Luke Grogatch must scrape up and return into the hopper. Behind Luke two reinforcement men flung steel hoops into place, flash-welding them to longitudinal bars with quick pinches of the fingers, contact-plates in their gauntlets discharging the requisite gout of energy. Behind came the concrete-spray man, mix hissing out of his revolving spider, followed by two finishers, nervous men working with furious energy, stroking the concrete into a glossy polish. Fedor Miskitman marched back and forth, testing the reinforcement, gauging the thickness of the concrete, making frequent progress checks on the chart to the rear of the rotary cutter, where an electronic device traced the course of the tunnel, guiding it through the system of conduits, ducts, passages, pipes, tubes for water, air, gas, steam, transportation, freight and communication which knit the City into an Organized unit.

The night shift ended at four o'clock in the morning. Miskitman made careful entries in his log; the concrete-spray man blew out his nozzles; the reinforcement workers removed their gauntlets, power packs and insulating garments. Luke Grogatch straightened, rubbed his sore back, stood glowering at the shovel. He felt Miskitman's ox-calm scrutiny. If he threw the shovel to the side of the tunnel as usual and marched off about his business, he would be guilty of Disorganized Conduct. The penalty, as Luke knew well, was declassification. Luke stared at the shovel, fuming with humiliation. Conform, or be declassified. Submit — or become a Junior Executive.

Luke heaved a deep sigh. The shovel was clean enough; one or two swipes with a rag would remove the dust. But there was the ride by crowded man-belt to the warehouse, the queue at the window, the check-in, the added distance to his dormitory. Tomorrow the process must be repeated. Why the necessity for this added effort? Luke knew well enough. An obscure functionary somewhere along the chain of bureaus and commissions had been at a loss for a means to display his diligence. What better method than concern for valuable City property? Consequently the absurd directive, filtering down to Fedor Miskitman and ultimately Luke Grogatch, the victim. What joy to meet this obscure functionary face to face, to tweak his sniveling nose, to kick his craven rump along the corridors of his own office.

Fedor Miskitman's voice disturbed his reverie. "Clean your shovel. It is the end of the shift."

Luke made token resistance. "The shovel is clean," he growled. "This is the most absurd antic I've ever been coerced into. If only I —"

Fedor Miskitman, in a voice as calm and unhurried as a deep river, said, "If you do not like the policy, you should put a petition in the Suggestion Box. That is the privilege of all. Until the policy is changed you must conform. That is the way we live. That is Organization, and we are Organized men."

"Let me see that directive," Luke barked. "I'll get it changed. I'll cram it down somebody's throat. I'll —"

"You must wait until it is logged. Then you may have it; it is useless to me."

"I'll wait," said Luke between clenched teeth.

With method and deliberation Fedor Miskitman made a final check of the job: inspecting machinery, the teeth of the cutter-head, the nozzles of the spider, the discharge belt. He went to his little desk at the rear of the rotary drill, noted progress, signed expense-account vouchers, finally registered the policy directive on mini-film. Then with a ponderous sweep of his arm, he tendered the yellow sheet to Luke. "What will you do with it?"

"I'll find who formed this idiotic policy. I'll tell him what I think of it and what I think of him, to boot."

Miskitman shook his head in disapproval. "That is not the way such things should be done."

"How would you do it?" asked Luke with a wolfish grin.

Miskitman considered, pursing his lips, perking his bristling eyebrows. At last with great simplicity of manner he said, "I would not do it."

Luke threw up his hands, set off down the tunnel. Miskitman's voice boomed against his back. "You must take the shovel!"

Luke halted. Slowly he faced about, glared back at the hulking figure of the foreman. Obey the policy directive, or be declassified. With slow steps, a hanging head and averted eyes, he retraced his path. Snatching the shovel, he stalked back down the tunnel. His bony shoulder blades were exposed and sensitive, and Fedor Miskitman's mild blue gaze, following him, seemed to scrape the nerves of his back.

Ahead the tunnel extended, a glossy pale sinus, dwindling back along the distance they had bored. Through some odd trick of refraction alternate bright and dark rings circled the tube, confusing the eye, creating a hypnotic semblance of two-dimensionality. Luke shuffled drearily into this illusory bull's-eye, dazed with shame and helplessness, the shovel a load of despair. Had he come to this — Luke

Grogatch, previously so arrogant in his cynicism and barely concealed Nonconformity? Must he cringe at last, submit slavishly to witless regulations?...If only he were a few places farther up the list! Drearily he pictured the fine incredulous shock with which he would have greeted the policy directive, the sardonic nonchalance with which he would have let the shovel fall from his limp hands...Too late, too late! Now he must toe the mark, must carry his shovel dutifully to the warehouse. In a spasm of rage he flung the blameless implement clattering down the tunnel ahead of him. Nothing he could do! Nowhere to turn! No way to strike back! Organization: smooth and relentless; Organization, massive and inert, tolerant of the submissive, serenely cruel to the unbeliever...Luke came to his shovel and whispering an obscenity snatched it up and half-ran down the pallid tunnel.

He climbed through a manhole, emerged upon the deck of the 1123rd Avenue Hub, where he was instantly absorbed in the crowds trampling between the man-belts, which radiated like spokes, and the various escalators. Clasping the shovel to his chest, Luke struggled aboard the Fontego Man-belt and rushed south, in a direction opposite to that of his dormitory. He rode ten minutes to Astoria Hub, dropped a dozen levels on the Grimesby College Escalator, crossed a gloomy dank area smelling of old rock to a local feeder-belt which carried him to the District 8892 Sewer Maintenance Warehouse.

Luke found the warehouse brightly lit, and the center of considerable activity, with several hundred men coming and going. Those coming, like Luke, carried tools; those going went empty-handed.

Luke joined the line which had formed in front of the tool storeroom. Fifty or sixty men preceded him, a drab centipede of arms, shoulders, heads, legs, the tools projecting to either side. The centipede moved slowly, the men exchanging badinage and quips.

Observing their patience, Luke's normal irascibility asserted itself. Look at them, he thought, standing like sheep, jumping to attention at the rustle of an unfolding directive. Did they inquire the reason for the order? Did they question the necessity for their inconvenience? No! The louts stood chuckling and chatting, accepting the directive as one of life's incalculable vicissitudes, something elemental and arbitrary, like the changing of the seasons...And he, Luke Grogatch, was he better or worse? The question burned in Luke's throat like the aftertaste of vomit.

Still, better or worse, where was his choice? Conform or declassify. A poor choice. There was always the recourse of the Suggestion Box, as Fedor Miskitman, perhaps in bland jest, had pointed out. Luke growled in disgust. Weeks later he might receive a printed form with one statement of a multiple-choice list checked off by some clerical flunky or junior executive: "The situation described by your petition is already under study by responsible officials. Thank you for your interest." Or "The situation described by your petition is temporary and may shortly be altered. Thank you for your interest." Or "The situation described by your petition is the product of established policy and is not subject to change. Thank you for your interest."

A novel thought occurred to Luke: he might exert himself and reclassify *up* the list... As soon as the idea arrived he dismissed it. In the first place he was close to middle age; too many young men were pushing up past him. Even if he could goad himself into the competition...

The line moved slowly forward. Behind Luke a plump little man sagged under the weight of a Velstro inchskip. A forelock of light brown floss dangled into his moony face; his mouth was puckered into a rosebud of concentration; his eyes were absurdly serious. He wore a rather dapper pink and brown coverall with orange ankle-boots and a blue beret with the three orange pom-poms affected by the Velstro technicians.

Between shabby sour-mouthed Luke and this short moony man in the dandy's coveralls existed so basic a difference that an immediate mutual dislike was inevitable. The short man's prominent hazel eyes rested on Luke's shovel, traveled thoughtfully over Luke's dirt-stained trousers and jacket. He turned his eyes to the side.

"Come a long way?" Luke asked maliciously.

"Not far," said the moon-faced man.

"Worked overtime, eh?" Luke winked. "A bit of quiet beavering, nothing like it — or so I'm told."

"We finished the job," said the plump man with dignity. "Beavering doesn't enter into it. Why spend half tomorrow's shift on five minutes work we could do tonight?"

"I know a reason," said Luke wisely. "To do your fellow man a good one in the eye."

The moon-faced man twisted his mouth in a quick uncertain smile, then decided that the remark was not humorous. "That's not my way of working," he said stiffly.

"That thing must be heavy," said Luke, noting how the plump little arms struggled and readjusted to the irregular contours of the tool.

"Yes," came the reply. "It is heavy."

"An hour and a half," intoned Luke. "That's how long it's taking me to park this shovel. Just because somebody up the list has a nightmare. And we poor hoodlums at the bottom suffer."

"I'm not at the bottom of the list. I'm a Technical Tool Operator."

"No difference," said Luke. "The hour and a half is the same. Just for somebody's silly notion."

"It's not really so silly," said the moon-faced man. "I fancy there is a good reason for the policy."

Luke shook the handle of the shovel. "And so I have to carry this back and forth along the man-belt three hours a day?"

The little man pursed his lips. "The author of the directive undoubtedly knows his business very well. Otherwise he'd not hold his classification."

"Just who is this unsung hero?" sneered Luke. "I'd like to meet him. I'd like to learn why he wants me to waste three hours a day."

The short man now regarded Luke as he might an insect in his victual ration. "You talk like a Nonconformist. Excuse me if I seem offensive."

"Why apologize for something you can't help?" asked Luke and turned his back.

He flung his shovel to the clerk behind the wicket and received a check. Elaborately Luke turned to the moon-faced man, tucked the check into his breast pocket. "You keep this; you'll be using that shovel before I will."

He stalked proudly out of the warehouse. A grand gesture, but — he hesitated before stepping on the man-belt — was it sensible? The moony technical tool operator in the pink and brown coveralls came out of the warehouse behind him, turned him a queer glance, and hurried away.

Luke looked back into the warehouse. If he returned now he could set things right and tomorrow there'd be no trouble. If he stormed off to his dormitory, it meant another declassification. Luke Grogatch, Junior Executive... Luke reached into his jumper, took out the policy directive he had acquired from Fedor Miskitman: a bit of yellow paper, printed with a few lines of type, a trivial thing in itself—but it symbolized the Organization: massive force in irresistible operation. Nervously Luke plucked at the paper and looked back into the warehouse. The tool operator had called him a Nonconformist; Luke's mouth squirmed in a brief weary grimace. It wasn't true. Luke was not a Nonconformist; Luke was nothing in particular. And he needed his bed, his nutrition ticket, his meager expense account. Luke groaned quietly—almost a whisper. The end of the road. He had gone as far as he could go; had he ever thought he could defeat the Organization? Maybe he was wrong and everyone else was right. Possible, thought Luke without conviction. Miskitman seemed content enough; the technical tool operator seemed not only content but complacent. Luke leaned against the warehouse wall, eyes burning and moist with self-pity. Nonconformist. Misfit. What was he going to do?

He curled his lip spitefully, stepped forward onto the man-belt. Devil take them all! They could declassify him; he'd become a junior executive and laugh!

In subdued spirits Luke rode back to the Grimesby Hub. Here, about to board the escalator, he stopped short, blinking and rubbing his long sallow chin, considering still another aspect to the matter. It seemed to offer a chance of—but no. Hardly likely... and yet, why not? Once again he examined the directive. Lavester Limon, Manager of the District Office of Procurement, presumably had issued the policy; Lavester Limon could rescind it. If Luke could so persuade Limon, his troubles, while not dissipated, at least would be lessened. He could report shovel-less to his job; he could return sardonic grin for bland hidden grin with Fedor Miskitman. He might even go to the trouble of locating the moon-faced little technical tool operator with the inchskip...

Luke sighed. Why continue this futile daydream? First Lavester Limon must be induced to rescind the directive—and what were the odds of this?...Perhaps not astronomical after all, mused Luke as he rode the man-belt back to his dormitory. The directive clearly was impractical. It worked an inconvenience on many people, while accomplishing very little. If Lavester Limon could be persuaded of this, if he could be shown that his own prestige and reputation were suffering, he might agree to recall the ridiculous directive.

Luke arrived at his dormitory shortly after seven. He went immediately to the communication booth, called the District 8892 Office of Procurement. Lavester Limon, he was told, would be arriving at eight-thirty.

Luke made a careful toilet, and after due consideration invested four Special Coupons in a fresh set of fibers: a tight black jacket and blue trousers of somewhat martial cut, of considerably better quality than his usual costume. Surveying himself in the washroom mirror, Luke felt that he cut not so poor a figure.

He took his morning quota of nutrition at a nearby Type RP Victualing Service, then ascended to Sublevel 14 and rode the man-belt to District 8892 Bureau of Sewer Construction and Maintenance.

A pert office girl, dark hair pulled forward over her face in the modish 'Robber Baron' style, conducted Luke into Lavester Limon's office. At the door she glanced demurely backward, and Luke was glad that he had invested in new clothes. Responding to the stimulus, he threw back his shoulders, marched confidently into Lavester Limon's office.

Lavester Limon, sitting at his desk, bumped briefly to his feet in courteous acknowledgement — an amiable-seeming man of middle stature, golden-brown hair brushed carefully across a freckled and sun-tanned bald spot; golden-brown eyes, round and easy; a golden-brown lounge jacket and trousers of fine golden-brown corduroy. He waved his arm to a chair. "Won't you sit down, Mr. Grogatch?"

In the presence of so much cordiality Luke relaxed his truculence, and even felt a burgeoning of hope. Limon seemed a decent sort; perhaps the directive was, after all, an administrative error.

Limon raised his golden-brown eyebrows inquiringly.

Luke wasted no time on preliminaries. He brought forth the directive. "My business concerns this, Mr. Limon: a policy which you seem to have formulated."

Limon took the directive, read, nodded. "Yes, that's my policy. Something wrong?"

Luke felt surprise and a pang of premonition: surely so reasonable-seeming a man must instantly perceive the folly of the directive!

"It's simply not a workable policy," said Luke earnestly. "In fact, Mr. Limon, it's completely unreasonable!"

Lavester Limon seemed not at all offended. "Well, well! And why do you say that? Incidentally, Mr. Grogatch, you're…" Again the golden-brown eyebrows arched inquiringly.

"I'm a flunky, Class D, on a tunnel gang," said Luke. "Today it took me an hour and a half to check my shovel. Tomorrow, there'll be another hour and a half checking the shovel out. All on my own time. I don't think that's reasonable."

Lavester Limon reread the directive, pursed his lips, nodded his head once or twice. He spoke into his desk phone. "Miss Rab, I'd like to see —" he consulted the directive's reference number "— Item 7542, File G98." To Luke he said in rather an absent voice: "Sometimes these things become a trifle complicated…"

"But can you change the policy?" Luke burst out. "Do you agree that it's unreasonable?"

Limon cocked his head to the side, made a doubtful grimace. "We'll see what's on the reference. If my memory serves me…" His voice faded away.

Twenty seconds passed. Limon tapped his fingers on his desk. A soft chime sounded. Limon touched a button; his desk-screen exhibited the item he had requested: another policy directive similar in form to the first.

PUBLIC WORKS DEPARTMENT, PUBLIC UTILITIES DIVISION

AGENCY OF SANITARY WORKS, DISTRICT 8892

SEWAGE DISPOSAL SECTION
. . . .
Director's Office

    Policy Directive: 2888 Series BQ008
        Order Code: GZP — AAR — REF

Reference: OR9 — 123
Date Code: BR — EQ — LLT
Authorized: JR D-SDS
Checked: AC
Counterchecked: CX McD

From: Judiath Ripp, Director
Through:
To: Lavester Limon, Manager, Office of Procurement
Attention:
Subject: Economies of operation
Instant of Application: Immediate
Duration of Relevance: Permanent
Substance: Your monthly quota of supplies for disbursement Type A, B,
D, F, H is hereby reduced 2.2%. It is suggested that you advise
affected personnel of this reduction, and take steps to insure most
stringent economies. It has been noticed that department use of
supplies Type D in particular is in excess of calculated norm.

Suggestion: Greater care by individual users of tools, including warehouse
storage at night.

"Type D supplies," said Lavester Limon wryly, "are hand-tools. Old Ripp wants stringent economies. I merely pass along the word. That's the story behind 6511." He returned the directive in question to Luke, leaned back in his seat. "I can see how you're exercised, but —" he raised his hands in a careless, almost flippant gesture "— that's the way the Organization works."

Luke sat rigid with disappointment. "Then you won't revoke the directive?"

"My dear fellow! How can I?"

Luke made an attempt at reckless nonchalance. "Well, there's always room for me among the junior executives. I told them where to put their shovel."

"Mmmf. Rash. Sorry I can't help." Limon surveyed Luke curiously, and his lips curved in a faint grin. "Why don't you tackle old Ripp?"

Luke squinted sidewise in suspicion. "What good will that do?"

"You never know," said Limon breezily. "Suppose lightning strikes —

suppose he rescinds his directive? I can't agitate with him myself; I'd get in trouble — but there's no reason why you can't." He turned Luke a quick knowing smile, and Luke understood that Lavester Limon's amiability, while genuine, served as a useful camouflage for self-interest and artful playing of the angles.

Luke rose abruptly to his feet. He played cat's-paw for no one, and he opened his mouth to tell Lavester Limon as much. In that instant a recollection crossed his mind: the scene in the warehouse, where he had contemptuously tossed the check for his shovel to the technical tool operator. Always Luke had been prone to the grand gesture, the reckless commitment which left him no scope for retreat. When would he learn self-control? In a subdued voice Luke asked, "Who is this Ripp again?"

"Judiath Ripp, Director of the Sewage Disposal Section. You may have difficulty getting in to see him; he's a troublesome old brute. Wait, I'll find out if he's at his office."

He made inquiries into his desk phone. Information returned to the effect that Judiath Ripp had just arrived at the Section office on Sublevel 3, under Bramblebury Park.

Limon gave Luke tactical advice. "He's choleric, something of a barker. Here's the secret: pay no attention to him. He respects firmness. Pound the table. Roar back at him. If you pussyfoot he'll sling you out. Give him tit for tat and he'll listen."

Luke looked hard at Lavester Limon, well aware that the twinkle in the golden-brown eyes was malicious glee. He said, "I'd like a copy of that directive, so he'll know what I'm talking about."

Limon sobered instantly. Luke could read his mind: *Will Ripp hold it against me if I send up this crackpot? It's worth the chance.* "Sure," said Limon. "Pick it up from the girl."

Luke ascended to Sublevel 3 and walked through the pleasant tri-level arcade below Bramblebury Park. He passed the tall glass-walled fish tank open to the sky and illuminated by sunlight, boarded the local man-belt, and after a ride of two or three minutes alighted in front of the District 8892 Agency of Sanitary Works.

The Sewage Disposal Section occupied a rather pretentious suite off a small courtyard garden. Luke walked along a passage tiled with blue, gray and green mosaic, entered a white room furnished in pale gray and pink. A long mural of cleverly twisted gold, black and white tubing decorated one wall; another was swathed in heavy green leaves growing from a chest-high planter. At a desk sat the receptionist, a plump pouty blonde girl with a simulated bone through her nose and a shark's-tooth necklace dangling around her neck. She wore her hair tied up over her head like a sheaf of wheat, and an amusing black and brown primitive symbol decorated her forehead.

Luke explained that he wished a few words with Mr. Judiath Ripp, Director of the Section.

Perhaps from uneasiness, Luke spoke brusquely. The girl blinked in surprise, examined him curiously. After a moment's hesitation the girl shook her head doubtfully. "Won't someone else do? Mr. Ripp's day is tightly scheduled. What did you want to see him about?"

Luke, attempting a persuasive smile, achieved a leer of sinister significance. The girl was frankly startled.

"Perhaps you'll tell Mr. Ripp I'm here," said Luke. "One of his policy directives... well, there have been irregularities, or rather a misapplication —"

"Irregularities?" The girl seemed to hear only the single word. She gazed at Luke with new eyes, observing the crisp new black and blue garments with their quasi-military cut. Some sort of inspector? "I'll call Mr. Ripp," she said nervously. "Your name, sir, and status?"

"Luke Grogatch. My status —" Luke smiled once more, and the girl averted her eyes. "It's not important."

"I'll call Mr. Ripp, sir. One moment, if you please." She swung around, murmured anxiously into her screen, looked at Luke and spoke again. A thin voice rasped a reply. The girl swung back around, nodded at Luke. "Mr. Ripp can spare a few minutes. The first door, please."

Luke walked with stiff shoulders into a tall wood-paneled room, one wall of which displayed green-glowing tanks of darting red and yellow fish. At the desk sat Judiath Ripp, a tall heavy man, himself resembling a large fish. His head was narrow, pale as mackerel, and rested backward-tilting on his shoulders. He had no perceptible chin; the neck ran up to his carplike mouth. Pale eyes stared at Luke over small round nostrils; a low brush of hair thrust up from the rear of his head like dry grass over a sand dune. Luke remembered Lavester Limon's verbal depiction of Ripp: "choleric". Hardly appropriate. Had Limon a grudge against Ripp? Was he using Luke as an instrument of mischievous revenge? Luke suspected as much; he felt uncomfortable and awkward.

Judiath Ripp surveyed him with cold unblinking eyes. "What can I do for you, Mr. Grogatch? My secretary tells me you are an investigator of some sort."

Luke considered the situation, his narrow black eyes fixed on Ripp's face. He told the exact truth. "For several weeks I have been working in the capacity of a Class D Flunky on a tunnel gang."

"What the devil do you investigate on a tunnel gang?" Ripp asked in chilly amusement.

Luke made a slight gesture, signifying much or nothing, as one might choose to take it. "Last night the foreman of this gang received a policy directive issued by Lavester Limon of the Office of Procurement. For sheer imbecility this policy caps any of my experience."

"If it's Limon's doing, I can well believe it," said Ripp between his teeth.

"I sought him out in his office. He refused to accept responsibility and referred me to you."

Ripp sat a trifle straighter in his chair. "What policy is this?"

Luke passed the two directives across the desk. Ripp read slowly, then reluctantly returned the directives. "I fail to see exactly —" He paused. "I should say, these directives merely reflect instructions received by me which I have implemented. Where is the difficulty?"

"Let me cite my personal experience," said Luke. "This morning — as I say, in my temporary capacity as a flunky — I carried a shovel from tunnel head to warehouse and checked it. The operation required an hour and a half. If I were working steadily on a job of this sort, I'd be quite demoralized."

Ripp appeared untroubled. "I can only refer you to my superiors." He spoke aside into his desk phone. "Please transmit File OR9, Item 123." He turned back to Luke. "I can't take responsibility, either for the directive or for revoking it. May I ask what sort of investigation takes you down into the tunnels? And to whom you report?"

At a loss for words at once evasive and convincing, Luke conveyed an attitude of contemptuous silence.

Judiath Ripp contracted the skin around his blank round eyes in a frown. "As I consider this matter I become increasingly puzzled. Why is this subject a matter for investigation? Just who —"

From a slot appeared the directive Ripp had requested. He glanced at it, tossed it to Luke. "You'll see that this relieves me totally of responsibility," he said curtly.

The directive was the standard form:

PUBLIC WORKS DEPARTMENT, PUBLIC UTILITIES DIVISION

· ·

Office of the Commissioner of Public Utilities

Policy Directive:	449 Series UA-14-G2
Order Code:	GZP — AAR — REF
Reference:	TQ9 — 1422
Date Code:	BP — EQ — LLT
Authorized:	PU-PUD-Org.
Checked:	G. Evan
Counterchecked:	Hernon Klanech

From:	Parris deVicker, Commissioner of Public Utilities
Through:	All District Agencies of Sanitary Works
To:	All Department Heads
Attention:	
Subject:	The urgent need for sharp and immediate economies in the use of equipment and consumption of supplies.
Instant of Application:	Immediate
Duration of Relevance:	Permanent
Substance:	All department heads are instructed to initiate, effect and enforce rigid economies in the employment of supplies and equipment, especially those items comprised of or manufactured from alloy metals or requiring the functional consumption of same, in those areas in which official authority is exercised. A decrement of 2% will be considered minimal. Status augmentation will in some measure be affected by economies achieved.

Directive reviewed and transmitted:	Lee Jon Smith, District Agent of Sanitary Works 8892

Luke rose to his feet, concerned now only to depart from the office as quickly as possible. He indicated the directive. "This is a copy?"

"Yes."

"I'll take it, if I may." He included it with the previous two.

Judiath Ripp watched with a faint but definite suspicion. "I fail to understand whom you represent."

"Sometimes the less one knows the better," said Luke.

The suspicion faded from Judiath Ripp's piscine face. Only a person secure in his status could afford to use language of this sort to a member of the low High Echelon. He nodded slightly. "Is that all you require?"

"No," said Luke, "but it's all I can get here."

He turned toward the door, feeling the rake of Ripp's eyes on his back.

Ripp's voice cut at him suddenly and sharply. "Just a moment."

Luke slowly turned.

"Who are you? Let me see your credentials."

Luke laughed coarsely. "I don't have any."

Judiath Ripp rose to his feet, stood towering with knuckles pressed on the desk. Suddenly Luke saw that, after all, Judiath Ripp *was* choleric. His face, mackerel-pale, became suffused with salmon-pink. "Identify yourself," he said throatily, "before I call the watchman."

"Certainly," said Luke. "I have nothing to hide. I am Luke Grogatch. I work as Class D Flunky on Tunnel Gang No. 3 out of the Bureau of Sewer Construction and Maintenance."

"What are you doing here, misrepresenting yourself, wasting my time?"

"Where did I misrepresent myself?" demanded Luke in a contentious voice. "I came here to find out why I had to carry my shovel to the warehouse this morning. It cost me an hour and a half. It doesn't make sense. You've been ordered to economize two percent, so I spend three hours a day carrying a shovel back and forth."

Judiath Ripp stared at Luke for ten seconds, then abruptly sat down. "You're a Class D Flunky?"

"That's right."

"Hmm. You've been to the Office of Procurement. The manager sent you here?"

"No. He gave me a copy of his directive, just as you did."

The salmon-pink flush had died from Ripp's flat cheeks. The carp-like mouth twitched in infinitesimal amusement. "No harm in that, certainly. What do you hope to achieve?"

"I don't want to carry that blasted shovel back and forth. I'd like you to issue orders to that effect."

Judiath Ripp spread his pale mouth in a cold drooping smile. "Bring me a policy directive to that effect from Parris deVicker and I'll be glad to oblige you. Now —"

"Will you make an appointment for me?"

"An appointment?" Ripp was puzzled. "With whom?"

"With the Commissioner of Public Utilities."

"Pffah." Ripp waved his hand in cold dismissal. "Get out."

Luke stood in the blue-mosaic entry seething with hate for Ripp, Limon, Miskitman and every intervening functionary. If he were only Chairman of the Board for a brief two hours — went the oft-repeated daydream — how they'd quick-step! In his mind's eye he saw Judiath Ripp shoveling wads of 'wet waste' with a leaden shovel while a rotary driller, twice as noisy and twice as violent, blew back gales of hot dust and rock chips across his neck. Lavester Limon would be forced to change the smoking teeth of the drill with a small and rusty monkey wrench, while Fedor Miskitman, before and after the shift, carried shovel, monkey wrench and all the worn teeth to and from the warehouse.

Luke stood moping in the passage for five minutes, then escalated to the surface, which at this point, by virtue of Bramblebury Park, could clearly be distinguishable as the surface and not just another level among co-equal levels. He walked slowly along the gravel paths, ignoring the open sky for the immediacy of his problems. He faced a dead end. There was no further scope of action. Judiath Ripp mockingly had suggested that he consult the Commissioner of Public Utilities. Even if by some improbable circumstance he secured an appointment with the Commissioner, what good would ensue? Why should the Commissioner revoke a policy directive of such evident importance? Unless he could be persuaded — by some instrumentality

Luke was unable to define or even imagine — to issue a special directive exempting Luke from the provision of the policy...

Luke chuckled hollowly, a noise which alarmed the pigeons strutting along the walk. Now what? Back to the dormitory. His dormitory privileges included twelve hours use of his cot per day, and he was not extracting full value from his expense account unless he made use of it. But Luke had no desire for sleep. As he glanced up at the perspective of the towers surrounding the park he felt a melancholy exhilaration. The sky, the wonderful clear open sky, blue and brilliant! Luke shivered, for the sun here was hidden by the Morgenthau Moonspike, and the air was brisk.

Luke crossed the park, thinking to sit where a band of hazy sunlight slashed down between the towers. The benches were crowded with blinking old men and women, but Luke presently found a seat. He sat looking up into the sky, enjoying the mild natural sun-warmth. How seldom did he see the sun! In his youth he had frequently set forth on long cross-city hikes, rambling high along the skyways, with space to right and left, the clouds near enough for intimate inspection, the sunlight sparkling and stinging his skin. Gradually the hikes had spread apart, coming at ever longer intervals, and now he could hardly remember when last he'd tramped the wind-lanes. What dreams he had had in those early days, what exuberant visions! Obstacles seemed trivial; he had seen himself clawing up the list, winning a good expense account, the choicest of perquisites, unnumbered Special Coupons! He had planned a private air-car, unrestricted nutrition, an apartment far above the surface, high and remote...Dreams. Luke had been victimized by his tongue, his quick temper, his obstinacy. At heart, he was no Nonconformist — no, cried Luke, never! Luke had been born of tycoon stock, and through influence, a word here, a hint there, had been launched into the Organization on a high status. But circumstances and Luke's chronic truculence had driven him into opposition with established ways, and down the Status List he had gone: through professional scholarships, technical trainee appointments, craft apprenticeships, all the varieties of semiskills and machine operation. Now he was Luke Grogatch, flunky, unskilled, Class D, facing the final declassification. But still too vain to carry a shovel. No: Luke corrected himself. His vanity was not at stake. Vanity he had discarded long ago, along with his youthful dreams. All he had left was pride, his right to use the word "I" in connection with himself. If he submitted to Policy Directive 6511 he relinquished this right; he combined with the masses of the Organization as a spatter of foam falls back and is absorbed into the ocean... Luke jerked nervously to his feet. He wasted time sitting here. Judiath Ripp, with conger-like malice, had suggested a directive from the Commissioner of Public Utilities. Very well, Luke would obtain that directive and fling it down under Ripp's pale round nostrils.

How?

Luke rubbed his chin dubiously. He walked to a communication booth, checked the directory. As he had surmised, the Commission of Public Utilities was housed in the Organization Central Tower, in Silverado, District 3666, ninety miles to the north.

Luke stood in the watery sunlight, hoping for inspiration. The aged idlers, huddling on the benches like winterbound sparrows, watched him incuriously. Once again Luke was obscurely pleased with his purchase of new clothes. A fine figure he cut, he assured himself.

How? wondered Luke. How to gain an appointment with the Commissioner? How to persuade him to change his views?

No inkling of a solution presented itself.

He looked at his watch: still only middle morning. Ample time to visit Organization Central and return in time to report for duty... Luke grimaced wanly. Was his resolution so feeble, then? Was he, after all, to slink back into the tunnel tonight carrying the hated shovel? Luke shook his head slowly. He did not know.

At the Bramblebury Interchange Luke boarded an express highline northbound for Silverado Station. With a hiss and a whine, the shining metal worm darted forward, sliding up to Level 13, flashing north at great speed, in and out of the sunlight, through tunnels, across intertower chasms, with far below the nervous seethe of the City. Four times the express sighed to a halt: at IBM University, at Braemar, at Great Northern Junction, and finally, thirty minutes out of Bramblebury, at Silverado Central. Luke disembarked; the express slid away through the towers, lithe as an eel through waterweed.

Luke entered the tenth-level foyer of the Central Tower, a vast cave of marble and bronze. Throngs of men and women thrust past him: grim striding tycoons, stamped with the look of destiny, High Echelon personnel, their assistants, the assistants to their assistants, functionaries on down the list, all dutifully wearing high-status garments, the lesser folk hoping to be mistaken for their superiors. All hurried, tense-faced and abrupt, partly from habit, partly because only a person of low status had no need to hurry. Luke thrust and elbowed with the best of them, and made his way to the central kiosk where he consulted a directory.

Parris deVicker, Commissioner of Public Utilities, had his office on Level 59. Luke passed him by and located the Secretary of Public Affairs, Mr. Sewell Sepp, on Level 81. No more underlings, thought Luke. This time I'm going to the top. If anyone can resolve this matter, it's Sewell Sepp.

He put himself aboard the lift and emerged into the lobby of the Department of Public Affairs — a splendid place, glittering with disciplined color and ornament after that mock-antique décor known as Second Institutional. The walls were of polished milk glass inset with medallions of shifting kaleidoscopic flashes. The floor was diapered in blue and white sparkle-stone. A dozen bronze statues dominated the room, massive figures symbolizing the basic public services: communication, transport, education, water, energy and sanitation. Luke skirted the pedestals, crossed to the reception counter, where ten young women in handsome brown and black uniforms stood with military precision, each to her six feet of counter top. Luke selected one of these girls, who curved her lips in an automatic empty smile. "Yes sir?"

"I want to see Mr. Sepp," said Luke brazenly.

The girl's smile remained frozen while she looked at him with startled eyes. "Mr. who?"

"Sewell Sepp, the Secretary of Public Affairs."

The girl asked gently, "Do you have an appointment, sir?"

"No."

"It's impossible, sir."

Luke nodded sourly. "Then I'll see Commissioner Parris deVicker."

"Do you have an appointment to see Mr. deVicker?"

"No, I'm afraid not."

The girl shook her head with a trace of amusement. "Sir, you can't just walk in on these people. They're extremely busy. Everyone must have an appointment."

"Oh come now," said Luke. "Surely it's conceivable that —"

"Definitely not, sir."

"Then," said Luke, "I'll make an appointment. I'd like to see Mr. Sepp some time today, if possible."

The girl lost interest in Luke. She resumed her manner of impersonal courtesy. "I'll call the office of Mr. Sepp's appointment secretary."

She spoke into a mesh, turned back to Luke. "No appointments are open this month, sir. Will you speak to someone else? Some underofficial?"

"No," said Luke. He gripped the edge of the counter for a moment, started to turn away, then asked, "Who authorizes these appointments?"

"The secretary's first aide, who screens the list of applications."

"I'll speak to the first aide, then."

The girl sighed. "You need an appointment, sir."

"I need an appointment to make an appointment?"

"Yes, sir."

"Do I need an appointment to make an appointment for an appointment?"

"No, sir. Just walk right in."

"Where?"

"Suite 42, inside the rotunda, sir."

Luke passed through twelve-foot crystal doors, walked down a short hall. Scurrying patterns of color followed him like shadows along both the walls, grotesque cubistic shapes parodying the motion of his body: a whimsy which surprised Luke and might have pleased him under less critical circumstances.

He passed through another pair of crystal portals into the rotunda. Six levels above, a domed ceiling depicted scenes of legend in stained glass. Behind a ring of leather couches doors gave into surrounding offices; one of these doors, directly across from the entrance, bore the words:

OFFICES OF THE SECRETARY
Department of Public Affairs

On the couches half a hundred men and women waited, with varying degrees of patience. The careful disdain with which they surveyed each other suggested that their status was high; the frequency with which they consulted their watches conveyed the impression that they were momentarily on the point of departure.

A mellow voice sounded over a loudspeaker: "Mr. Artur Coff, please, to the Office of the Secretary." A plump gentleman threw down the periodical he had fretfully been examining, jumped to his feet. He crossed to the bronze and black glass door, passed through.

Luke watched him enviously, then turned aside through an arch marked *Suite 42*. An usher in a brown and black uniform stepped forward; Luke stated his business and was conducted into a small cubicle.

A young man behind a metal desk peered intently at him. "Sit down, please." He motioned to a chair. "Your name?"

"Luke Grogatch."

"Ah, Mr. Grogatch. May I inquire your business?"

"I have something to say to the Secretary of Public Affairs."

"Regarding what subject?"

"A personal matter."

"I'm sorry, Mr. Grogatch. The Secretary is more than busy. He's swamped with important Organization business. But if you'll explain the situation to me, I'll recommend you to an appropriate member of the staff."

"That won't help," said Luke. "I want to consult the Secretary in relation to a recently issued policy directive."

"Issued by the Secretary?"

"Yes."

"You wish to object to this directive?"

Luke grudgingly admitted as much.

"There are appropriate channels for this process," said the aide decisively. "If you will fill out this form — not here, but in the rotunda — drop it into the Suggestion Box to the right of the door as you go out —"

In sudden fury Luke wadded up the form, flung it down on the desk. "Surely he has five minutes free —"

"I'm afraid not, Mr. Grogatch," the aide said in a voice of ice. "If you will look through the rotunda you will see a number of very important people who have waited, some of them for months, for five minutes with the Secretary. If you wish to fill out an application, stating your business in detail, I will see that it receives due consideration."

Luke stalked out of the cubicle. The aide watched him go with a bleak smile of dislike. The man obviously had Nonconformist tendencies, he thought…probably should be watched.

Luke stood in the rotunda, muttering, "What now? What now? What now?" in a half-mesmerized undertone. He stared around the rotunda, at the pompous High Echelon folk, arrogantly consulting their watches and tapping their feet. "Mr. Jepper Prinn!" called the mellow voice over the loudspeaker. "The Office of the Secretary, if you please." Luke watched Jepper Prinn walk to the bronze and black glass portal.

Luke slumped into a chair, scratched his long nose, looked cautiously around the rotunda. Nearby sat a big, bull-necked man with a red face, protruding lips, a shock of rank blond hair — a tycoon, judging from his air of absolute authority.

Luke rose and went to a desk placed for the convenience of those waiting. He took several sheets of paper with the Tower letterhead, unobtrusively circled the rotunda to the entrance into Suite 42. The bull-necked tycoon paid him no heed.

Luke girded himself, closing his collar, adjusting the set of his jacket. He took a deep breath, then, when the florid man glanced in his direction, came forward officiously. He looked briskly around the circle of couches, consulting his papers; then catching the eye of the tycoon, frowned, squinted, walked forward.

"Your name, sir?" asked Luke in an official voice.

"I'm Hardin Arthur," rasped the tycoon. "Why?"

Luke nodded, consulted his paper. "The time of your appointment?"

"Eleven-ten. What of it?"

"The Secretary would like to know if you can conveniently lunch with him at one-thirty?"

Arthur considered. "I suppose it's possible," he grumbled. "I'll have to rearrange some other business…An inconvenience — but I can do it, yes."

"Excellent," said Luke. "At lunch the Secretary feels that he can discuss your business more informally and at greater length than at eleven-ten, when he can only allow you seven minutes."

"Seven minutes!" rumbled Arthur indignantly. "I can hardly spread my plans out in seven minutes."

"Yes sir," said Luke. "The Secretary realizes this, and suggests that you lunch with him."

Arthur petulantly hauled himself to his feet. "Very well. Lunch at one-thirty, correct?"

"Correct, sir. If you will walk directly into the Secretary's office at that time."

Arthur departed the rotunda, and Luke settled into the seat Arthur had vacated.

Time passed very slowly. At ten minutes after eleven the mellow voice called out, "Mr. Hardin Arthur, please. To the Office of the Secretary."

Luke rose to his feet, stalked with great dignity across the rotunda and through the bronze and black glass door.

Behind a long black desk sat the Secretary, a rather undistinguished man with gray hair and snapping gray eyes. He raised his eyebrows as Luke came forward: Luke evidently did not fit his preconception of Hardin Arthur.

The Secretary spoke. "Sit down, Mr. Arthur. I may as well tell you bluntly and frankly that we think your scheme is impractical. By 'we' I mean myself and the Board of Policy Evaluation—who of course have referred to the Files. First, the costs are excessive. Second, there's no guarantee that you can phase your program into that of our other tycoons. Third, the Board of Policy Evaluation tells me that Files doubts whether we'll need that much new capacity."

"Ah," Luke nodded wisely. "I see. Well, no matter. It's not important."

"Not important?" The Secretary sat up in his chair, stared at Luke in wonder. "I'm surprised to hear you say so."

Luke made an airy gesture. "Forget it. Life's too short to worry about these things. Actually there's another matter I want to discuss with you."

"Ah?"

"It may seem trivial, but the implications are large. A former employee called the matter to my attention. He's now a flunky on one of the sewer maintenance tunnel gangs, an excellent chap. Here's the situation. Some idiotic jack-in-office has issued a directive which forces this man to carry a shovel back and forth to the warehouse every day, before and after work. I've taken the trouble to follow up the matter and the chain leads here." He displayed his three policy directives.

Frowningly the Secretary glanced through them. "These all seem perfectly regular. What do you want me to do?"

"Issue a directive clarifying the policy. After all, we can't have these poor devils working three hours overtime for tomfoolishness."

"Tomfoolishness?" The Secretary was displeased. "Hardly that, Mr. Arthur. The economy directive came to me from the Board of Directors, from the Chairman himself, and if—"

"Don't mistake me," said Luke hastily. "I've no quarrel with economy; I merely want the policy applied sensibly. Checking a shovel into the warehouse—where's the economy in that?"

"Multiply that shovel by a million, Mr. Arthur," said the Secretary coldly.

"Very well, multiply it," argued Luke. "We have a million shovels. How many of these million shovels are conserved by this order? Two or three a year?"

The Secretary shrugged. "Obviously in a general directive of this sort, inequalities occur. So far as I'm concerned, I issued the directive because I was instructed to do so. If you want it changed you'll have to consult the Chairman of the Board."

"Very well. Can you arrange an appointment for me?"

"Let's settle the matter even sooner," said the Secretary. "Right now. We'll talk to him across the screen, although, as you say, it seems a trivial matter…"

"Demoralization of the working force isn't trivial, Secretary Sepp."

The Secretary shrugged, touched a button, spoke into a mesh. "The Chairman of the Board, if he's not occupied."

The screen glowed. The Chairman of the Board of Directors looked out at them. He sat in a lounge chair on the deck of his penthouse at the pinnacle of the tower. In one hand he held a glass of pale effervescent liquid; beyond him opened sunlight and blue air and a wide glimpse of the miraculous City.

"Good morning, Sepp," said the Chairman cordially, and nodded toward Luke. "Good morning to you, sir."

"Chairman, Mr. Arthur here is protesting the economy directive you sent down a few days ago. He claims that strict application is causing hardship among the labor force: demoralization, actually. Something to do with shovels."

The Chairman considered. "Economy directive? I hardly recall the exact case."

Secretary Sepp described the directive, citing code and reference numbers, explaining the provisions, and the Chairman nodded in recollection. "Yes, the metal-shortage thing. Afraid I can't help you, Sepp, or you, Mr. Arthur. Policy Evaluation sent it up. Apparently we're running short of minerals; what else can we do? Cinch in the old belts, eh? Hard on all of us. What's this about shovels?"

"It's the whole matter," cried Luke in sudden shrillness, evoking startled glances from Secretary and Chairman. "Carrying a shovel back and forth to the warehouse three hours a day! It's not economy, it's a disorganized farce!"

"Come now, Mr. Arthur," the Chairman chided humorously. "So long as you're not carrying the shovel yourself why the excitement? It works the very devil with one's digestion. Until Policy Evaluation changes its collective mind — as it often does — then we've got to string along. Can't go counter to Policy Evaluation, you know. They're the people with the facts and figures."

"Neither here nor there," mumbled Luke. "Carrying a shovel three hours —"

"Perhaps a bit of bother for the men concerned," said the Chairman with a hint of impatience, "but they've got to see the thing from the long view. Sepp, perhaps you'll lunch with me? A marvelous day, lazy weather."

"Thank you, Mr. Chairman. I'll be pleased indeed."

"Excellent. At one or one-thirty, whenever convenient for you."

The screen went blank. Secretary Sepp rose to his feet. "There it is, Mr. Arthur. I can't do any more."

"Very well, Mr. Secretary," said Luke in a hollow voice.

"Sorry I can't be of more help in the other matter, but as I say —"

"It's inconsequential."

Luke turned, left the elegant office, passed through the bronze and black glass doors into the rotunda. Through the arch into Suite 42 he saw a large bull-necked man, tomato-red in the face, hunched forward across a counter. Luke stepped forward smartly, leaving the rotunda just as the authentic Mr. Arthur and the aide came forth, deep in agitated conversation.

Luke stopped by the information desk. "Where is the Policy Evaluation Board?"

"Level 29, sir, this building."

In Policy Evaluation on Level 29 Luke talked with a silk-mustached young man, courtly and elegant, with the status classification *Plan Coordinator*. "Certainly!" exclaimed the young man in response to Luke's question. "Authoritative information is the basis of authoritative organization. Material from Files is collated, digested in the Bureau of Abstracts and sent up to us. We shape it and present it to the Board of Directors in the form of a daily précis."

Luke expressed interest in the Bureau of Abstracts, and the young man quickly became bored. "Grubbers among the statistics, barely able to compose an intelligible sentence. If it weren't for us —" His eyebrows, silken as his mustache, hinted of the disasters which in the absence of Policy Evaluation would overtake the Organization. "They work in a suite down on the Sixth Level."

Luke descended to the Bureau of Abstracts, and found no difficulty gaining admission to the general office. In contrast to the rather nebulous intellectualism of Policy Evaluation, the Bureau of Abstracts seemed workaday and matter-of-fact. A middle-aged woman, cheerfully fat, inquired Luke's business, and when Luke professed himself a journalist, conducted him about the premises. They went from the main lobby, walled in antique cream-colored plaster with gold scrollwork, past the small fusty cubicles, where clerks sat at projection-desks scanning ribbons of words, extracting idea-sequences, emending, excising, condensing, cross-referring, finally producing the abstract to be submitted to Policy Evaluation. Luke's fat and cheerful guide brewed them a pot of tea; she asked questions which Luke answered in general terms, straining his voice and pursing his mouth in the effort to seem agreeable and hearty. He himself asked questions. "I'm interested in a set of statistics on the scarcity of metals, or ores, or something similar which recently went up to Policy Evaluation. Would you know anything about this?"

"Heavens no," the woman responded. "There's just too much material coming in — the business of the entire Organization."

"Where does this material come from? Who sends it to you?"

The woman made a humorous little grimace of distaste. "From Files, down on Sublevel 12. I can't tell you much, because we don't associate with the personnel. They're low status: clerks and the like. Sheer automatons."

Luke expressed an interest in the source of the Bureau of Abstracts' information. The woman shrugged, as if to say, everyone to his own taste. "I'll call down to the Chief File Clerk; I know him, very slightly."

The Chief File Clerk, Mr. Sidd Boatridge, was self-important and brusque, as if aware of the low esteem in which he was held by the Bureau of Abstracts. He dismissed Luke's questions with a stony face of indifference. "I really have no idea, sir. We file, index, and cross-index material into the Information Bank, but concern ourselves very little with outgoing data. My duties in fact are mainly administrative. I'll call in one of the under-clerks; he can tell you more than I can."

The under-clerk who answered Boatridge's summons was a short turnip-faced man with matted red hair. "Take Mr. Grogatch into the outer office," said the Chief File Clerk testily. "He wants to ask you a few questions."

In the outer office, out of the Chief File Clerk's hearing, the under-clerk became rather surly and pompous, as if he had divined the level of Luke's status. He referred to himself as a "line-tender" rather than a "file clerk", the latter apparently being a classification of lesser prestige. His "line-tending" consisted of sitting beside a panel which glowed and blinked with a thousand orange and green lights. "The orange lights indicate information going down into the Bank," said the file clerk. "The green lights show where somebody up-level is drawing information out — generally at the Bureau of Abstracts."

Luke observed the orange and green flickers for a moment. "What information is being transmitted now?"

"Couldn't say," the file clerk grunted. "It's all coded. Down in the old office we had a monitoring machine and never used it. Too much else to do."

Luke considered. The file clerk showed signs of restiveness. Luke's mind worked hurriedly. He asked, "So — as I understand it — you file information, but have nothing further to do with it?"

"We file it and code it. Whoever wants information puts a program into the works and the information goes out to him. We never see it, unless we went and looked in the old monitoring machine."

"Which is still down at your old office?"

The file clerk nodded. "They call it the staging chamber now. Nothing there but input and output pipes, the monitor, and the custodian."

"Where is the staging chamber?"

"Way down the levels, behind the Bank. Too low for me to work. I got more ambition." For emphasis he spat on the floor.

"A custodian is there, you say?"

"An old junior executive named Dodkin. He's been there a hundred years."

Luke dropped thirty levels aboard an express lift, then rode the down escalator another six levels to Sublevel 48. He emerged on a dingy landing, a low-perquisite nutrition hall to one side, a lift-attendants dormitory to the other. The air carried the familiar reek of the deep underground, a compound of dank concrete, phenol, mercaptans, a discreet but pervasive human smell. Luke realized with bitter amusement that he had returned to familiar territory.

Following instructions grudgingly detailed by the under-file clerk, Luke stepped aboard a chattering man-belt labeled '902 — Tanks'. Presently he came to a brightly-lit landing marked by a black and yellow sign:

INFORMATION TANKS: TECHNICAL STATION.

Inside the door a number of mechanics sat on stools, dangling their legs, lounging, chaffering.

Luke changed to a side-belt, even more dilapidated, almost in a state of disrepair. At the second junction — this unmarked — he left the man-belt, turned down a narrow passage toward a far yellow bulb. The passage was silent, almost sinister in its disassociation from the life of the City.

Below the single yellow bulb a dented metal door was daubed with a sign:

Information Tanks: Staging Chamber
NO ADMITTANCE

Luke tested the door and found it locked. He rapped and waited.

Silence shrouded the passage, broken only by a faint sound from the distant man-belt.

Luke rapped again, and now from within came a shuffle of movement. The door slid back, a pale placid eye looked forth. A rather weak voice inquired, "Yes sir?"

Luke attempted a manner of easy authority. "You're Dodkin the custodian?"

"Yes, sir, I'm Dodkin."

"Open up, please, I'd like to come in."

The pale eye blinked in mild wonder. "This is only the staging room, sir. There's nothing here to see. The storage complexes are around to the front; if you'll go back to the junction —"

Luke broke into the flow of words. "I've just come down from Files; it's you I want to see."

The pale eye blinked once more; the door slid open. Luke entered the long narrow concrete-floored staging room. Conduits dropped from the ceiling by the thousands, bent, twisted and looped, entered the wall, each conduit labeled with a dangling metal tag. At one end of the room was a grimy cot where Dodkin apparently slept; at the other end was a long black desk: the monitoring machine? Dodkin himself was small and stooped, but moved nimbly in spite of his evident age. His white hair was stained but well brushed; his gaze, weak and watery, was without guile, and fixed on Luke with an astronomer's detachment. He opened his mouth, and words quavered forth in spate, with Luke vainly seeking to interrupt.

"Not often do visitors come from above. Is something wrong?"

"No, nothing wrong."

"They should tell me if aught isn't correct, or perhaps there's been new policies of which I haven't been notified."

"Nothing like that, Mr. Dodkin. I'm just a visitor —"

"I don't move out as much as I used to, but last week I —"

Luke pretended to listen while Dodkin maundered on in obbligato to Luke's bitter thoughts. The continuity of directives leading from Fedor Miskitman to Lavester Limon to Judiath Ripp, by-passing Parris deVicker to Sewell Sepp and the Chairman of the Board, then returning down the classifications, down the levels through the Policy Evaluation Board, the Bureau of Abstracts, the File Clerk's Office — the continuity had finally ended; the thread he had traced with such forlorn hope seemed about to lose itself. Well, Luke told himself, he had accepted Miskitman's challenge; he had failed, and now was faced with his original choice. Submit, carry the wretched shovel back and forth to the warehouse, or defy the order, throw down his shovel, assert himself as a free-willed man, and be declassified, to become a junior executive like old Dodkin — who, sucking and wheezing, still rambled on in compulsive loquacity.

"...something incorrect, I'd never know, because who ever tells me? From year end to year end I'm quiet down here and there's no one to relieve me, and I only get to the up-side rarely, once a fortnight or so, but then once you've seen the sky, does it ever change? And the sun, the marvel of it, but once you've seen a marvel —"

Luke drew a deep breath. "I'm investigating an item of information which reached the File Clerk's Office. I wonder if you can help me."

Dodkin blinked his pale eyes. "What item is this, sir? Naturally I'll be glad to help in any way, even though —"

"The item dealt with economy in the use of metals and metal tools."

Dodkin nodded. "I remember the item perfectly."

It was Luke's turn to stare. "You *remember* this item?"

"Certainly. It was, if I may say so, one of my little interpolations. A personal observation which I included among the other material."

"Would you be kind enough to explain?"

Dodkin would be only too pleased to explain. "Last week I had occasion to visit an old friend over by Claxton Abbey, a fine Conformist, well adapted and cooperative, even if, alas, like myself, a junior executive. Of course, I mean no disrespect to good Davy Evans, like myself about ready for the pension — though little enough they allow nowadays..."

"The interpolation?"

"Yes, indeed. On my way home along the man-belt — on Sublevel 32, as I recall — I saw a workman of some sort — perhaps an electrical technician — toss several tools into a crevice on his way off-shift. I thought, now there's a slovenly act — disgraceful! Suppose the man forgot where he had hidden his tools? They'd be lost! Our reserves of raw metallic ore are very low — that's common knowledge — and every year the ocean water becomes weaker and more dilute. That man had no regard for the future of Organization. We should cherish our natural resources, do you not agree, sir?"

"I agree, naturally. But —"

"In any event, I returned here and added a memorandum to that effect into the material which goes up to the Assistant File Clerk. I thought that perhaps he'd be impressed and say a word to someone with influence — perhaps the Head File Clerk. In any event, there's the tale of my interpolation. Naturally I attempted to give it weight by citing the inevitable diminution of our natural resources."

"I see," said Luke. "And do you frequently include interpolations into the day's information?"

"Occasionally," said Dodkin, "and sometimes, I'm glad to say, people more important than I share my views. Only three weeks ago I was delayed several minutes on my way between Claxton Abbey and Kittsville on Sublevel 30. I made a note of it, and last week I noticed that construction has commenced on a new eight-lane man-belt between the two points, a really magnificent and modern undertaking. A month ago I noticed a shameless group of girls daubed like savages with cosmetic. What a waste! I told myself, what vanity and folly! I hinted as much in a little message to the Under-File Clerk. I seem to be just one of the many with these views, for two days later a general order discouraging these petty vanities was issued by the Secretary of Education."

"Interesting," Luke muttered. "Interesting indeed. How do you include these 'interpolations' into the information?"

Dodkin hobbled nimbly to the monitoring machine, beckoned. "The output from the tanks comes through here. I print a bit on the typewriter and tuck it in where the Under-Clerk will see it."

"Admirable," sighed Luke. "A man with your intelligence should have ranked higher in the Status List."

Dodkin shook his placid old head. "I don't have the ambition nor the ability. I'm fit for just this simple job, and only barely. I'd take my pension tomorrow, only the Chief File Clerk asked me to stay on a bit until he could find a man to take my place. No one seems to like the quiet down here."

"Perhaps you'll have your pension sooner than you think," said Luke.

Luke strolled along the glossy tube, ringed with alternate pale and dark refractions like a bull's-eye. Ahead was motion, the glint of metal, the mutter of voices. The entire crew of Tunnel Gang No. 3 stood idle and restless.

Fedor Miskitman waved his arm with uncharacteristic vehemence. "Grogatch! At your post! You've held up the entire crew!" His heavy face was suffused with pink. "Four minutes already we're behind schedule."

Luke strolled closer.

"Hurry!" bellowed Miskitman. "What do you think this is, a blasted promenade?"

If anything Luke slackened his pace. Fedor Miskitman lowered his big bull-head, staring balefully. Luke halted in front of him.

"Where's your shovel?" Fedor Miskitman asked.

"I don't know," said Luke. "I'm here on the job. It's up to you to provide tools."

Fedor Miskitman stared unbelievingly. "Didn't you take it to the warehouse?"

"Yes," said Luke. "I took it there. If you want it, go get it."

Fedor Miskitman opened his mouth. He roared, "Get off the job!"

"Just as you like," said Luke. "You're the foreman."

"Don't come back!" bellowed Miskitman. "I'll report you before the day is out. You won't gain status from me, I tell you that!"

" 'Status'?" Luke laughed. "Go ahead. Cut me down to junior executive. Do you think I care? No. And I'll tell you why. There's going to be a change or two made. When things seem different to you, think of me."

Luke Grogatch, Junior Executive, said good-by to the retiring custodian of the staging chamber. "Don't thank me, not at all," said Luke. "I'm here by my own doing. In fact — well, never mind all that. Go up-side, sit in the sun, enjoy the air."

Finally Dodkin, in mingled joy and sorrow, hobbled for the last time down the musty passageway to the chattering man-belt.

Luke was alone in the staging chamber. Around his ears hummed the near-inaudible rush of information. From behind the wall came the sense of a million relays clicking, twitching, meshing; of cylinders and trace-tubes and memory-lanes whirring with activity. At the monitoring machine the output streamed forth on a reel of yellow tape. Nearby rested the typewriter.

Luke seated himself. His first interpolation…what should it be? Freedom for the Nonconformists? Tunnel-gang foremen to carry tools for the entire crew? A higher expense account for junior executives?

Luke rose to his feet and scratched his chin. Power…to be subtly applied. How should he use it? To secure rich perquisites for himself? Yes, of course, this he would accomplish, by devious means. And then — what? Luke thought of the billions of men and women living and working in the Organization. He looked at the typewriter. He could shape their lives, change their thoughts, disorganize the Organization. Was this wise? Or right? Or even amusing?

Luke sighed. In his mind's eye he saw himself standing on a high terrace overlooking the city. Luke Grogatch, Chairman of the Board. Not impossible, quite feasible. A little at a time, the correct interpolations…Luke Grogatch, Chairman of the Board. Yes. This for a starter. But it was necessary to move cautiously, with great delicacy…

Luke seated himself at the typewriter and began to pick out his first interpolation.

THE MOON MOTH

THE HOUSEBOAT HAD BEEN BUILT to the most exacting standards of Sirenese craftsmanship, which is to say, as close to the absolute as human eye could detect. The planking of waxy dark wood showed no joints, the fastenings were platinum rivets countersunk and polished flat. In style, the boat was massive, broad-beamed, steady as the shore itself, without ponderosity or slackness of line. The bow bulged like a swan's breast, the stem rising high, then crooking forward to support an iron lantern. The doors were carved from slabs of a mottled black-green wood; the windows were many-sectioned, paned with squares of mica, stained rose, blue, pale green and violet. The bow was given to service facilities and quarters for the slaves; amidships were a pair of sleeping cabins, a dining saloon and a parlor saloon, opening upon an observation deck at the stern.

Such was Edwer Thissell's houseboat, but ownership brought him neither pleasure nor pride. The houseboat had become shabby. The carpeting had lost its pile; the carved screens were chipped; the iron lantern at the bow sagged with rust. Seventy years ago the first owner, on accepting the boat, had honored the builder and had been likewise honored; the transaction (for the process represented a great deal more than simple giving and taking) had augmented the prestige of both. That time was far gone; the houseboat now commanded no prestige whatever. Edwer Thissell, resident on Sirene only three months, recognized the lack but could do nothing about it: this particular houseboat was the best he could get. He sat on the rear deck practising the *ganga*, a zither-like instrument not much larger than his hand. A hundred yards inshore, surf defined a strip of white beach; beyond rose jungle, with the silhouette of craggy black hills against the sky. Mireille shone hazy and white overhead, as if through a tangle of spider-web; the face of the ocean pooled and puddled with mother-of-pearl luster. The scene had become as familiar, though not as boring, as the *ganga*, at which he had worked two hours, twanging out the Sirenese scales, forming chords, traversing simple progressions. Now he put down the *ganga* for the *zachinko*, this a small sound-box studded with keys, played with the right hand. Pressure on the keys forced air through reeds in the keys themselves, producing a concertina-like tone. Thissell ran off a dozen quick scales, making very few mistakes. Of the six instruments he had set himself to learn, the *zachinko* had proved the least refractory (with the exception, of course, of the *hymerkin*, that clacking, slapping, clattering device of wood and stone used exclusively with the slaves).

Thissell practised another ten minutes, then put aside the *zachinko*. He flexed his arms, wrung his aching fingers. Every waking moment since his arrival had been given to the instruments: the *hymerkin*, the *ganga*, the *zachinko*, the *kiv*, the *strapan*, the *gomapard*. He had practised scales in nineteen keys and four modes, chords without number, intervals never imagined on the Home Planets. Trills, arpeggios, slurs, click-stops and nasalization; damping and augmentation of overtones; vibratos and wolf-tones; concavities and convexities. He practised with a dogged, deadly diligence, in which his original concept of music as a source of pleasure had long become lost. Looking over the instruments Thissell resisted an urge to fling all six into the Titanic.

He rose to his feet, went forward through the parlor saloon, the dining-saloon, along a corridor past the galley and came out on the fore-deck. He bent over the rail, peered down into the underwater pens where Toby and Rex, the slaves, were harnessing the dray-fish for the weekly trip to Fan, eight miles north. The youngest fish, either playful or captious, ducked and plunged. Its streaming black muzzle broke water, and Thissell, looking into its face felt a peculiar qualm: the fish wore no mask!

Thissell laughed uneasily, fingering his own mask, the Moon Moth. No question about it, he was becoming acclimated to Sirene! A significant stage had been reached when the naked face of a fish caused him shock!

The fish were finally harnessed; Toby and Rex climbed aboard, red bodies glistening, black cloth masks clinging to their faces. Ignoring Thissell they stowed the pen, hoisted anchor. The dray-fish strained, the harness tautened, the houseboat moved north.

Returning to the after-deck, Thissell took up the *strapan* — this a circular sound-box eight inches in diameter. Forty-six wires radiated from a central hub to the circumference where they connected to either a bell or a tinkle-bar. When plucked, the bells rang, the bars chimed; when strummed, the instrument gave off a twanging, jingling sound. When played with competence, the pleasantly acid dissonances produced an expressive effect; in an unskilled hand, the results were less felicitous, and might even approach random noise. The *strapan* was Thissell's weakest instrument and he practised with concentration during the entire trip north.

In due course the houseboat approached the floating city. The dray-fish were curbed, the houseboat warped to a mooring. Along the dock a line of idlers weighed and gauged every aspect of the houseboat, the slaves and Thissell himself, according to Sirenese habit. Thissell, not yet accustomed to such penetrating inspection, found the scrutiny unsettling, all the more so for the immobility of the masks. Self-consciously adjusting his own Moon Moth, he climbed the ladder to the dock.

A slave rose from where he had been squatting, touched knuckles to the black cloth at his forehead, and sang on a three-tone phrase of interrogation: "The Moon Moth before me possibly expresses the identity of Ser Edwer Thissell?"

Thissell tapped the *hymerkin* which hung at his belt and sang: "I am Ser Thissell."

"I have been honored by a trust," sang the slave. "Three days from dawn to dusk I have waited on the dock; three nights from dusk to dawn I have crouched on a raft below this same dock listening to the feet of the Night-men. At last I behold the mask of Ser Thissell."

Thissell evoked an impatient clatter from the *hymerkin*. "What is the nature of this trust?"

"I carry a message, Ser Thissell. It is intended for you."

Thissell held out his left hand, playing the *hymerkin* with his right. "Give me the message."

"Instantly, Ser Thissell."

The message bore a heavy superscription:

EMERGENCY COMMUNICATION!
RUSH!

Thissell ripped open the envelope. The message was signed by Castel Cromartin, Chief Executive of the Interworld Policies Board, and after the formal salutation read:

> **ABSOLUTELY URGENT** the following orders be
> executed! Aboard *Carina Cruzeiro*, destination Fan,
> date of arrival January 10 U.T., is notorious assassin,
> Haxo Angmark. Meet landing with adequate
> authority, effect detention and incarceration of
> this man. These instructions must be successfully
> implemented. Failure is unacceptable.
> **ATTENTION!** Haxo Angmark is superlatively
> dangerous. Kill him without hesitation at any show of
> resistance.

Thissell considered the message with dismay. In coming to Fan as Consular Representative he had expected nothing like this; he felt neither inclination nor competence in the matter of dealing with dangerous assassins. Thoughtfully he rubbed the fuzzy gray cheek of his mask. The situation was not completely dark; Esteban Rolver, Director of the Space-Port, would doubtless cooperate, and perhaps furnish a platoon of slaves.

More hopefully, Thissell reread the message. January 10, Universal Time. He consulted a conversion calendar. Today, 40th in the Season of Bitter Nectar — Thissell ran his finger down the column, stopped. January 10. Today.

A distant rumble caught his attention. Dropping from the mist came a dull shape: the lighter returning from contact with the *Carina Cruzeiro*.

Thissell once more re-read the note, raised his head, studied the descending lighter. Aboard would be Haxo Angmark. In five minutes he would emerge upon the soil of Sirene. Landing formalities would detain him possibly twenty minutes. The landing field lay a mile and a half distant, joined to Fan by a winding path through the hills.

Thissell turned to the slave. "When did this message arrive?"

The slave leaned forward uncomprehendingly. Thissell reiterated his question, singing to the clack of the *hymerkin*: "This message: you have enjoyed the honor of its custody how long?"

The slave sang: "Long days have I waited on the wharf, retreating only to the raft at the onset of dusk. Now my vigil is rewarded; I behold Ser Thissell."

Thissell turned away, walked furiously up the dock. Ineffective, inefficient Sirenese! Why had they not delivered the message to his houseboat? Twenty-five minutes — twenty-two now...

At the esplanade Thissell stopped, looked right, left, hoping for a miracle: some sort of air-transport to whisk him to the space-port, where with Rolver's aid, Haxo Angmark might still be detained. Or better yet, a second message canceling the first. Something, anything... But air-cars were not to be found on Sirene, and no second message appeared.

Across the esplanade rose a meager row of permanent structures, built of stone and iron and so proof against the efforts of the Nightmen. A hostler occupied one of these structures, and as Thissell watched a man in a splendid pearl and silver mask emerged riding one of the lizard-like mounts of Sirene.

Thissell sprang forward. There was still time; with luck he might yet intercept Haxo Angmark. He hurried across the esplanade.

Before the line of stalls stood the hostler, inspecting his stock with solicitude, occasionally burnishing a scale or whisking away an insect. There were five of the beasts in prime condition, each as tall as a man's shoulder, with massive legs, thick bodies, heavy wedge-shaped heads. From their fore-fangs, which had been artificially lengthened and curved into near-circles, gold rings depended. Their scales had been stained in diaper-pattern: purple and green, orange and black, red and blue, brown and pink, yellow and silver.

Thissell came to a breathless halt in front of the hostler. He reached for his *kiv**, then hesitated. Could this be considered a casual personal encounter? The *zachinko* perhaps? But the statement of his needs hardly seemed to demand the formal approach. Better the *kiv* after all. He struck a chord, but by error found himself stroking the *ganga*. Beneath his mask Thissell grinned apologetically; his relationship with this hostler was by no means on an intimate basis. He hoped that the hostler was of sanguine disposition, and in any event the urgency of the occasion allowed no time to select an exactly appropriate instrument. He struck a second chord, and playing as well as agitation, breathlessness and lack of skill allowed, sang out a request: "Ser Hostler, I have immediate need of a swift mount. Allow me to select from your herd."

The hostler wore a mask of considerable complexity which Thissell could not identify: a construction of varnished brown cloth, pleated gray leather and high on the forehead two large green and scarlet globes, minutely segmented like insect eyes. He inspected Thissell a long moment, then, rather ostentatiously selecting his *stimic*†, executed a brilliant progression of trills and rounds, of an import Thissell failed to grasp. The hostler sang, "Ser Moon Moth, I fear that my steeds are unsuitable to a person of your distinction."

Thissell earnestly twanged at the *ganga*. "By no means: they all seem adequate. I am in great haste and will gladly accept any of the group."

The hostler played a brittle cascading crescendo. "Ser Moon Moth," he sang, "the steeds are ill and dirty. I am flattered that you consider them adequate to your use. I cannot accept the merit you offer me. And —" here, switching instruments, he struck a cool tinkle from his *krodatch*‡ "— somehow I fail to recognize the boon

---

* *Kiv*: five banks of resilient metal strips, fourteen to the bank, played by touching, twisting, twanging.

† *Stimic*: three flute-like tubes equipped with plungers. Thumb and forefinger squeeze a bag to force air across the mouth-pieces; the second, third and fourth little fingers manipulate the slide. The *stimic* is an instrument well-adapted to the sentiments of cool withdrawal, or even disapproval.

‡ *Krodatch*: a small square sound-box strung with resined gut. The musician scratches the strings with his fingernail, or strokes them with his fingertips, to produce a variety of quietly formal sounds. The *krodatch* is also used as an instrument of insult.

companion and co-craftsman who accosts me so familiarly with his *ganga*."

The implication was clear. Thissell would receive no mount. He turned, set off at a run for the landing field. Behind him sounded a clatter of the hostler's *hymerkin* — whether directed toward the hostler's slaves, or toward himself Thissell did not pause to learn.

The previous Consular Representative of the Home Planets on Sirene had been killed at Zundar. Masked as a Tavern Bravo he had accosted a girl beribboned for the Equinoctial Attitudes, a solecism for which he had been instantly beheaded by a Red Demiurge, a Sun Sprite and a Magic Hornet. Edwer Thissell, recently graduated from the Institute, had been named his successor, and allowed three days to prepare himself. Normally of a contemplative, even cautious disposition, Thissell had regarded the appointment as a challenge. He learned the Sirenese language by sub-cerebral techniques, and found it uncomplicated. Then, in the Journal of Universal Anthropology, he read:

> The population of the Titanic littoral is highly individualistic, possibly in response to a bountiful environment which puts no premium upon group activity. The language, reflecting this trait, expresses the individual's mood, his emotional attitude toward a given situation. Factual information is regarded as a secondary concomitant. Moreover, the language is sung, characteristically to the accompaniment of a small instrument. As a result, there is great difficulty in ascertaining fact from a native of Fan, or the forbidden city Zundar. One will be regaled with elegant arias and demonstrations of astonishing virtuosity upon one or another of the numerous musical instruments. The visitor to this fascinating world, unless he cares to be treated with the most consummate contempt, must therefore learn to express himself after the approved local fashion.

Thissell made a note in his memorandum book: *Procure small musical instrument, together with directions as to use.* He read on.

There is everywhere and at all times a plenitude, not to say, a superfluity, of food, and the climate is benign. With a fund of racial energy and a great deal of leisure time, the population occupies itself with intricacy. Intricacy in all things: intricate craftsmanship, such as the carved panels which adorn the houseboats; intricate symbolism, as exemplified in the masks worn by everyone; the intricate half-musical language which admirably expresses subtle moods and emotions, and above all the fantastic intricacy of inter-personal relationships. Prestige, face, *mana*, repute, glory: the Sirenese word is *strakh*. Every man has his characteristic *strakh*, which determines whether, when he needs a houseboat, he will be urged to avail himself of a floating palace, rich with gems, alabaster lanterns, peacock faience and carved wood, or grudgingly permitted an abandoned shack on a raft. There is no medium of exchange on Sirene; the single and sole currency is *strakh*...

Thissell rubbed his chin and read further.

Masks are worn at all times, in accordance with the philosophy that a man should not be compelled to use a similitude foisted upon him by factors beyond his control; that he should be at liberty to choose that semblance most consonant with his *strakh*. In the civilized areas of Sirene — which is to say the Titanic littoral — a man literally never shows his face; it is his basic secret.

Gambling, by this token, is unknown on Sirene; it would be catastrophic to Sirenese self-respect to gain advantage by means other than the exercise of *strakh*. The word 'luck' has no counterpart in the Sirenese language.

Thissell made another note: *Get mask. Museum? Drama guild?*

He finished the article, hastened forth to complete his preparations, and the next day embarked aboard the *Robert Astroguard* for the first leg of the passage to Sirene.

✳

The lighter settled upon the Sirenese space-port, a topaz disk isolated among the black, green and purple hills. The lighter grounded, and Edwer Thissell stepped forth. He was met by Esteban Rolver, the local agent for Spaceways. Rolver threw up his hands, stepped back. "Your mask," he cried huskily. "Where is your mask?"

Thissell held it up rather self-consciously. "I wasn't sure —"

"Put it on," said Rolver, turning away. He himself wore a fabrication of dull green scales, blue-lacquered wood. Black quills protruded at the cheeks, and under his chin hung a black and white checked pom-pom, the total effect creating a sense of sardonic supple personality.

Thissell adjusted the mask to his face, undecided whether to make a joke about the situation or to maintain a reserve suitable to the dignity of his post.

"Are you masked?" Rolver inquired over his shoulder.

Thissell replied in the affirmative and Rolver turned. The mask hid the expression of his face, but his hand unconsciously flicked a set of keys strapped to his thigh. The instrument sounded a trill of shock and polite consternation. "You can't wear that mask!" sang Rolver. "In fact — how, where, did you get it?"

"It's copied from a mask owned by the Polypolis museum," declared Thissell stiffly. "I'm sure it's authentic."

Rolver nodded, his own mask more sardonic-seeming than ever. "It's authentic enough. It's a variant of the type known as the Sea-Dragon Conqueror, and is worn on ceremonial occasions by persons of enormous prestige: princes, heroes, master craftsmen, great musicians."

"I wasn't aware —"

Rolver made a gesture of languid understanding. "It's something you'll learn in due course. Notice my mask. Today I'm wearing a Tarn Bird. Persons of minimal prestige — such as you, I, any other out-worlder — wear this sort of thing."

"Odd," said Thissell, as they started across the field toward a low concrete blockhouse. "I assumed that a person wore whatever he liked."

"Certainly," said Rolver. "Wear any mask you like — if you can make it stick. This Tarn Bird for instance. I wear it to indicate that I presume nothing. I make no claims to wisdom, ferocity, versatility, musicianship, truculence, or any of a dozen other Sirenese virtues."

"For the sake of argument," said Thissell, "what would happen if I walked through the streets of Zundar in this mask?"

Rolver laughed, a muffled sound behind his mask. "If you walked along the docks of Zundar — there are no streets — in any mask, you'd be killed within the hour. That's what happened to Benko, your predecessor. He didn't know how to act. None of us out-worlders know how to act. In Fan we're tolerated — so long as we keep our place. But you couldn't even walk around Fan in that regalia you're sporting now. Somebody wearing a Fire Snake or a Thunder Goblin — masks, you understand — would step up to you. He'd play his *krodatch*, and if you failed to challenge his audacity with a passage on the *skaranyi**, a devilish instrument, he'd play his *hymerkin* — the instrument we use with the slaves. That's the ultimate expression of contempt. Or he might ring his dueling-gong and attack you then and there."

"I had no idea that people here were quite so irascible," said Thissell in a subdued voice.

Rolver shrugged and swung open the massive steel door into his office. "Certain acts may not be committed on the Concourse at Polypolis without incurring criticism."

"Yes, that's quite true," said Thissell. He looked around the office. "Why the security? The concrete, the steel?"

"Protection against the savages," said Rolver. "They come down from the mountains at night, steal what's available, kill anyone they find ashore." He went to a closet, brought forth a mask. "Here. Use this Moon Moth; it won't get you in trouble."

Thissell unenthusiastically inspected the mask. It was constructed of mouse-colored fur; there was a tuft of hair at each side of the mouth-hole, a pair of feather-like antennae at the forehead. White lace flaps dangled beside the temples and under the eyes hung a series of red folds, creating an effect at once lugubrious and comic.

Thissell asked, "Does this mask signify any degree of prestige?"

"Not a great deal."

"After all, I'm Consular Representative," said Thissell. "I represent the Home Planets, a hundred billion people —"

---

* *Skaranyi*: a miniature bag-pipe, the sac squeezed between thumb and palm, the four fingers controlling the stops along four tubes.

"If the Home Planets want their representative to wear a Sea-Dragon Conqueror mask, they'd better send out a Sea-Dragon Conqueror type of man."

"I see," said Thissell in a subdued voice. "Well, if I must..."

Rolver politely averted his gaze while Thissell doffed the Sea-Dragon Conqueror and slipped the more modest Moon Moth over his head. "I suppose I can find something just a bit more suitable in one of the shops," Thissell said. "I'm told a person simply goes in and takes what he needs, correct?"

Rolver surveyed Thissell critically. "That mask — temporarily, at least — is perfectly suitable. And it's rather important not to take anything from the shops until you know the *strakh* value of the article you want. The owner loses prestige if a person of low *strakh* makes free with his best work."

Thissell shook his head in exasperation. "Nothing of this was explained to me! I knew of the masks, of course, and the painstaking integrity of the craftsmen, but this insistence on prestige — *strakh*, whatever the word is..."

"No matter," said Rolver. "After a year or two you'll begin to learn your way around. I suppose you speak the language?"

"Oh, indeed. Certainly."

"And what instruments do you play?"

"Well — I was given to understand that any small instrument was adequate, or that I could merely sing."

"Very inaccurate. Only slaves sing without accompaniment. I suggest that you learn the following instruments as quickly as possible: the *hymerkin* for your slaves. The *ganga* for conversation between intimates or one a trifle lower than yourself in *strakh*. The *kiv* for casual polite intercourse. The *zachinko* for more formal dealings. The *strapan* or the *krodatch* for your social inferiors — in your case, should you wish to insult someone. The *gomapard** or the *double-kamanthil†* for

---

* *Gomapard*: one of the few electric instruments used on Sirene. An oscillator produces an oboe-like tone which is modulated, choked, vibrated, raised and lowered in pitch by four keys.

† *Double-kamanthil*: an instrument similar to the *ganga*, except the tones are produced by twisting and inclining a disk of resined leather against one or more of the forty-six strings.

ceremonials." He considered a moment. "The *crebarin*, the water-lute and the *slobo* are highly useful also — but perhaps you'd better learn the other instruments first. They should provide at least a rudimentary means of communication."

"Aren't you exaggerating?" suggested Thissell. "Or joking?"

Rolver laughed his saturnine laugh. "Not at all. First of all, you'll need a houseboat. And then you'll want slaves."

Rolver took Thissell from the landing field to the docks of Fan, a walk of an hour and a half along a pleasant path under enormous trees loaded with fruit, cereal pods, sacs of sugary sap.

"At the moment," said Rolver, "there are only four out-worlders in Fan, counting yourself. I'll take you to Welibus, our Commercial Factor. I think he's got an old houseboat he might let you use."

Cornely Welibus had resided fifteen years in Fan, acquiring sufficient *strakh* to wear his South Wind mask with authority. This consisted of a blue disk inlaid with cabochons of lapis-lazuli, surrounded by an aureole of shimmering snake-skin. Heartier and more cordial than Rolver, he not only provided Thissell with a houseboat, but also a score of various musical instruments and a pair of slaves.

Embarrassed by the largesse, Thissell stammered something about payment, but Welibus cut him off with an expansive gesture. "My dear fellow, this is Sirene. Such trifles cost nothing."

"But a houseboat —"

Welibus played a courtly little flourish on his *kiv*. "I'll be frank, Ser Thissell. The boat is old and a trifle shabby. I can't afford to use it; my status would suffer." A graceful melody accompanied his words. "Status as yet need not concern you. You require merely shelter, comfort and safety from the Night-men."

"'Night-men'?"

"The cannibals who roam the shore after dark."

"Oh yes. Ser Rolver mentioned them."

"Horrible things. We won't discuss them." A shuddering little trill issued from his *kiv*. "Now, as to slaves." He tapped the blue disk of his mask with a thoughtful forefinger. "Rex and Toby should serve you well." He raised his voice, played a swift clatter on the hymerkin. *"Avan esx trobu!"*

A female slave appeared wearing a dozen tight bands of pink cloth, and a dainty black mask sparkling with mother-of-pearl sequins.

"Fascu etz Rex ae Toby."

Rex and Toby appeared, wearing loose masks of black cloth, russet jerkins. Welibus addressed them with a resonant clatter of *hymerkin*, enjoining them to the service of their new master, on pain of return to their native islands. They prostrated themselves, sang pledges of servitude to Thissell in soft husky voices. Thissell laughed nervously and essayed a sentence in the Sirenese language. "Go to the houseboat, clean it well, bring aboard food."

Toby and Rex stared blankly through the holes in their masks. Welibus repeated the orders with *hymerkin* accompaniment. The slaves bowed and departed.

Thissell surveyed the musical instruments with dismay. "I haven't the slightest idea how to go about learning these things."

Welibus turned to Rolver. "What about Kershaul? Could he be persuaded to give Ser Thissell some basic instruction?"

Rolver nodded judicially. "Kershaul might undertake the job."

Thissell asked, "Who is Kershaul?"

"The fourth of our little group of expatriates," replied Welibus, "an anthropologist. You've read *Zundar the Splendid*? *Rituals of Sirene*? *The Faceless Folk*? No? A pity. All excellent works. Kershaul is high in prestige, and I believe visits Zundar from time to time. Wears a Cave Owl, sometimes a Star Wanderer or even a Wise Arbiter."

"He's taken to an Equatorial Serpent," said Rolver. "The variant with the gilt tusks."

"Indeed!" marveled Welibus. "Well, I must say he's earned it. A fine fellow, good chap indeed." And he strummed his *zachinko* thoughtfully.

Three months passed. Under the tutelage of Mathew Kershaul, Thissell practised the *hymerkin*, the *ganga*, the *strapan*, the *kiv*, the *gomapard*, and the *zachinko*. The *double-kamanthil*, the *krodatch*, the *slobo*, the water-lute and a number of others could wait, said Kershaul, until Thissell had mastered the six basic instruments. He lent Thissell recordings of noteworthy Sirenese conversing in various moods and to various accompaniments, so that Thissell might learn the melodic conventions currently in vogue, and perfect himself in the niceties of intonation, the various rhythms, cross-rhythms, compound rhythms, implied rhythms and suppressed rhythms. Kershaul professed to find Sirenese music a fascinating study, and Thissell admitted that it was a subject not readily exhausted. The quarter-tone tuning of the instruments admitted the use of twenty-four tonalities which, multiplied by the five modes in general use, resulted in one hundred and twenty separate scales. Kershaul, however, advised that Thissell primarily concentrate on learning each instrument in its fundamental tonality, using only two of the modes.

With no immediate business at Fan except the weekly visits to Mathew Kershaul, Thissell took his houseboat eight miles south and moored it in the lee of a rocky promontory. Here, if it had not been for the incessant practising, Thissell lived an idyllic life. The sea was calm and crystal-clear; the beach, ringed by the gray, green and purple foliage of the forest, lay close at hand if he wanted to stretch his legs.

Toby and Rex occupied a pair of cubicles forward, Thissell had the after-cabins to himself. From time to time he toyed with the idea of a third slave, possibly a young female, to contribute an element of charm and gaiety to the menage, but Kershaul advised against the step, fearing that the intensity of Thissell's concentration might somehow be diminished. Thissell acquiesced and devoted himself to the study of the six instruments.

The days passed quickly. Thissell never became bored with the pageantry of dawn and sunset; the white clouds and blue sea of noon; the night sky blazing with the twenty-nine stars of Cluster SI 1-715. The weekly trip to Fan broke the tedium, Toby and Rex foraged for food; Thissell visited the luxurious houseboat of Mathew Kershaul for instruction and advice. Then, three months after Thissell's arrival, came the message completely disorganizing the routine: Haxo Angmark, assassin, *agent provocateur*, ruthless and crafty criminal, had come to Sirene. *Effect detention and incarceration of this man!* read the orders. *Attention! Haxo Angmark is superlatively dangerous. Kill without hesitation!*

Thissell was not in the best of condition. He trotted fifty yards until his breath came in gasps, then walked: through low hills crowned with white bamboo and black tree-ferns; across meadows yellow with grass-nuts, through orchards and wild vineyards. Twenty minutes passed, twenty-five minutes passed, twenty-five minutes; with a heavy sensation in his stomach Thissell knew that he was too late. Haxo Angmark had landed, and might be traversing this very road toward Fan. But along the way Thissell met only four persons: a boy-child in a mock-fierce Alk Islander mask; two young women wearing the Red Bird and the Green Bird; a man masked as a Forest Goblin. Coming upon the man, Thissell stopped short. Could this be Angmark?

Thissell essayed a stratagem. He went boldly to the man, stared into the hideous mask. "Angmark," he called in the language of the Home Planets, "you are under arrest!"

The Forest Goblin stared uncomprehendingly, then started forward along the track.

Thissell put himself in the way. He reached for his *ganga*, then recalling the hostler's reaction, instead struck a chord on the *zachinko*. "You travel the road from the space-port," he sang. "What have you seen there?"

The Forest Goblin grasped his hand-bugle, an instrument used to deride opponents on the field of battle, to summon animals, or occasionally to evince a rough and ready truculence. "Where I travel and what I see are the concern solely of myself. Stand back or I walk upon your face." He marched forward, and had not Thissell leapt aside the Forest Goblin might well have made good his threat.

Thissell stood gazing after the retreating back. Angmark? Not likely, with so sure a touch on the hand-bugle. Thissell hesitated, then turned and continued on his way.

Arriving at the space-port, he went directly to the office. The heavy door stood ajar; as Thissell approached, a man appeared in the doorway. He wore a mask of dull green scales, mica plates, blue-lacquered wood and black quills — the Tarn Bird.

"Ser Rolver," Thissell called out anxiously, "who came down from the *Carina Cruzeiro*?"

Rolver studied Thissell a long moment. "Why do you ask?"

"Why do I ask?" demanded Thissell. "You must have seen the space-gram I received from Castel Cromartin!"

"Oh yes," said Rolver. "Of course. Naturally."

"It was delivered only half an hour ago," said Thissell bitterly. "I rushed out as fast as I could. Where is Angmark?"

"In Fan, I assume," said Rolver.

Thissell cursed softly. "Why didn't you hold him up, delay him in some way?"

Rolver shrugged. "I had neither authority, inclination nor the capability to stop him."

Thissell fought back his annoyance. In a voice of studied calm he said, "On the way I passed a man in rather a ghastly mask — saucer eyes, red wattles."

"A Forest Goblin," said Rolver. "Angmark brought the mask with him."

"But he played the hand-bugle," Thissell protested. "How could Angmark —"

"He's well-acquainted with Sirene; he spent five years here in Fan."

Thissell grunted in annoyance. "Cromartin made no mention of this."

"It's common knowledge," said Rolver with a shrug. "He was Commercial Representative before Welibus took over."

"Were he and Welibus acquainted?"

Rolver laughed shortly. "Naturally. But don't suspect poor Welibus of anything more venal than juggling his accounts; I assure you he's no consort of assassins."

"Speaking of assassins," said Thissell, "do you have a weapon I might borrow?"

Rolver inspected him in wonder. "You came out here to take Angmark bare-handed?"

"I had no choice," said Thissell. "When Cromartin gives orders he expects results. In any event you were here with your slaves."

"Don't count on me for help," Rolver said testily. "I wear the Tarn Bird and make no pretensions of valor. But I can lend you a power pistol. I haven't used it recently; I won't guarantee its charge."

Rolver went into the office and a moment later returned with the gun. "What will you do now?"

Thissell shook his head wearily. "I'll try to find Angmark in Fan. Or might he head for Zundar?"

Rolver considered. "Angmark might be able to survive in Zundar. But he'd want to brush up on his musicianship. I imagine he'll stay in Fan a few days."

"But how can I find him? Where should I look?"

"That I can't say," replied Rolver. "You might be safer not finding him. Angmark is a dangerous man."

Thissell returned to Fan the way he had come.

Where the path swung down from the hills into the esplanade a thick-walled *pisé-de-terre* building had been constructed. The door was carved from a solid black plank; the windows were guarded by enfoliated bands of iron. This was the office of Cornely Welibus, Commercial Factor, Importer and Exporter. Thissell found Welibus sitting at his ease on the tiled verandah, wearing a modest adaptation of the Waldemar mask. He seemed lost in thought and might or might not have recognized Thissell's Moon Moth; in any event he gave no signal of greeting.

Thissell approached the porch. "Good morning, Ser Welibus."

Welibus nodded abstractedly and said in a flat voice, plucking at his *krodatch*, "Good morning."

Thissell was rather taken aback. This was hardly the instrument to use toward a friend and fellow out-worlder, even if he did wear the Moon Moth.

Thissell said coldly, "May I ask how long you have been sitting here?"

Welibus considered half a minute, and now when he spoke he accompanied himself on the more cordial *crebarin*. But the recollection of the *krodatch* chord still rankled in Thissell's mind.

"I've been here fifteen or twenty minutes. Why do you ask?"

"I wonder if you noticed a Forest Goblin pass?"

Welibus nodded. "He went on down the esplanade — turned into that first mask shop, I believe."

Thissell hissed between his teeth. This would naturally be Angmark's first move. "I'll never find him once he changes masks," he muttered.

"Who is this Forest Goblin?" asked Welibus, with no more than casual interest.

Thissell could see no reason to conceal the name. "A notorious criminal: Haxo Angmark."

"Haxo Angmark!" croaked Welibus, leaning back in his chair. "You're sure he's here?"

"Reasonably sure."

Welibus rubbed his shaking hands together. "This is bad news — bad news indeed! He's an unscrupulous scoundrel."

"You knew him well?"

"As well as anyone." Welibus was now accompanying himself with the *kiv*. "He held the post I now occupy. I came out as an inspector and found that he was embezzling some four thousand UMIs a month. I'm sure he feels no great gratitude toward me." Welibus glanced nervously up the esplanade. "I hope you catch him."

"I'm doing my best. He went into the mask shop, you say?"

"I'm sure of it."

Thissell turned away. As he went down the path he heard the black plank door thud shut behind him.

He walked down the esplanade to the mask-maker's shop, paused outside as if admiring the display: a hundred miniature masks, carved from rare woods and minerals, dressed with emerald flakes, spider-web silk, wasp wings, petrified fish scales and the like. The shop was empty except for the mask-maker, a gnarled knotty man in a yellow robe, wearing a deceptively simple Universal Expert mask, fabricated from over two thousand bits of articulated wood.

Thissell considered what he would say, how he would accompany himself, then entered. The mask-maker, noting the Moon Moth and Thissell's diffident manner, continued with his work.

Thissell, selecting the easiest of his instruments, stroked his *strapan* — possibly not the most felicitous choice, for it conveyed a certain degree of condescension. Thissell tried to counteract this flavor by singing in warm, almost effusive, tones, shaking the *strapan* whimsically when he struck a wrong note: "A stranger is an interesting person to deal with; his habits are unfamiliar, he excites curiosity. Not twenty minutes ago a stranger entered this fascinating shop, to exchange his drab Forest Goblin for one of the remarkable and adventurous creations assembled on the premises."

The mask-maker turned Thissell a side glance, and without words he played a progression of chords on an instrument Thissell had never seen before: a flexible sac gripped in the palm with three short tubes leading between the fingers. When the tubes were squeezed almost shut and air forced through the slit, an oboe-like tone ensued. To Thissell's developing ear the instrument seemed difficult, the mask-maker expert, and the music conveyed a profound sense of disinterest.

Thissell tried again, laboriously manipulating the *strapan*. He sang, "To an out-worlder on a foreign planet, the voice of one from his home is like water to a wilting plant. A person who could unite two such persons might find satisfaction in such an act of mercy."

The mask-maker casually fingered his own *strapan*, and drew forth a set of rippling scales, his fingers moving faster than the eyes could follow. He sang in the formal style: "An artist values his moments of concentration; he does not care to spend time exchanging banalities with persons of at best average prestige." Thissell attempted to insert a counter melody, but the mask-maker struck a new set of complex chords whose portent evaded Thissell's understanding, and continued: "Into the shop comes a person who evidently has picked up for the first time an instrument of unparalleled complication, for the execution of his music is open to criticism. He sings of home-sickness and longing for the sight of others like himself. He dissembles his enormous *strakh* behind a Moon Moth, for he plays the *strapan* to a Master Craftsman, and sings in a voice of contemptuous raillery. The refined and creative artist ignores the provocation. He plays a polite instrument, remains noncommittal, and trusts that the stranger will tire of his sport and depart."

Thissell took up his *kiv*. "The noble mask-maker completely misunderstands me —"

He was interrupted by staccato rasping of the mask-maker's *strapan*. "The stranger now sees fit to ridicule the artist's comprehension."

Thissell scratched furiously at his *strapan*: "To protect myself from the heat, I wander into a small and unpretentious mask-shop. The artisan, though still distracted by the novelty of his tools, gives promise of development. He works zealously to perfect his skill, so much so that he refuses to converse with strangers, no matter what their need."

The mask-maker carefully laid down his carving tool. He rose to his feet, went behind a screen, and shortly returned wearing a mask of gold and iron, with simulated flames licking up from the scalp. In one hand he carried a *skaranyi*, in the other a scimitar. He struck off a brilliant series of wild tones, and sang: "Even the most accomplished artist can augment his *strakh* by killing sea-monsters, Night-men and importunate idlers. Such an occasion is at hand. The artist delays his attack exactly ten seconds, because the offender wears a Moon Moth." He twirled his scimitar, spun it in the air.

Thissell desperately pounded the *strapan*. "Did a Forest Goblin enter the shop? Did he depart with a new mask?"

"Five seconds have elapsed," sang the mask-maker in steady ominous rhythm.

Thissell departed in frustrated rage. He crossed the square, stood looking up and down the esplanade. Hundreds of men and women sauntered along the docks, or stood on the decks of their houseboats, each wearing a mask chosen to express his mood, prestige and special attributes, and everywhere sounded the twitter of musical instruments.

Thissell stood at a loss. The Forest Goblin had disappeared. Haxo Angmark walked at liberty in Fan, and Thissell had failed the urgent instructions of Castel Cromartin.

Behind him sounded the casual notes of a *kiv*. "Ser Moon Moth Thissell, you stand engrossed in thought."

Thissell turned, to find beside him a Cave Owl, in a somber cloak of black and gray. Thissell recognized the mask, which symbolized erudition and patient exploration of abstract ideas; Mathew Kershaul had worn it on the occasion of their meeting a week before.

"Good morning, Ser Kershaul," muttered Thissell.

"And how are the studies coming? Have you mastered the C-Sharp Plus scale on the *gomapard*? As I recall, you were finding those inverse intervals puzzling."

"I've worked on them," said Thissell in a gloomy voice. "However, since I'll probably be recalled to Polypolis, it may be all time wasted."

"Eh? What's this?"

Thissell explained the situation in regard to Haxo Angmark. Kershaul nodded gravely. "I recall Angmark. Not a gracious personality, but an excellent musician, with quick fingers and a real talent for new instruments." Thoughtfully he twisted the goatee of his Cave Owl mask. "What are your plans?"

"They're non-existent," said Thissell, playing a doleful phrase on the *kiv*. "I haven't any idea what masks he'll be wearing, and if I don't know what he looks like, how can I find him?"

Kershaul tugged at his goatee. "In the old days he favored the Exo Cambian Cycle, and I believe he used an entire set of Nether Denizens. Now of course his tastes may have changed."

"Exactly," Thissell complained. "He might be twenty feet away and I'd never know it." He glanced bitterly across the esplanade toward the mask-maker's shop. "No one will tell me anything. I doubt if they care that a murderer is walking their docks."

"Quite correct," Kershaul agreed. "Sirenese standards are different from ours."

"They have no sense of responsibility," declared Thissell. "I doubt if they'd throw a rope to a drowning man."

"It's true that they dislike interference," Kershaul agreed. "They emphasize individual responsibility and self-sufficiency."

"Interesting," said Thissell, "but I'm still in the dark about Angmark."

Kershaul surveyed him gravely. "And should you locate Angmark, what will you do then?"

"I'll carry out the orders of my superior," said Thissell doggedly.

"Angmark is a dangerous man," mused Kershaul. "He's got a number of advantages over you."

"I can't take that into account. It's my duty to send him back to Polypolis. He's probably safe, since I haven't the remotest idea how to find him."

Kershaul reflected. "An out-worlder can't hide behind a mask, not from the Sirenese at least. There are four of us here at Fan — Rolver, Welibus, you and me. If another out-worlder tries to set up housekeeping the news will get around in short order."

"What if he heads for Zundar?"

Kershaul shrugged. "I doubt if he'd dare. On the other hand —" Kershaul paused, then noting Thissell's sudden inattention, turned to follow Thissell's gaze.

A man in a Forest Goblin mask came swaggering toward them along the esplanade. Kershaul laid a restraining hand on Thissell's arm, but Thissell stepped out into the path of the Forest Goblin, his borrowed gun ready. "Haxo Angmark," he cried, "don't make a move, or I'll kill you. You're under arrest."

"Are you sure this is Angmark?" asked Kershaul in a worried voice.

"I'll find out," said Thissell. "Angmark, turn around, hold up your hands."

The Forest Goblin stood rigid with surprise and puzzlement. He reached to his *zachinko*, played an interrogatory arpeggio, and sang, "Why do you molest me, Moon Moth?"

Kershaul stepped forward and played a placatory phrase on his *slobo*. "I fear that a case of confused identity exists, Ser Forest Goblin. Ser Moon Moth seeks an out-worlder in a Forest Goblin mask."

The Forest Goblin's music became irritated, and he suddenly switched to his *stimic*. "He asserts that I am an out-worlder? Let him prove his case, or he has my retaliation to face."

Kershaul glanced in embarrassment around the crowd which had gathered and once more struck up an ingratiating melody. "I am positive that Ser Moon Moth—"

The Forest Goblin interrupted with a fanfare of *skaranyi* tones. "Let him demonstrate his case or prepare for the flow of blood."

Thissell said, "Very well, I'll prove my case." He stepped forward, grasped the Forest Goblin's mask. "Let's see your face, that'll demonstrate your identity!"

The Forest Goblin sprang back in amazement. The crowd gasped, then set up an ominous strumming and toning of various instruments.

The Forest Goblin reached to the nape of his neck, jerked the cord to his duel-gong, and with his other hand snatched forth his scimitar.

Kershaul stepped forward, playing the *slobo* with great agitation. Thissell, now abashed, moved aside, conscious of the ugly sound of the crowd.

Kershaul sang explanations and apologies; the Forest Goblin answered; Kershaul spoke over his shoulder to Thissell: "Run for it, or you'll be killed! Hurry!"

Thissell hesitated; the Forest Goblin put up his hand to thrust Kershaul aside. "Run!" screamed Kershaul. "To Welibus' office, lock yourself in!"

Thissell took to his heels. The Forest Goblin pursued him a few yards, then stamped his feet, sent after him a set of raucous and derisive blasts of the hand-bugle, while the crowd produced a contemptuous counterpoint of clacking *hymerkins*.

There was no further pursuit. Instead of taking refuge in the Import-Export office, Thissell turned aside and after cautious reconnaissance proceeded to the dock where his houseboat was moored.

The hour was not far short of dusk when he finally returned aboard. Toby and Rex squatted on the forward deck, surrounded by the provisions they had brought back: reed baskets of fruit and cereal, blue-glass jugs containing wine, oil and pungent sap, three young pigs in a wicker pen. They were cracking nuts between their teeth, spitting the shells over the side. They looked up at Thissell, and it seemed that they rose to their feet with a new casualness. Toby muttered something under his breath; Rex smothered a chuckle.

Thissell clacked his *hymerkin* angrily. He sang, "Take the boat offshore; tonight we remain at Fan."

In the privacy of his cabin he removed the Moon Moth, stared into a mirror at his almost unfamiliar features. He picked up the Moon Moth, examined the detested lineaments: the furry gray skin, the blue spines, the ridiculous lace flaps. Hardly a dignified presence for the Consular Representative of the Home Planets. If, in fact, he still held the position when Cromartin learned of Angmark's winning free!

Thissell flung himself into a chair, stared moodily into space. Today he'd suffered a series of setbacks, but he wasn't defeated yet; not by any means. Tomorrow he'd visit Mathew Kershaul; they'd discuss how best to locate Angmark. As Kershaul had pointed out, another out-world establishment could not be camouflaged; Haxo Angmark's identity would soon become evident. Also, tomorrow he must procure another mask. Nothing extreme or vainglorious, but a mask which expressed a modicum of dignity and self-respect.

At this moment one of the slaves tapped on the door-panel, and Thissell hastily pulled the hated Moon Moth back over his head.

Early next morning, before the dawn-light had left the sky, the slaves sculled the houseboat back to that section of the dock set aside for the use of out-worlders. Neither Rolver nor Welibus nor Kershaul had yet arrived and Thissell waited impatiently. An hour passed, and Welibus brought his boat to the dock. Not wishing to speak to Welibus, Thissell remained inside his cabin.

A few moments later Rolver's boat likewise pulled in alongside the dock. Through the window Thissell saw Rolver, wearing his usual Tarn Bird, climb to the dock. Here he was met by a man in a yellow-tufted Sand Tiger mask, who played a formal accompaniment on his *gomapard* to whatever message he brought Rolver.

Rolver seemed surprised and disturbed. After a moment's thought he manipulated his own *gomapard*, and as he sang he indicated Thissell's houseboat. Then, bowing, he went on his way.

The man in the Sand Tiger mask climbed with rather heavy dignity to the float and rapped on the bulwark of Thissell's houseboat.

Thissell presented himself. Sirenese etiquette did not demand that he invite a casual visitor aboard, so he merely struck an interrogation on his *zachinko*.

The Sand Tiger played his *gomapard* and sang. "Dawn over the bay of Fan is customarily a splendid occasion; the sky is white with yellow and green colors; when Mireille rises, the mists burn and writhe like flames. He who sings derives a greater enjoyment from the hour when the floating corpse of an out-worlder does not appear to mar the serenity of the view."

Thissell's *zachinko* gave off a startled interrogation almost of its own accord; the Sand Tiger bowed with dignity. "The singer acknowledges no peer in steadfastness of disposition; however, he does not care to be plagued by the antics of a dissatisfied ghost. He therefore has ordered his slaves to attach a thong to the ankle of the corpse, and while we have conversed they have linked the corpse to the stern of your houseboat. You will wish to administer whatever rites are prescribed in the Outworld. He who sings wishes you a good morning and now departs."

Thissell rushed to the stern of his houseboat. There, near-naked and mask-less, floated the body of a mature man, supported by air trapped in his pantaloons.

Thissell studied the dead face, which seemed characterless and vapid — perhaps in direct consequence of the mask-wearing habit. The body appeared of medium stature and weight, and Thissell estimated the age as between forty-five and fifty. The hair was nondescript brown, the features bloated by the water. There was nothing to indicate how the man had died.

This must be Haxo Angmark, thought Thissell. Who else could it be? Mathew Kershaul? Why not? Thissell asked himself uneasily. Rolver and Welibus had already disembarked and gone about their business. He searched across the bay to locate Kershaul's houseboat, and discovered it already tying up to the dock. Even as he watched, Kershaul jumped ashore, wearing his Cave Owl mask.

He seemed in an abstracted mood, for he passed Thissell's houseboat without lifting his eyes from the dock.

Thissell turned back to the corpse. Angmark then, beyond a doubt. Had not three men disembarked from the houseboats of Rolver, Welibus and Kershaul, wearing masks characteristic of these men? Obviously, the corpse of Angmark…The easy solution refused to sit quiet in Thissell's mind. Kershaul had pointed out that another outworlder would be quickly identified. How else could Angmark maintain himself unless he…Thissell brushed the thought aside. The corpse was obviously Angmark.

And yet…

Thissell summoned his slaves, gave orders that a suitable container be brought to the dock, that the corpse be transferred therein, and conveyed to a suitable place of repose. The slaves showed no enthusiasm for the task and Thissell was forced to thunder forcefully, if not skillfully, on the *hymerkin* to emphasize his orders.

He walked along the dock, turned up the esplanade, passed the office of Cornely Welibus and set out along the pleasant little lane to the landing field.

When he arrived, he found that Rolver had not yet made an appearance. An over-slave, given status by a yellow rosette on his black cloth mask, asked how he might be of service. Thissell stated that he wished to dispatch a message to Polypolis.

There was no difficulty here, declared the slave. If Thissell would set forth his message in clear block-print it would be dispatched immediately.

Thissell wrote:

Out-worlder found dead, possibly Angmark. Age
48, medium physique, brown hair. Other means of
identification lacking. Await acknowledgement
and/or instructions.

He addressed the message to Castel Cromartin at Polypolis and
handed it to the over-slave. A moment later he heard the characteristic
sputter of trans-space discharge.

An hour passed. Rolver made no appearance. Thissell paced rest-
lessly back and forth in front of the office. There was no telling how long
he would have to wait: trans-space transmission time varied unpre-
dictably. Sometimes the message snapped through in micro-seconds;
sometimes it wandered through unknowable regions for hours; and
there were several authenticated examples of messages being received
before they had been transmitted.

Another half-hour passed, and Rolver finally arrived, wearing his
customary Tarn Bird. Coincidentally Thissell heard the hiss of the
incoming message.

Rolver seemed surprised to see Thissell. "What brings you out so
early?"

Thissell explained. "It concerns the body which you referred to me
this morning. I'm communicating with my superiors about it."

Rolver raised his head and listened to the sound of the incoming
message. "You seem to be getting an answer. I'd better attend to it."

"Why bother?" asked Thissell. "Your slave seems efficient."

"It's my job," declared Rolver. "I'm responsible for the accurate
transmission and receipt of all space-grams."

"I'll come with you," said Thissell. "I've always wanted to watch the
operation of the equipment."

"I'm afraid that's irregular," said Rolver. He went to the door which
led into the inner compartment. "I'll have your message in a moment."

Thissell protested, but Rolver ignored him and went into the inner
office.

Five minutes later he reappeared, carrying a small yellow envelope.
"Not too good news," he announced with unconvincing commiseration.

Thissell glumly opened the envelope. The message read:

Body not Angmark. Angmark has black hair. Why
did you not meet landing? Serious infraction, highly
dissatisfied. Return to Polypolis next opportunity.

Castel Cromartin

Thissell put the message in his pocket. "Incidentally, may I inquire
the color of your hair?"

Rolver played a surprised little trill on his *kiv*. "I'm quite blond. Why
do you ask?"

"Mere curiosity."

Rolver played another run on the *kiv*. "Now I understand. My dear
fellow, what a suspicious nature you have! Look!" He turned and
parted the folds of his mask at the nape of his neck. Thissell saw that
Rolver was blond indeed.

"Are you reassured?" asked Rolver jocularly.

"Oh, indeed," said Thissell. "Incidentally, have you another mask
you could lend me? I'm sick of this Moon Moth."

"I'm afraid not," said Rolver. "But you need merely go into a mask-
maker's shop and make a selection."

"Yes, of course," said Thissell. He took his leave of Rolver and
returned along the trail to Fan. Passing Welibus' office he hesitated,
then turned in. Today Welibus wore a dazzling confection of green
glass prisms and silver beads, a mask Thissell had never seen before.

Welibus greeted him cautiously to the accompaniment of a *kiv*.
"Good morning, Ser Moon Moth."

"I won't take too much of your time," said Thissell, "but I have a
rather personal question to put to you. What color is your hair?"

Welibus hesitated a fraction of a second, then turned his back,
lifted the flap of his mask. Thissell saw heavy black ringlets. "Does that
answer your question?" inquired Welibus.

"Completely," said Thissell. He crossed the esplanade, went out
on the dock to Kershaul's houseboat. Kershaul greeted him without
enthusiasm, and invited him aboard with a resigned wave of the hand.

"A question I'd like to ask," said Thissell; "What color is your hair?"

Kershaul laughed woefully. "What little remains is black. Why do
you ask?"

"Curiosity."

"Come, come," said Kershaul with an unaccustomed bluffness. "There's more to it than that."

Thissell, feeling the need of counsel, admitted as much. "Here's the situation. A dead out-worlder was found in the harbor this morning. His hair was brown. I'm not entirely certain, but the chances are — let me see, yes, two out of three that Angmark's hair is black."

Kershaul pulled at the Cave Owl's goatee. "How do you arrive at that probability?"

"The information came to me through Rolver's hands. He has blond hair. If Angmark has assumed Rolver's identity, he would naturally alter the information which came to me this morning. Both you and Welibus admit to black hair."

"Hm," said Kershaul. "Let me see if I follow your line of reasoning. You feel that Haxo Angmark has killed either Rolver, Welibus or myself and assumed the dead man's identity. Right?"

Thissell looked at him in surprise. "You yourself emphasized that Angmark could not set up another out-world establishment without revealing himself! Don't you remember?"

"Oh, certainly. To continue. Rolver delivered a message to you stating that Angmark was dark, and announced himself to be blond."

"Yes. Can you verify this? I mean for the old Rolver?"

"No," said Kershaul sadly. "I've seen neither Rolver nor Welibus without their masks."

"If Rolver is not Angmark," Thissell mused, "if Angmark indeed has black hair, then both you and Welibus come under suspicion."

"Very interesting," said Kershaul. He examined Thissell warily. "For that matter, you yourself might be Angmark. What color is your hair?"

"Brown," said Thissell curtly. He lifted the gray fur of the Moon Moth mask at the back of his head.

"But you might be deceiving me as to the text of the message," Kershaul put forward.

"I'm not," said Thissell wearily. "You can check with Rolver if you care to."

Kershaul shook his head. "Unnecessary. I believe you. But another matter: what of voices? You've heard all of us before and after Angmark arrived. Isn't there some indication there?"

"No. I'm so alert for any evidence of change that you all sound rather different. And the masks muffle your voices."

Kershaul tugged the goatee. "I don't see any immediate solution to the problem." He chuckled. "In any event, need there be? Before Angmark's advent, there were Rolver, Welibus, Kershaul and Thissell. Now — for all practical purposes — there are still Rolver, Welibus, Kershaul and Thissell. Who is to say that the new member may not be an improvement upon the old?"

"An interesting thought," agreed Thissell, "but it so happens that I have a personal interest in identifying Angmark. My career is at stake."

"I see," murmured Kershaul. "The situation then becomes an issue between yourself and Angmark."

"You won't help me?"

"Not actively. I've become pervaded with Sirenese individualism. I think you'll find that Rolver and Welibus will respond similarly." He sighed. "All of us have been here too long."

Thissell stood deep in thought. Kershaul waited patiently a moment, then said, "Do you have any further questions?"

"No," said Thissell. "I have merely a favor to ask you."

"I'll oblige if I possibly can," Kershaul replied courteously.

"Give me, or lend me, one of your slaves, for a week or two."

Kershaul played an exclamation of amusement on the *ganga*. "I hardly like to part with my slaves; they know me and my ways —"

"As soon as I catch Angmark you'll have him back."

"Very well," said Kershaul. He rattled a summons on his *hymerkin*, and a slave appeared. "Anthony," sang Kershaul, "you are to go with Ser Thissell and serve him for a short period."

The slave bowed, without pleasure.

Thissell took Anthony to his houseboat, and questioned him at length, noting certain of the responses upon a chart. He then enjoined Anthony to say nothing of what had passed, and consigned him to the care of Toby and Rex. He gave further instructions to move the houseboat away from the dock and allow no one aboard until his return.

He set forth once more along the way to the landing field, and found

Rolver at a lunch of spiced fish, shredded bark of the salad tree, and a bowl of native currants. Rolver clapped an order on the *hymerkin*, and a slave set a place for Thissell. "And how are the investigations proceeding?"

"I'd hardly like to claim any progress," said Thissell. "I assume that I can count on your help?"

Rolver laughed briefly. "You have my good wishes."

"More concretely," said Thissell, "I'd like to borrow a slave from you. Temporarily."

Rolver paused in his eating. "Whatever for?"

"I'd rather not explain," said Thissell. "But you can be sure that I make no idle request."

Without graciousness Rolver summoned a slave and consigned him to Thissell's service.

On the way back to his houseboat, Thissell stopped at Welibus' office.

Welibus looked up from his work. "Good afternoon, Ser Thissell."

Thissell came directly to the point. "Ser Welibus, will you lend me a slave for a few days?"

Welibus hesitated, then shrugged. "Why not?" He clacked his *hymerkin*; a slave appeared. "Is he satisfactory? Or would you prefer a young female?" He chuckled — rather offensively, to Thissell's way of thinking.

"He'll do very well. I'll return him in a few days."

"No hurry." Welibus made an easy gesture and returned to his work.

Thissell continued to his houseboat, where he separately interviewed each of his two new slaves and made notes upon his chart.

Dusk came soft over the Titanic Ocean. Toby and Rex sculled the houseboat away from the dock, out across the silken waters. Thissell sat on the deck listening to the sound of soft voices, the flutter and tinkle of musical instruments. Lights from the floating houseboats glowed yellow and wan watermelon-red. The shore was dark; the Night-men would presently come slinking to paw through refuse and stare jealously across the water.

In nine days the *Buenaventura* came past Sirene on its regular schedule; Thissell had his orders to return to Polypolis. In nine days, could he locate Haxo Angmark?

Nine days weren't too many, Thissell decided, but they might possibly be enough.

Two days passed, and three and four and five. Every day Thissell went ashore and at least once a day visited Rolver, Welibus and Kershaul.

Each reacted differently to his presence. Rolver was sardonic and irritable; Welibus formal and at least superficially affable; Kershaul mild and suave, but ostentatiously impersonal and detached in his conversation.

Thissell remained equally bland to Rolver's dour jibes, Welibus' jocundity, Kershaul's withdrawal. And every day, returning to his houseboat he made marks on his chart.

The sixth, the seventh, the eighth day came and passed. Rolver, with rather brutal directness, inquired if Thissell wished to arrange for passage on the *Buenaventura*. Thissell considered, and said, "Yes, you had better reserve passage for one."

"Back to the world of faces," shuddered Rolver. "Faces! Everywhere pallid, fish-eyed faces. Mouths like pulp, noses knotted and punctured; flat, flabby faces. I don't think I could stand it after living here. Luckily you haven't become a real Sirenese."

"But I won't be going back," said Thissell.

"I thought you wanted me to reserve passage."

"I do. For Haxo Angmark. He'll be returning to Polypolis in the brig."

"Well, well," said Rolver. "So you've picked him out."

"Of course," said Thissell. "Haven't you?"

Rolver shrugged. "He's either Welibus or Kershaul, that's as close as I can make it. So long as he wears his mask and calls himself either Welibus or Kershaul, it means nothing to me."

"It means a great deal to me," said Thissell. "What time tomorrow does the lighter go up?"

"Eleven twenty-two sharp. If Haxo Angmark's leaving, tell him to be on time."

"He'll be here," said Thissell.

He made his usual call upon Welibus and Kershaul, then returning to his houseboat, put three final marks on his chart.

The evidence was here, plain and convincing. Not absolutely incontrovertible evidence, but enough to warrant a definite move. He checked over his gun. Tomorrow: the day of decision. He could afford no errors.

The day dawned bright white, the sky like the inside of an oyster shell; Mireille rose through iridescent mists. Toby and Rex sculled the houseboat to the dock. The remaining three out-world houseboats floated somnolently on the slow swells.

One boat Thissell watched in particular, that whose owner Haxo Angmark had killed and dropped into the harbor. This boat presently moved toward the shore, and Haxo Angmark himself stood on the front deck, wearing a mask Thissell had never seen before: a construction of scarlet feathers, black glass and spiked green hair.

Thissell was forced to admire his poise. A clever scheme, cleverly planned and executed — but marred by an insurmountable difficulty.

Angmark returned within. The houseboat reached the dock. Slaves flung out mooring lines, lowered the gang-plank. Thissell, his gun ready in the pocket flap of his robes, walked down the dock, went aboard. He pushed open the door to the saloon. The man at the table raised his red, black and green mask in surprise.

Thissell said, "Angmark, please don't argue or make any —"

Something hard and heavy tackled him from behind; he was flung to the floor, his gun wrested expertly away.

Behind him the *hymerkin* clattered; a voice sang, "Bind the fool's arms."

The man sitting at the table rose to his feet, removed the red, black and green mask to reveal the black cloth of a slave. Thissell twisted his head. Over him stood Haxo Angmark, wearing a mask Thissell recognized as a Dragon Tamer, fabricated from black metal, with a knife-blade nose, socketed eyelids, and three crests running back over the scalp.

The mask's expression was unreadable, but Angmark's voice was triumphant. "I trapped you very easily."

"So you did," said Thissell. The slave finished knotting his wrists together. A clatter of Angmark's *hymerkin* sent him away. "Get to your feet," said Angmark. "Sit in that chair."

"What are we waiting for?" inquired Thissell.

"Two of our fellows still remain out on the water. We won't need them for what I have in mind."

"Which is?"

"You'll learn in due course," said Angmark. "We have an hour or so on our hands."

Thissell tested his bonds. They were undoubtedly secure.

Angmark seated himself. "How did you fix on me? I admit to being curious…Come, come," he chided as Thissell sat silently. "Can't you recognize that I have defeated you? Don't make affairs unpleasant for yourself."

Thissell shrugged. "I operated on a basic principle. A man can mask his face, but he can't mask his personality."

"Aha," said Angmark. "Interesting. Proceed."

"I borrowed a slave from you and the other two out-worlders, and I questioned them carefully. What masks had their masters worn during the month before your arrival? I prepared a chart and plotted their responses. Rolver wore the Tarn Bird about eighty percent of the time, the remaining twenty percent divided between the Sophist Abstraction and the Black Intricate. Welibus had a taste for the heroes of Kan Dachan Cycle. He wore the Chalekun, the Prince Intrepid, the Seavain most of the time: six days out of eight. The other two days he wore his South Wind or his Gay Companion. Kershaul, more conservative, preferred the Cave Owl, the Star Wanderer, and two or three other masks he wore at odd intervals.

"As I say, I acquired this information from possibly its most accurate source, the slaves. My next step was to keep watch upon the three of you. Every day I noted what masks you wore and compared it with my chart. Rolver wore his Tarn Bird six times, his Black Intricate twice. Kershaul wore his Cave Owl five times, his Star Wanderer once, his Quincunx once and his Ideal of Perfection once. Welibus wore the Emerald Mountain twice, the Triple Phoenix three times, the Prince Intrepid once and the Shark God twice."

Angmark nodded thoughtfully. "I see my error. I selected from Welibus' masks, but to my own taste — and as you point out, I revealed myself. But only to you." He rose and went to the window. "Kershaul and Rolver are now coming ashore; they'll soon be past and about their business — though I doubt if they'd interfere in any case; they've both become good Sirenese."

Thissell waited in silence. Ten minutes passed. Then Angmark reached to a shelf and picked up a knife. He looked at Thissell. "Stand up."

Thissell slowly rose to his feet. Angmark approached from the side, reached out, lifted the Moon Moth from Thissell's head. Thissell gasped and made a vain attempt to seize it. Too late; his face was bare and naked.

Angmark turned away, removed his own mask, donned the Moon Moth. He struck a call on his *hymerkin*. Two slaves entered, stopped in shock at the sight of Thissell.

Angmark played a brisk tattoo, sang, "Carry this man up to the dock."

"Angmark," cried Thissell. "I'm maskless!"

The slaves seized him and in spite of Thissell's desperate struggles, conveyed him out on the deck, along the float and up on the dock.

Angmark fixed a rope around Thissell's neck. He said, "You are now Haxo Angmark, and I am Edwer Thissell. Welibus is dead, you shall soon be dead. I can handle your job without difficulty. I'll play musical instruments like a Night-man and sing like a crow. I'll wear the Moon Moth till it rots and then I'll get another. The report will go to Polypolis, Haxo Angmark is dead. Everything will be serene."

Thissell barely heard. "You can't do this," he whispered. "My mask, my face…" A large woman in a blue and pink flower mask walked down the dock. She saw Thissell and emitted a piercing shriek, flung herself prone on the dock.

"Come along," said Angmark brightly. He tugged at the rope, and pulled Thissell down the dock. A man in a Pirate Captain mask coming up from his houseboat stood rigid in amazement.

Angmark played the *zachinko* and sang, "Behold the notorious criminal Haxo Angmark. Through all the outer-worlds his name is reviled. Now he is captured and led in shame to his death. Behold Haxo Angmark!"

They turned into the esplanade. A child screamed in fright, a man called hoarsely. Thissell stumbled; tears tumbled from his eyes; he could see only disorganized shapes and colors. Angmark's voice belled out richly: "Everyone behold: the criminal of the out-worlds, Haxo Angmark! Approach and observe his execution!"

Thissell feebly cried out, "I'm not Angmark; I'm Edwer Thissell; he's Angmark." But no one listened to him; there were only cries of dismay, shock, disgust at the sight of his face. He called to Angmark, "Give me my mask, a slave-cloth…"

Angmark sang jubilantly, "In shame he lived, in maskless shame he dies."

A Forest Goblin stood before Angmark. "Moon Moth, we meet once more."

Angmark sang, "Stand aside, friend Goblin, I must execute this criminal. In shame he lived, in shame he dies!"

A crowd had formed around the group; masks stared in morbid titillation at Thissell.

The Forest Goblin jerked the rope from Angmark's hand, threw it to the ground. The crowd roared. Voices cried, "No duel, no duel! Execute the monster!"

A cloth was thrown over Thissell's head. Thissell awaited the thrust of a blade. But instead his bonds were cut. Hastily he adjusted the cloth, hiding his face, peering between the folds.

Four men clutched Haxo Angmark. The Forest Goblin confronted him, playing the *skaranyi*. "A week ago you reached to divest me of my mask; you have now achieved your perverse aim!"

"But he is a criminal," cried Angmark. "He is notorious, infamous!"

"What are his misdeeds?" sang the Forest Goblin.

"He has murdered, betrayed; he has wrecked ships; he has tortured, blackmailed, robbed, sold children into slavery; he has —"

The Forest Goblin stopped him. "Your religious differences are of no importance. We can vouch however for your present crimes!"

The hostler stepped forward. He sang fiercely, "This insolent Moon Moth nine days ago sought to pre-empt my choicest mount!"

Another man pushed close. He wore a Universal Expert, and sang, "I am a Master Mask-maker; I recognize this Moon Moth out-worlder! Only recently he entered my shop and derided my skill. He deserves death!"

"Death to the out-world monster!" cried the crowd. A wave of men surged forward. Steel blades rose and fell, the deed was done.

Thissell watched, unable to move. The Forest Goblin approached, and playing the *stimic* sang sternly, "For you we have pity, but also contempt. A true man would never suffer such indignities!"

Thissell took a deep breath. He reached to his belt and found his *zachinko*. He sang, "My friend, you malign me! Can you not appreciate true courage? Would you prefer to die in combat or walk maskless along the esplanade?"

The Forest Goblin sang, "There is only one answer. First I would die in combat; I could not bear such shame."

Thissell sang. "I had such a choice. I could fight with my hands tied, and so die — or I could suffer shame, and through this shame conquer my enemy. You admit that you lack sufficient *strakh* to achieve this deed. I have proved myself a hero of bravery! I ask, who here has courage to do what I have done?"

"Courage?" demanded the Forest Goblin. "I fear nothing, up to and beyond death at the hands of the Night-men!"

"Then answer."

The Forest Goblin stood back. He played his *double-kamanthil*. "Bravery indeed, if such were your motives."

The hostler struck a series of subdued *gomapard* chords and sang, "Not a man among us would dare what this maskless man has done."

The crowd muttered approval.

The mask-maker approached Thissell, obsequiously stroking his *double-kamanthil*. "Pray, Lord Hero, step into my nearby shop, exchange this vile rag for a mask befitting your quality."

Another mask-maker sang, "Before you choose, Lord Hero, examine my magnificent creations!"

A man in a Bright Sky Bird mask approached Thissell reverently. "I have only just completed a sumptuous houseboat; seventeen years of toil have gone into its fabrication. Grant me the good fortune of accepting and using this splendid craft; aboard waiting to serve you are alert slaves and pleasant maidens; there is ample wine in storage and soft silken carpets on the decks."

"Thank you," said Thissell, striking the *zachinko* with vigor and confidence. "I accept with pleasure. But first a mask."

The mask-maker struck an interrogative trill on the *gomapard*.

"Would the Lord Hero consider a Sea-Dragon Conqueror beneath his dignity?"

"By no means," said Thissell. "I consider it suitable and satisfactory. We shall go now to examine it."

Green Magic

Howard Fair, looking over the relicts of his great-uncle Gerald McIntyre, found a large ledger entitled:

WORKBOOK & JOURNAL
Open at Peril!

Fair read the journal with interest, although his own work went far beyond ideas treated only gingerly by Gerald McIntyre.

"The existence of disciplines concentric to the elementary magics must now be admitted without further controversy," wrote McIntyre. "Guided by a set of analogies from the white and black magics (to be detailed in due course), I have delineated the basic extension of purple magic, as well as its corollary, Dynamic Nomism."

Fair read on, remarking the careful charts, the projections and expansions, the transpolations and transformations by which Gerald McIntyre had conceived his systemology. So swiftly had the technical arts advanced that McIntyre's expositions, highly controversial sixty years before, now seemed pedantic and overly rigorous.

"Whereas benign creatures: angels, white sprites, merrihews, sandestins — are typical of the white cycle; whereas demons, magners, trolls and warlocks are evinced by black magic; so do the purple and green cycles sponsor their own particulars, but these are neither good nor evil, bearing, rather, the same relation to the black and white provinces that these latter do to our own basic realm."

Fair re-read the passage. The 'green cycle'? Had great-uncle McIntyre wandered into regions overlooked by modern workers?

He reviewed the journal in the light of this suspicion, and discovered additional hints and references. Especially provocative was a bit of scribbled marginalia: "More concerning my latest researches I may not state, having been promised an infinite reward for this forbearance."

The passage was dated a day before Gerald McIntyre's death, which had occurred on March 21, 1898, the first day of spring. McIntyre had enjoyed very little of his 'infinite reward', whatever had been its nature... Fair returned to a consideration of the journal, which, in a sentence or two, had opened a chink on an entire new panorama. McIntyre provided no further illumination, and Fair set out to make a fuller investigation.

His first steps were routine. He performed two divinations, searched the standard indexes, concordances, handbooks and formularies, evoked a demon whom he had previously found knowledgeable: all without success. He found no direct reference to cycles beyond the purple; the demon refused even to speculate.

Fair was by no means discouraged; if anything, the intensity of his interest increased. He re-read the journal, with particular care to the justification for purple magic, reasoning that McIntyre, groping for a lore beyond the purple, might well have used the methods which had yielded results before. Applying stains and ultraviolet light to the pages, Fair made legible a number of notes McIntyre had jotted down, then erased.

Fair was immensely stimulated. The notes assured him that he was on the right track and further indicated a number of blind alleys from which Fair profited by avoiding. He applied himself so successfully that before the week was out he had evoked a sprite of the green cycle. It appeared in the semblance of a man with green glass eyes and a thatch of young eucalyptus leaves in the place of hair. It greeted Fair with cool courtesy, would not seat itself, and ignored Fair's proffer of coffee. After wandering around the apartment inspecting Fair's books and curios with an air of negligent amusement, it agreed to respond to Fair's questions.

Fair asked permission to use his tape-recorder, which the sprite allowed, and Fair set the apparatus in motion. (When subsequently he replayed the interview, no sound could be heard.)

"What realms of magic lie beyond the green?" asked Fair.

"I can't give you an exact answer," replied the sprite, "because I don't know. There are at least two more, corresponding to the colors we call rawn and pallow, and very likely others."

Fair arranged the microphone where it would more directly intercept the voice of the sprite. "What," he asked, "is the green cycle like? What is its physical semblance?"

The sprite paused to consider. Glistening mother-of-pearl films wandered across its face, reflecting the tinge of its thoughts. "I'm rather severely restricted by your use of the word 'physical'. And 'semblance' involves a subjective interpretation, which changes with the rise and fall of the seconds."

"By all means," Fair said hastily, "describe it in your own words."

"Well—we have four different regions, two of which floresce from the basic skeleton of the universe, and so subsede the others. The first of these is compressed and isthiated, but is notable for its wide pools of mottle which we use sometimes for deranging stations. We've transplanted club-mosses from Earth's Devonian and a few ice-fires from Perdition. They climb among the rods which we call devil-hair—" he went on for several minutes but the meaning almost entirely escaped Fair. And it seemed as if the question by which he had hoped to break the ice might run away with the entire interview. He introduced another idea.

"Can we freely manipulate the physical extensions of Earth?"

The sprite seemed amused. "You refer, so I assume, to the various aspects of space, time, mass, energy, life, thought and recollection."

"Exactly."

The sprite raised its green cornsilk eyebrows. "I might as sensibly ask, can you break an egg by striking it with a club? The response is on a similar level of seriousness."

Fair had expected a certain amount of condescension and impatience, and was not abashed. "How may I learn these techniques?"

"In the usual manner: through diligent study."

"Ah, indeed—but where could I study, and who would teach me?"

The sprite made an easy gesture, and whorls of green smoke trailed from his fingers to spin through the air. "I could arrange the matter, but since I bear you no particular animosity, I'll do nothing of the sort. And now, I must be gone."

"Where do you go?" Fair asked in wonder and longing. "May I go with you?"

The sprite, swirling a drape of bright green dust over its shoulders, shook his head. "You would be less than comfortable."

"Other men have explored the worlds of magic!"

"True: your uncle Gerald McIntyre, for instance."

"My uncle Gerald learned green magic?"

"To the limit of his capabilities. He found no pleasure in his learning. You would do well to profit by his experience and modify your ambitions." The sprite turned and walked away.

Fair watched it depart. The sprite receded in space and dimension, but never reached the wall of Fair's room. At a distance which might have been fifty yards, the sprite glanced back, as if to make sure that Fair was not following, then stepped off at another angle and disappeared.

Fair's first impulse was to take heed and limit his explorations. He was an adept in white magic, and had mastered the black art — occasionally he evoked a demon to liven a social gathering which otherwise threatened to become dull — but he had by no means illuminated every mystery of purple magic, which is the realm of Incarnate Symbols.

Howard Fair might have turned away from the green cycle except for three factors.

First was his physical appearance. He stood rather under medium height, with a swarthy face, sparse black hair, a gnarled nose, a small heavy mouth. He felt no great sensitivity about his appearance, but realized that it might be improved. In his mind's eye he pictured the personified ideal of himself: he was taller by six inches, his nose thin and keen, his skin cleared of its muddy undertone. A striking figure, but still recognizable as Howard Fair. He wanted the love of women, but he wanted it without the interposition of his craft. Many times he had brought beautiful girls to his bed, lips wet and eyes shining; but purple magic had seduced them rather than Howard Fair, and he took limited satisfaction in such conquests.

Here was the first factor which drew Howard Fair back to the green lore; the second was his yearning for extended, perhaps eternal, life; the third was simple thirst for knowledge.

The fact of Gerald McIntyre's death, or dissolution, or disappearance — whatever had happened to him — was naturally a matter of concern. If he had won to a goal so precious, why had he died so quickly? Was the 'infinite reward' so miraculous, so exquisite, that the mind failed under its possession? (If such were the case, the reward was hardly a reward.)

Fair could not restrain himself, and by degrees returned to a study of green magic. Rather than again invoke the sprite whose air of indulgent contempt he had found exasperating, he decided to seek knowledge by an indirect method, employing the most advanced concepts of technical and cabalistic science.

He obtained a portable television transmitter which he loaded into his panel truck along with a receiver. On a Monday night in early May, he drove to an abandoned graveyard far out in the wooded hills, and there, by the light of a waning moon, he buried the television camera in graveyard clay until only the lens protruded from the soil. With a sharp alder twig he scratched on the ground a monstrous outline. The television lens served for one eye, a beer bottle pushed neck-first into the soil the other.

During the middle hours, while the moon died behind wisps of pale cloud, he carved a word on the dark forehead; then, standing back, recited the activating incantation.

The ground rumbled and moaned, the golem heaved up to blot out the stars.

The glass eyes stared down at Fair, secure in his pentagon.

"Speak!" called out Fair. "*Enteresthes, Akmai Adonai Bidemgir! Elohim, pa rahulli! Enteresthes, HVOI!* Speak!"

"Return me to earth, return my clay to the quiet clay from whence you roused me."

"First you must serve."

The golem stumbled forward to crush Fair, but was halted by the pang of protective magic.

"Serve you I will, if serve you I must."

Fair stepped boldly forth from the pentagon, strung forty yards of green ribbon down the road in the shape of a narrow V. "Go forth into the realm of green magic," he told the monster. "The ribbons reach forty miles; walk to the end, turn about, return, and then fall back, return to the earth from which you rose."

The golem turned, shuffled into the V of green ribbon, shaking off clods of mold, jarring the ground with its ponderous tread. Fair watched the squat shape dwindle, recede, yet never reach the angle of the magic V. He returned to his panel truck, tuned the television receiver to the golem's eye, and surveyed the fantastic vistas of the green realm.

Two elementals of the green realm met on a spun-silver landscape. They were Jaadian and Misthemar, and they fell to discussing the earthen monster which had stalked forty miles through the region known as Cil; which then, turning in its tracks, had retraced its steps, gradually increasing its pace until at the end it moved in a shambling rush, leaving a trail of clods on the fragile moth-wing mosaics.

"Events, events, events," Misthemar fretted, "they crowd the chute of time till the bounds bulge. Or then again, the course is as lean and spare as a stretched tendon…But in regard to this incursion…" He paused for a period of reflection, and silver clouds moved over his head and under his feet.

Jaadian remarked, "You are aware that I conversed with Howard Fair; he is so obsessed to escape the squalor of his world that he acts with recklessness."

"The man Gerald McIntyre was his uncle," mused Misthemar. "McIntyre besought, we yielded; as perhaps now we must yield to Howard Fair."

Jaadian uneasily opened his hand, shook off a spray of emerald fire. "Events press, both in and out. I find myself unable to act in this regard."

"I likewise do not care to be the agent of tragedy."

A Meaning came fluttering up from below: "A disturbance among the spiral towers! A caterpillar of glass and metal has come clanking; it has thrust electric eyes into the Portinone and broke open the Egg of Innocence. Howard Fair is the fault."

Jaadian and Misthemar consulted each other with wry disinclination. "Very well, both of us will go; such a duty needs two souls in support."

They impinged upon Earth and found Howard Fair in a wall booth at a cocktail bar. He looked up at the two strangers. One of them asked, "May we join you?"

Fair examined the two men. Both wore conservative suits and carried cashmere topcoats over their arms. Fair noticed that the left thumb-nail of each man glistened green, in accordance with precept.

Fair rose politely to his feet. "Will you sit down?"

The green sprites hung up their overcoats and slid into the booth. Fair looked from one to the other. He addressed Jaadian. "Aren't you he whom I interviewed several weeks ago?"

Jaadian assented. "You have not accepted my advice."

Fair shrugged. "You asked me to remain ignorant, to accept my stupidity and ineptitude."

"And why should you not?" asked Jaadian gently. "You are a primitive in a primitive realm; nevertheless not one man in a thousand can match your achievements."

Fair agreed, smiling faintly. "But knowledge creates a craving for further knowledge. Where is the harm in knowledge?"

Misthemar, the more mercurial of the sprites, spoke angrily. "Where is the harm? Consider your earthen monster! It befouled forty miles of delicacy, the record of ten million years. Consider your caterpillar! It trampled our pillars of carved milk, our dreaming towers, damaged the nerve-skeins which extrude and waft us our Meanings."

"I'm dreadfully sorry," said Fair. "I meant no destruction."

The sprites nodded. "But your apology conveys no guarantee of restraint."

Fair toyed with his glass. A waiter approached the table, addressed the two sprites. "Something for you two gentlemen?"

Jaadian ordered a glass of charged water, as did Misthemar. Fair called for another highball.

"What do you hope to gain from this activity?" inquired Misthemar. "Destructive forays teach you nothing!"

Fair agreed. "I have learned little. But I have seen miraculous sights. I am more than ever anxious to learn."

The green sprites glumly watched the bubbles rising in their glasses. Jaadian at last drew a deep sigh. "Perhaps we can obviate toil on your part and disturbance on ours. Explicitly, what gains or advantages do you hope to derive from green magic?"

Fair, smiling, leaned back into the red imitation-leather cushions. "I want many things. Extended life — mobility in time — comprehensive memory — augmented perception, with vision across the whole spectrum. I want physical charm and magnetism, the semblance of youth, muscular endurance…Then there are qualities more or less speculative, such as —"

Jaadian interrupted. "These qualities and characteristics we will confer upon you. In return you will undertake never again to disturb the green realm. You will evade centuries of toil; we will be spared the nuisance of your presence, and the inevitable tragedy."

"Tragedy?" inquired Fair in wonder. "Why tragedy?"

Jaadian spoke in a deep reverberating voice. "You are a man of Earth. Your goals are not our goals. Green magic makes you aware of our goals."

Fair thoughtfully sipped his highball. "I can't see that this is a disadvantage. I am willing to submit to the discipline of instruction. Surely a knowledge of green magic will not change me into a different entity?"

"No. And this is the basic tragedy!"

Misthemar spoke in exasperation. "We are forbidden to harm lesser creatures, and so you are fortunate; for to dissolve you into air would end all the annoyance."

Fair laughed. "I apologize again for making such a nuisance of myself. But surely you understand how important this is to me?"

Jaadian asked hopefully, "Then you agree to our offer?"

Fair shook his head. "How could I live, forever young, capable of extended learning, but limited to knowledge which I already see bounds to? I would be bored, restless, miserable."

"That well may be," said Jaadian. "But not so bored, restless and miserable as if you were learned in green magic."

Fair drew himself erect. "I must learn green magic. It is an opportunity which only a person both torpid and stupid could refuse."

Jaadian sighed. "In your place I would make the same response." The sprites rose to their feet. "Come then, we will teach you."

"Don't say we didn't warn you," said Misthemar.

✳

Time passed. Sunset waned and twilight darkened. A man walked up the stairs, entered Howard Fair's apartment. He was tall, unobtrusively muscular. His face was sensitive, keen, humorous; his left thumb-nail glistened green.

Time is a function of vital processes. The people of Earth had perceived the motion of their clocks. On this understanding, two hours had elapsed since Howard Fair had followed the green sprites from the bar.

Howard Fair had perceived other criteria. For him the interval had been seven hundred years, during which he had lived in the green realm, learning to the utmost capacity of his brain.

He had occupied two years training his senses to the new conditions. Gradually he learned to walk in the six basic three-dimensional directions, and accustomed himself to the fourth-dimensional short-cuts. By easy stages the blinds over his eyes were removed, so that the dazzling over-human intricacy of the landscape never completely confounded him.

Another year was spent training him to the use of a code-language — an intermediate step between the vocalizations of Earth and the meaning-patterns of the green realm, where a hundred symbol-flakes (each a flitting spot of delicate iridescence) might be displayed in a single swirl of import. During this time Howard Fair's eyes and brain were altered, to allow him the use of the many new colors, without which the meaning-flakes could not be recognized.

These were preliminary steps. For forty years he studied the flakes, of which there were almost a million. Another forty years was given to elementary permutations and shifts, and another forty to parallels, attenuations, diminishments and extensions; and during this time he was introduced to flake patterns, and certain of the more obvious displays.

Now he was able to study without recourse to the code-language, and his progress became more marked. Another twenty years found him able to recognize more complicated Meanings, and he was introduced to a more varied program. He floated over the field of moth-wing mosaics, which still showed the footprints of the golem. He sweated in embarrassment, the extent of his wicked willfulness now clear to him.

So passed the years. Howard Fair learned as much green magic as his brain could encompass.

He explored much of the green realm, finding so much beauty that he feared his brain might burst. He tasted, he heard, he felt, he sensed, and each one of his senses was a hundred times more discriminating than before. Nourishment came in a thousand different forms: from pink eggs which burst into a hot sweet gas, suffusing his entire body; from passing through a rain of stinging metal crystals; from simple contemplation of the proper symbol.

Homesickness for Earth waxed and waned. Sometimes it was insupportable and he was ready to forsake all he had learned and abandon his hopes for the future. At other times the magnificence of the green realm permeated him, and the thought of departure seemed like the threat of death itself.

By stages so gradual he never realized them he learned green magic.

But the new faculty gave him no pride: between his crude ineptitudes and the poetic elegance of the sprites remained a tremendous gap — and he felt his innate inferiority much more keenly than he ever had in his old state. Worse, his most earnest efforts failed to improve his technique, and sometimes, observing the singing joy of an improvised manifestation by one of the sprites, and contrasting it to his own labored constructions, he felt futility and shame.

The longer he remained in the green realm, the stronger grew the sense of his own maladroitness, and he began to long for the easy environment of Earth, where each of his acts would not shout aloud of vulgarity and crassness. At times he would watch the sprites (in the gossamer forms natural to them) at play among the pearl-petals, or twining like quick flashes of music through the forest of pink spirals. The contrast between their verve and his brutish fumbling could not be borne and he would turn away. His self-respect dwindled with each passing hour, and instead of pride in his learning, he felt a sullen ache for what he was not and could never become. The first few hundred years he worked with the enthusiasm of ignorance, for the next few he was buoyed by hope. During the last part of his time, only dogged obstinacy kept him plodding through what now he knew for infantile exercises.

In one terrible bitter-sweet spasm, he gave up. He found Jaadian weaving tinkling fragments of various magics into a warp of shining long splines. With grave courtesy, Jaadian gave Fair his attention, and Fair laboriously set forth his meaning.

Jaadian returned a message. "I recognize your discomfort, and extend my sympathy. It is best that you now return to your native home."

He put aside his weaving and conveyed Fair down through the requisite vortices. Along the way they passed Misthemar. No flicker of meaning was expressed or exchanged, but Howard Fair thought to feel a tinge of faintly malicious amusement.

Howard Fair sat in his apartment. His perceptions, augmented and sharpened by his sojourn in the green realm, took note of the surroundings. Only two hours before, by the clocks of Earth, he had found them both restful and stimulating; now they were neither. His books: superstition, spuriousness, earnest nonsense. His private journals and workbooks: a pathetic scrawl of infantilisms. Gravity tugged at his feet, held him rigid. The shoddy construction of the house, which heretofore he never had noticed, oppressed him. Everywhere he looked he saw slipshod disorder, primitive filth. The thought of the food he must now eat revolted him.

He went out on his little balcony which overlooked the street. The air was impregnated with organic smells. Across the street he could look into windows where his fellow humans lived in stupid squalor.

Fair smiled sadly. He had tried to prepare himself for these reactions, but now was surprised by their intensity. He returned into his apartment. He must accustom himself to the old environment. And after all there were compensations. The most desirable commodities of the world were now his to enjoy.

Howard Fair plunged into the enjoyment of these pleasures. He forced himself to drink quantities of expensive wines, brandies, liqueurs, even though they offended his palate. Hunger overcame his nausea, he forced himself to the consumption of what he thought of as fried animal tissue, the hypertrophied sexual organs of plants. He experimented with erotic sensation, but found that beautiful women no longer seemed different from the plain ones, and that he could barely steel himself to the untidy contacts. He bought libraries of erudite books, glanced through them with contempt. He tried to amuse himself with his old magics; they seemed ridiculous.

He forced himself to enjoy these pleasures for a month; then he fled the city and established a crystal bubble on a crag in the Andes. To nourish himself, he contrived a thick liquid, which, while by no means as exhilarating as the substances of the green realm, was innocent of organic contamination.

After a certain degree of improvisation and make-shift, he arranged his life to its minimum discomfort. The view was one of austere grandeur; not even the condors came to disturb him. He sat back to ponder the chain of events which had started with his discovery of Gerald McIntyre's workbook. He frowned. Gerald McIntyre? He jumped to his feet, looked far over the crags.

He found Gerald McIntyre at a wayside service station in the heart of the South Dakota prairie. McIntyre was sitting in an old wooden chair, tilted back against the peeling yellow paint of the service station, a straw hat shading his eyes from the sun. He was a magnetically handsome man, blond of hair, brown of skin, with blue eyes whose gaze stung like the touch of an icicle. His left thumb-nail glistened green.

Fair greeted him casually; the two men surveyed each other with wry curiosity.

"I see you have adapted yourself," said Howard Fair.

McIntyre shrugged. "As well as possible. I balance between solitude and the pressure of humanity." He looked into the bright blue sky where crows flapped and called. "For many years I lived in isolation. I began to detest the sound of my own breathing."

Along the highway came a glittering automobile, rococo as a hybrid goldfish. With the perceptions now available to them, Fair and McIntyre could see the driver to be red-faced and truculent, his companion a peevish woman in expensive clothes.

"There are other advantages to residence here," said McIntyre. "For instance, I am able to enrich the lives of passers-by with an occasional trifle of novel adventure." He made a small gesture; two dozen crows swooped down and flew beside the automobile. They settled on the fenders, strutted back and forth along the hood, fouled the windshield.

The automobile squealed to a halt, the driver jumped out, put the birds to flight. He threw an ineffectual rock, waved his arms in outrage, returned to his car, proceeded.

"A paltry affair," said McIntyre with a sigh. "The truth of the matter is that I am bored." He pursed his mouth and blew forth three bright puffs of smoke: first red, then yellow, then blazing blue. "I have arrived at the estate of foolishness, as you can see."

Fair surveyed his great-uncle with a trace of uneasiness. McIntyre laughed. "Enough; no more pranks. I predict, however, that you will presently share my malaise."

"I share it already," said Fair. "Sometimes I wish I could abandon all my magic and return to my former innocence."

"I have toyed with the idea," McIntyre replied thoughtfully. "In fact I have made all the necessary arrangements. It is really a simple matter." He led Fair to a small room behind the station. Although the door was open, the interior showed only a thick darkness.

McIntyre, standing well back, surveyed the darkness with a quizzical curl to his lip. "You need only enter. All your magic, all your recollections of the green realm will depart. You will be no wiser than the next man you meet. And with your knowledge will go your boredom, your melancholy, your dissatisfaction."

Fair contemplated the dark doorway. A single step would resolve his discomfort.

He glanced at McIntyre; the two surveyed each other with sardonic amusement. They returned to the front of the building.

"Sometimes I stand by the door and look into the darkness," said McIntyre. "Then I am reminded how dearly I cherish my boredom, and what a precious commodity is so much misery."

Fair made himself ready for departure. "I thank you for this new wisdom, which a hundred more years in the green realm would not have taught me. And now — for a time, at least — I go back to my crag in the Andes."

McIntyre tilted his chair against the wall of the service station. "And I — for a time, at least — will wait for the next passer-by."

"Good-by, then, Uncle Gerald."

"Good-by, Howard."

Alfred's Ark

Ben Hixey, Editor of the Marketville, Iowa, *Weekly Courier*, leaned back in his chair, lit the stub of a dead cigar, inspected his visitor through the smoke. "Alfred, you look the picture of deep despair. Why the long face?"

Alfred Johnson, the local feed-and-grain merchant, made no immediate reply. He looked out the window, at his boots, at Ben, at his own thick hands. He rubbed his stiff brown hair, releasing a faint haze of dust and chaff. He said finally, "I don't hardly know how to tell you, Ben, without causing a lot of excitement."

"Begin at the beginning," said Ben. "I'm a hard man to excite. You're not getting married again?"

Alfred shook his head, grinning the painful grin of a man who has learned the hard way. "Twice was enough."

"Well, give. Let's hear the excitement."

"Do you read your Bible, Ben?"

"Bible?" Ben clapped his hand down on the latest issue of *Editor and Publisher*. "Here's my Bible."

"Seriously, now."

"No," said Ben, blowing a plume of smoke toward the ceiling. "I can't say as I'm a real deep-dyed student in such matters."

"You don't need the Bible to tell you there's wickedness in the world," Alfred said. "Lots of it."

Ben agreed. "I'd never vote for it, but it sure helps circulation."

"Six thousand years ago the world was like it is today — full of sin. You remember what happened?"

"Off-hand, no."

"The Lord sent a great flood. He washed the world clean of wickedness. Ben, there's going to be another flood."

"Now Alfred," said Ben briskly, "are you pulling my leg?"

"No sir. You study your Bible, you'll see for yourself. The day is coming and it's coming soon!"

Ben rearranged the papers on his desk. "I suppose you want me to print big headlines about this flood?"

Alfred hitched himself forward, struck the desk earnestly with his fist. "Here's my plan, Ben. I want the good citizens of this town to get together. I want us to build an ark, to put aboard two beasts of every kind, plenty of food and drink, a selection of good literature, and make ourselves ready. Don't laugh at me, Ben. It's coming."

"Just when is the big day?"

"June 20th. That gives us less than a year. Not much time, but enough."

"Alfred — are you serious?"

"I most surely am, Ben."

"I've always took you for a sensible man, Alfred. You can't believe something so fantastic as all this."

Alfred smiled. "I never expected you to take it on my say-so. I'm going to prove it to you." He took a Bible from his pocket, walked around the desk, held it in front of Ben's restless gaze. "Look here…"

For half an hour he argued his case, pointing out the significant passages, explaining implications which Ben might otherwise have missed. "Now," he said, "now do you believe me?"

Ben leaned back in his chair. "Alfred, you want my advice?"

"I'd like your *help*, Ben. I'd like you and your family aboard this ark I'm fixing to build."

"I'll give you my advice. Get yourself married again. It's the lesser of the evils, and it'll take your mind off this flood proposition."

Alfred rose to his feet. "I guess you won't run an announcement in the paper?"

"No sir. And do you know why? Because I don't want to make you the laughing-stock of the county. You go home and clean up, take a run into Davenport, get good and drunk, and forget all this stuff."

Alfred waved his hand in resignation, departed.

Ben Hixey sighed, shook his head, returned to work.

Alfred returned a moment or two later. "Here's something you can do for me, Ben. I want to put my business up for sale. I want to run a big ad on your front page. At the bottom I want you to print: 'Flood coming June 20th. Help and funds needed to build an ark.' Will you do that?"

"It's your advertisement," said Ben.

Two weeks later on a vacant lot next to his house, Alfred Johnson began construction of an ark. He had sold his business for a price his friends considered outrageous. "He stole it from you, Alfred!" Alfred shook his head. "I stole from him. In a year that business will be washed clean out of sight. I only took his money because in a year his money won't be any good either."

"Alfred," his friends told him in disgust, "you're making a fool of yourself!"

"Maybe so," said Alfred. "And maybe while you're swimming I'll be standing. Ever think of that?"

"You're really in earnest, Alfred?"

"Of course I'm in earnest. You ever hear of divine revelation? That's what I had. Now if you've only come to jaw, excuse me, I gotta get to work."

The ark took shape: a barge fifty feet long, thirty feet wide, ten feet deep. Alfred became something of a local celebrity, and the towns-people made it a practice to come past and check on progress. Alfred received a great deal of jocular advice.

"That barge sure ain't big enough, Alfred," called Bill Olafson. "Not when you consider the elephants and rhinoceroses and giraffes and lions and tigers and hippos and grizzly bears."

"I'm not taking savage beasts," said Alfred. "Just a few pedigreed cattle, cows, horses and sheep, nothing but good stock. If the Lord wanted the others saved he'd have sent me more money. I got just enough for what you see."

"What about a woman, Alfred? You ain't married. You planning to repopulate the world by this here immaculate conception idea?"

"If the right woman don't come along," said Alfred, "I'll just up and hire a woman for the day. When she sees I'm the only man left alive, she'll marry me quick enough."

The fall passed into winter; spring came, and the ark was complete. Alfred began loading aboard stores of all kinds.

Ben Hixey came out to see him one day. "Well, Alfred, I must say you got the courage of your conviction."

"It's not courage, Ben. It's cowardice. I don't want to drown. I'm sorry some of you other folks ain't cowards along with me."

"I'm more worried about the H-bomb, Alfred. That's what I'd like to build an ark against."

"In just about a month there won't be any H-bomb left, Ben. There won't be bombs of any kind, never again, if I got anything to say about it — and I guess I will, the way things look."

Ben surveyed the ark with wondering eyes. "You're really convinced of this business, aren't you, Alfred?"

"I sure am, Ben. There's a lot of good folk I'll hate to see go — but I gave you all warning. I wrote the President and the Governor and the head of *Reader's Digest*."

"Yeah? What did they say?"

"They wrote back thanks for my suggestions. But I could see they didn't believe me."

Ben Hixey smiled. "I don't either, Alfred."

"You'll see, Ben."

June arrived in a spell of wonderful summer weather. Never had the countryside looked so fresh and beautiful. Alfred bought his livestock, and on June 15th herded them aboard the ark. His friends and neighbors took photographs, and made a ceremonial presentation of a glass cage containing two fleas. The problem of securing a woman to become progenetrix of the future race solved itself: a press agent announced that his client, the beautiful movie starlet Maida Brent, had volunteered her services and would be aboard the ark on the morning of June 20th.

"No," said Alfred Johnson. "June 20th begins at midnight. She's got to be aboard on the night of June 19th."

The press agent, after consultation with Miss Brent, agreed.

June 18th dawned bright and sunny, although radio and TV weather reports mentioned peculiar kinks in the jet stream.

On the morning of June 19th, Alfred Johnson, wearing new shoes and a new suit, called in on Ben Hixey. "Last time around, Ben."

Ben looked up from an AP dispatch, grinning rather ruefully. "I've been reading the weather report."

Alfred nodded. "I know. Rain." He held out his hand. "Goodbye, Ben."

"Goodbye, Alfred. Happy landings."

At noon on June 19th, deep dull clouds began rolling in from the north. Miss Maida Brent arrived at seven o'clock in her Cadillac convertible, and amid the mingled flickers of lightning and flashbulbs went aboard the ark. The press agent attempted to come aboard also, but Alfred barred the way. "Sorry. Crew is complete now."

"But Miss Brent can't stay aboard all night, Mr. Johnson."

"She'll be aboard for forty days and forty nights. She might as well get used to it. Now scram."

The press agent shrugged, went to wait in the car. Miss Maida Brent would no doubt leave the ark when she was ready.

The rain began to fall during the evening, and at ten o'clock was coming down heavily. At eleven, the press agent sloshed over to the ark. "Maida! Hey Maida!"

Maida Brent appeared in the doorway of the cabin. "Well?"

"Let's go! We've got all the stuff we need."

Maida Brent sniffed, looked toward the massive black sky. "What's the weather report say?"

"Rain."

"Alfred and I are playing checkers. We're quite cozy. You go on. Bye."

The press agent turned up the collar to his coat, hopped stiff-legged back to the car, where he morosely tried to catnap. The thudding of the rain kept him awake.

Dawn failed to reveal itself. At nine o'clock, a wan wet gloom showed gutters ankle deep in water. The rain pelted down ever harder. Along the streets, cars driven by the curious began to appear, their radios turned to the weather report. Puzzled forecasters spoke of stationary cold fronts, occluded lows, cyclones and anti-cyclones. The forecast: rain.

The street became crowded. News came in that the Perry River Bridge had washed out, that Pewter Creek was in flood. Flood? Yes, flood!

Bill Olafson came splashing through the mud. "Hey Alfred! Where are you?"

THE MOON MOTH AND OTHER STORIES

Alfred looked calmly out of the cabin. "Hello, Bill."

"My wife and kids want to take a look at your ark. Okay if I bring 'em aboard for a spell?"

"Sorry, Bill. No can do."

Bill walked uncertainly back to the car. There was a tremendous rumble of thunder — he looked skyward in apprehension.

Alfred heard a sound from the rear of the ark. He pulled on his slicker, his boots, trudged back to find two teenaged boys and their girl friends mounting a ladder.

Alfred dislodged the ladder. "Keep clear, boys. Git away now. I don't wanta speak to you again."

"Alfred!" Maida's voice came thinly through the thrash of rain. "There's people coming aboard!"

Alfred ran back to meet a score of his friends and neighbors led by Bill Olafson carrying suitcases into the cabin. "Get off this ark, friends," said Alfred in a kindly voice. "There's not room aboard."

"We came to see how things were," said Bill.

"They're fine. Now git."

"I don't think so, Alfred." He reached over the side. "Okay Mama, pass up Joanne and the puppy. Quick. Before those others get here."

"If you don't go," said Alfred, "I'll have to make you git."

"Just don't try no funny stuff, Alfred."

Alfred stepped forward; Bill hit him in the nose. Others of Alfred's friends and neighbors lifted him, carried him kicking and cursing to the rail, threw him off the ark and into the mud.

From the street scores of people came running: men, women, children. They flung themselves up the rail, clambered aboard the ark. The cabin was crowded, the rails were thronged.

There was a clap of thunder; the rain lessened. Overhead appeared a thin spot in the clouds. The sun burst through. The rain stopped.

Alfred's friends and neighbors, crowded along the rail, looked down at Alfred. Alfred, still sitting in the mud, looked steadily back. Around them the sun glistened on the wet buildings, the flowing streets.

Sulwen's Planet

(A Canceling of Unknowns)

I

PROFESSOR JASON GENCH, Professor Victor Kosmin, Dr. Lawrence Drewe, and twenty-four others of equal note filed from the spaceship to contemplate the scene on Sulwen Plain below. The wondering mutters dwindled to silence; a hollow facetiousness met no response. Professor Gench glanced sidelong toward Professor Kosmin, to encounter Professor Kosmin's bland stare. Gench jerked his gaze away.

Boorish bumbling camel, thought Gench.

Piffling little jackanapes, thought Kosmin.

Each wished the other twelve hundred and four light-years distant: which is to say, back on Earth. Or twelve hundred and five light-years.

The first man on Sulwen Plain had been James Sulwen, an embittered Irish Nationalist turned space-wanderer. In his memoirs Sulwen wrote: "To say I was startled, awed, dumbfounded, is like saying the ocean is wet. Oh but it's a lonesome place, so far away, so dim and cold, the more so for the mystery. I stayed there three days and two nights, taking pictures, wondering about the history, all the histories of the universe. What had happened so long ago? What had brought these strange folk here to die? I became haunted; I had to leave…"

Sulwen returned to Earth with his photographs. His discovery was hailed as "the single most important event in human history". Public interest reached a level of dizzy excitement; here was cosmic drama at its most vivid: mystery, tragedy, cataclysm.

In such a perfervid atmosphere the 'Sulwen Planet Survey Commission' was nominated and instructed to perform a brief investigation upon which a full-scale program of research could be based. No one thought to point out that the function of Professor Victor Kosmin, in the field of comparative linguistics, and that of Professor Jason Gench, a philologist, overlapped. The Director of the commission was Dr. Lawrence Drewe, Fellow of Mathematical Philosophy at Vidmar Institute: a mild wry gentleman, superficially inadequate to the job of controlling the personalities of the other members of the commission.

Accompanied by four supply transports with men, materials, and machinery for the construction of a permanent base, the commission departed Earth.

II

Sulwen had understated the desolation of Sulwen's Plain. A dwarf white sun cast a wan glare double, or possibly triple, the intensity of full moonlight. Basalt crags rimmed the plain to north and east. A mile from the base of the crags was the first of the seven wrecked spaceships: a collapsed cylinder of black and white metal two hundred and forty feet long, a hundred and two feet in diameter. There were five such hulks. In and out of the ships, perfectly preserved in the scant atmosphere of frigid nitrogen, were the corpses of a squat pallid race, something under human size, with four arms, each terminating in two slender fingers.

The remaining two ships, three times the length and twice the diameter of the black and white ships, had been conceived and constructed on a larger, more flamboyant, scale. 'Big Purple', as it came to be known, was undamaged except for a gash down the length of its dorsal surface. 'Big Blue' had crashed nose first to the planet and stood in an attitude of precarious equilibrium, seemingly ready to topple at a touch. The design of 'Big Purple' and 'Big Blue' was eccentric, refined, and captious, implying esthetic intent or some analogous quality. These ships were manned by tall slender blue-black creatures with many-horned heads and delicate pinched faces half-concealed behind tufts of hair. They became known as 'Wasps' and their enemies, the pale creatures, were labeled 'Sea Cows', though in neither case was the metaphor particularly apt.

Sulwen Plain had been the site of a terrible battle between two space-faring races: so much was clear. Three questions occurred simultaneously to each of the commissioners:

Where did these peoples originate?

How long ago had the battle occurred?

How did the technology of the 'Wasps' and 'Sea Cows' compare with that of Earth?

There was no immediate answer to the first question. Sulwen's Star controlled no other planets.

As to the time of the battle, a first estimate, derived from the deposition of meteoric dust, suggested a figure of fifty thousand years. More accurate determinations ultimately put the time at sixty-two thousand years.

The third question was more difficult to answer. In some cases Wasp, Sea Cow, and Man had come by different routes to similar ends. In other cases, no comparison was possible.

There was endless speculation as to the course of the battle. The most popular theory envisioned the Sea Cow ships sweeping down upon Sulwen's Plain to find Big Blue and Big Purple at rest. Big Blue had lifted perhaps half a mile, only to be crippled and plunge nose first to the surface. Big Purple, with a mortal gash down the back, apparently had never left the ground. Perhaps other ships had been present; there was no way of knowing. By one agency or another five Sea Cow ships had been destroyed.

III

The ships from Earth landed on a rise to the southeast of the battle-field, where James Sulwen originally had put down. The commissioners, debarking in their out-suits, walked out to the nearest Sea Cow ship: Sea Cow D, as it became known. Sulwen's Star hung low to the horizon, casting a stark pallid light. Long black shadows lay across the putty-colored plain.

The commissioners studied the ruptured ship, inspected the

twisted Sea Cow corpses, then Sulwen's Star dropped below the horizon. Instant darkness came to the plain, and the commissioners, looking often over their shoulders, returned to their own ship.

After the evening meal, Director Drewe addressed the group: "This is a preliminary survey. I reiterate because we are scientists: we want to know! We are not so much interested in planning research as in the research itself. Well — we must practise restraint. For most of you, these wrecks will occupy many years to come. I myself, alas! am a formalist, a mathematical theorist, and as such will be denied your opportunity. Well, then, my personal problems aside: temporarily we must resign ourselves to ignorance. The mystery will remain a mystery, unless Professor Gench or Professor Kosmin instantly is able to read one of the languages." Here Drewe chuckled; he had intended the remark jocularly. Noticing the quick suspicious glance exchanged by Gench and Kosmin he decided that the remark had not been tactful. "For a day or two I suggest a casual inspection of the project, to orient ourselves. There is no pressure on us; we will achieve more if we relax, and try to realize a wide-angle view of the situation. And by all means, everyone be careful of the big blue ship. It looks as if it might topple at a breath!"

Professor Gench smiled bitterly. He was thin as a shrike, with a gaunt crooked face, a crag of a forehead, a black angry gaze. " 'No pressure on us'," he thought. "What a joke!"

" 'Relax'!" thought Kosmin, with a sardonic twitch of the lips. "With that preposterous Gench underfoot? Pah!" In contrast to Gench, Kosmin was massive, almost portly, with a big pale face, a tuft of yellow hair. His cheekbones were heavy, his forehead narrow and back-sloping. He made no effort to project an ingratiating personality; no more so did Gench. Of the two, Gench was perhaps the more gregarious, but his approach to any situation, social or professional, tended to be sharp and doctrinaire.

"I will perform some quick and brilliant exposition," Gench decided. "I must put Kosmin in his place."

"One man eventually will direct the linguistics program," mused Kosmin. "Who but a comparative linguist?"

Drewe concluded his remarks. "I need hardly urge all to caution. Be especially careful of your footing; do not venture into closed areas.

You naturally will be wearing out-suits; check your regenerators and energy levels before leaving the ship; keep your communications channels open at all times. Another matter: let us try to disturb conditions as little as possible. This is a monumental job, there is no point rushing forth, worrying at it like a dog with a rag. Well, then: a good night's rest and tomorrow, we'll have at it!"

IV

The commissioners stepped out upon the dreary surface of the plain, approached the wrecked ships. The closest at hand was Sea Cow D, a black and white vessel, battered, broken, littered with pale corpses. The metallurgists touched analyzers to various sections of hull and machinery, reading off alloy compositions; the biologists examined the corpses; the physicists and technicians peered into the engine compartments, marveling at the unfamiliar engineering of an alien race. Gench, walking under the hulk, found a strip of white fiber covered with rows of queer smears. As he lifted it, the fiber, brittle from cold and age, fell to pieces.

Kosmin, noticing, shook his head critically. "Precisely what you must not do!" he told Gench. "A valuable piece of information is lost forever."

Gench drew his lips back across his teeth. "That much is self-evident. Since the basic responsibility is mine, you need not trouble yourself with doubts or anxieties."

Kosmin ignored Gench's remarks as if he had never spoken. "In the future, please do not move or disturb an important item without consulting me."

Gench turned a withering glare upon his ponderous colleague. "As I interpret the scope of your work, you are to compare the languages after I have deciphered them. You are thus happily able to indulge your curiosity without incurring any immediate responsibility."

Kosmin did not trouble to refute Gench's proposition. "Please disturb no further data. You have carelessly destroyed an artifact. Consult me before you touch anything." And he moved off across the plain toward Big Purple.

Gench, hissing between his teeth, hesitated, then hastened in pursuit. Left to his own devices, Kosmin was capable of any excess. Gench told himself, "Two can play that game!"

Most of the group now stood about Big Purple, which, enormous and almost undamaged, dominated Sulwen Plain. The hull was a rough-textured lavender substance striped with four horizontal bands of corroded metal: apparently a component of the drive-system. Only a powdering of dust and crystals of frozen gas gave an intimation of its great age.

The commissioners walked around the hull, but the ports were sealed. The only access was by the gash along the top surface. A metallurgist found an exterior ladder welded to the hull: he tested the rungs: they seemed sound. While all watched he climbed to the ruptured spine of the ship, gave a jaunty wave of the hand and disappeared.

Gench glanced covertly at Kosmin, who was considering the handholds with lips pursed in distaste. Gench marched forward and climbed the ladder. Kosmin started as if he had been stung. He grimaced, took a step forward, put one of his big legs on the first rung.

Drewe came forward to counsel caution. "Better not risk it, Professor Kosmin; why take chances? I'll have technicians open the port, then we all can enter in safety. We are in no haste, none whatever."

Kosmin thought, "You're in no haste, of course not! And while you dither, that stick-insect walks inside pre-empting the best of everything!"

This indeed was Gench's intent. Clambering down through the torn hull with his dome-light on he found himself in a marvelous environment of shapes and colors which could only be characterized, if tritely, by the word 'weird'.* Certain functional details resembled those of Earth ships, but with odd distortions and differences of proportion that were subtly jarring. "Naturally, and to be expected," Gench told himself. "We alter environment to the convenience of our needs:

---

* In Drewe's book *Sulwen's Planet* he remarked: "Color is color and shape is shape; it would seem incorrect to speak of *human* shape and *human* color, and *Wasp* shape and *Wasp* color; but somehow, by some means, the distinction exists. Call me a mystic if you like…"

the length of our tread, the reach of our arms, the sensitivity of our retinas, many other considerations. And these other races, likewise... Fascinating... I suspect that a man confined for any length of time in this strange ship might become seriously disturbed, if not deranged." With great interest Gench inspected the Wasp corpses which lay sprawled along the corridors: blue-black husks, chitinous surfaces still glossy where dust had not settled. How long would corpses remain unaltered, Gench wondered. Forever? Why not? At 100 degrees K, in an inert atmosphere, it was difficult to imagine changes occurring except those stimulated by cosmic rays... But to work. No time now for speculation! He had stolen a march on the torpid Kosmin, and he meant to make the most of it.

One encouraging matter: there was no lack of writing. Everywhere were signs, plaques, notices in angular interweaving lines which at first glance offered no hope of decipherment. Gench was pleased rather than otherwise. The task would be challenging, but with the aid of computers, pattern-recognizing devices, keys and correlations derived from a study of the context in which the symbols occurred (here indeed lay the decipherer's basic contribution to the process) the language eventually would be elucidated. Another matter: aboard a ship of this size there might well exist not only a library, but rosters, inventories, service manuals pertaining to the various mechanisms: a wealth of material! And Gench saw his problem to be, not the decipherment, but the presence of Professor Kosmin.

Gench shook his head fretfully. A damnable nuisance! He must have a word with Director Drewe. Kosmin perhaps could be assigned to another task: indexing material to be transshipped to Earth, something of the sort.

Gench proceeded through the corridors and levels of Big Purple, trying to locate either a central repository of written materials, or failing this, the control center. But the ship's architecture was not instantly comprehensible and Gench was initially unsuccessful. Wandering back and forth, he found himself in what appeared to be a storage hold, stacked with cases and cartons, then, descending a ramp, he came to the base level and an entry foyer. The port had been forced; commissioners and technicians were passing in and out. Gench halted in disgust, then returned the way he had come: through the storage hold, along corridors, up and down ramps. He began meeting other members of the commission, and hurried his steps to such an extent that his colleagues turned to look after him in surprise. At last he came to the control room, though it bore no resemblance to the corresponding office of any Earth ship, and in fact Gench had passed through before without recognizing its function.

Professor Kosmin, already on hand, glanced around at Gench, then resumed the examination of what appeared to be a large book.

Gench marched indignantly forward. "Professor Kosmin, I prefer that you do not disturb the source materials, or move them, as the context in which they are found may be important."

Kosmin gave Gench a mild glance and returned to his scrutiny of the book.

"Please be extremely careful," said Professor Gench. "If any materials are damaged through mishandling—well, they are irreplaceable." Gench stepped forward. Kosmin moved slightly but somehow contrived to thrust his ample haunch into Gench, and thus barred his way.

Gench glared at his colleague's back, then swung around and departed the chamber in an ill-concealed huff.

He sought out Director Drewe. "Director, may I have a word with you?"

"Certainly."

"I fear that my investigations, and indeed the success of the entire translation program, are being compromised by the conduct of Professor Kosmin, who insists upon intruding into my scope of operation. I am sorry to trouble you with a complaint of this sort, but I feel that a decisive act now on your part will enormously facilitate my work."

Director Drewe sighed. "Professor Kosmin has taken a similar position. Something must be done. Where is he now?"

"In the control chamber, thumbing through an absolutely vital element of the investigation, as if it were a discarded magazine."

Drewe and Gench walked toward the control chamber. Gench said, "I suggest that you use Professor Kosmin in some administrative capacity: logging, indexing, compilation, or the like, until the translation program is sufficiently advanced that he may employ his specialized talents. As of now — ha ha! — there are no languages for him to compare!"

Drewe made no comment. In the control room they found Kosmin still absorbed in the book.

"What have we here?" inquired Drewe.

"Hmm. Umph… A highly important find. It appears to be — I may be over-optimistic — a dictionary, a word-book, a correspondence between the languages of the two races."

"If this is the case," declared Gench, "I had better take charge of it at once."

Drewe heaved a deep sigh. "Gentlemen, temporarily, at any rate, we must arrange a division of function so that neither you, Professor Kosmin, nor you, Professor Gench, are hampered. There are two races here, two languages. Professor Kosmin, which of the two interests you the more profoundly?"

"That is difficult to say," rumbled Kosmin. "I am not yet acquainted with either."

"What about you, Professor Gench?"

With his eyes fixed on the book, Gench said, "My first emphasis will be upon the records of this ship, though naturally, when the inquiry is expanded and I assemble a staff, I will devote equal effort to the other ships."

"Bah!" declared Kosmin, with as much emphasis as he ever permitted himself. "I will work first at this ship," he told Drewe. "It is more convenient. On the other hand, I would wish to ensure that source material elsewhere is handled competently. I have already reported the loss of one irreplaceable record."

Drewe nodded. "It seems that there is no possibility of agreement, let alone cooperation. Very well." He picked up a small metal disk. "We will consider this a coin. This side with the two nicks we will call heads. The other will be tails. Professor Gench, be so good as to call heads or tails while the disk is in the air. If you call correctly you may concentrate your research on the two large ships."

He tossed the disk.

"Heads," called Gench.

"The coin is 'tails'," said Drewe. "Professor Gench, you will survey the five black and white ships. Professor Kosmin, your responsibility will be the two larger ships. This seems a fair division of effort, and neither will inconvenience the other."

Kosmin made a guttural sound. Gench scowled and bit his lip. Neither was satisfied with the decision. With each familiar with only half of the program, a third man might be appointed to supervise and coordinate the labors of both.

Drewe said, "You both must remember that this is a survey expedition. What is required are suggestions as to how the research should be performed, not the research itself."

Kosmin turned to examine the book he had found. Gench threw his hands in the air and strode furiously away.

V

The season seemed to be summer. Sulwen's Star, a glittering sequin, rose far to the southeast, slanted up into the northern sky, slanted back down into the southwest, and black shadows shifted in consonance around the wrecked hulks. The construction crews erected a pair of polyhedric bubbles and the commission moved into more comfortable quarters.

On the fourth evening, as Sulwen's Star touched the edge of the plain, Drewe called his fellow-commissioners together.

"By now," he said, "I think we all have come to grips with the situation. I myself have done little but wander here and there. In fact I fear I am but excess baggage on the expedition. Well — as I have said before — enough of my personal hopes and fears. What have we learned? There seems a consensus that both races were technically more advanced than ourselves, though this may only be an intuition, a guess. As to their relative level — who knows? But let us have an inventory, an assessment of our mutual findings."

The physicists expressed astonishment at the radically different solutions to the problem of space-drive reached by the three races: Man, Sea Cow and Wasp. The chemists speculated as to the probable atmosphere breathed by Wasp and Sea Cow, and commented upon some of the new metallurgic compounds they had encountered aboard the ships. The engineers were somewhat non-plussed, having noticed unorthodox systems not readily susceptible to analysis which could not be dismissed out of hand as the result of incompetence. The biochemists could provide no immediate insight into the metabolic processes of either Wasp or Sea Cow.

Drewe called for an opinion on the languages, and the possibility of translation. Professor Gench rose to his feet, cleared his throat, only to hear the hated voice of Professor Kosmin issuing from another quarter of the room. "As of yet," said Kosmin, "I have given little attention to the Sea Cow language or system of writing. The Wasps, so I have learned from Professor Hideman and Dr. Miller, lack vocal cords, or equivalent organs. They seem to have produced sound by a scraping of certain bony parts behind a resonating membrane. Their conversation, it has been suggested, sounded like a cheap violin played by an idiot child." And Kosmin gave one of his rare oily chuckles. "The writing corresponds to this 'speech' as much as human writing corresponds to human speech. In other words, a vibrating, fluctuating sound is transcribed by a vibrating, fluctuating line: a difficult language to decipher. Naturally, not impossible. I have made one very important find: a compendium or dictionary of Sea Cow pictographs referred to their equivalent in the Wasp written system — a proof, incidentally, that the work of translating both languages must be entrusted to a single agency, and I will formulate a scheme to this end. I welcome the help of all of you; if anyone notices a clear-cut correspondence between symbol and idea, please call it to my attention. I have entrusted to Professor Gench the first cursory examination of the Sea Cow ships, but as of yet I have not checked through his findings." Kosmin continued a few minutes longer, then Drewe called on Professor Gench for his report. Gench leapt to his feet, lips twitching. He spoke with great care. "The program Professor Kosmin mentions is standard procedure. Professor Kosmin, a comparator of known languages, may well be excused for ignorance of deciphering techniques. With two such difficult languages no one need feel shame — ha, ha! — for working beyond his depth. The dictionary mentioned by Professor Kosmin is a valuable item indeed and I suggest that Director Drewe put it into safe custody or entrust it into my care. We cannot risk its abuse by untrained amateurs and dilettantes. I am pressing my search for a similar compendium aboard the Sea Cow ships.

"And I would like to announce a small but significant accomplishment. I have established the Sea Cow numerical system and it is much like our own. An unbroken black rectangle is 'zero'. A single bar is '1'. A cross-bar is '2'. An inverted 'u', conventionalized perhaps from a triangle, is '3'. A digit resembling our own '2' is the Sea Cow '4'. And so on. Perhaps Professor Kosmin has established the Wasp numeration?"

Kosmin, who had been listening without expression, said, "I have been busy with the work for which I was appointed: the formation and supervision of a decipherment program. Numbers at the moment are no great matter."

"I will look over your formulations," said Gench. "If any aspects seem well-conceived I will include them in the master program I am preparing. Here I wish to utter a testimonial to Professor Kosmin. He was urged into the commission against his better judgment, he was assigned a task for which he had no training; nonetheless he has uncomplainingly done his best, even though he is anxious to return to Earth and the work he so generously interrupted in our behalf." And Gench with a grin and bob of the head bowed toward Kosmin. From the other members of the commission came a spatter of dubious applause.

Kosmin rose ponderously to his feet. "Thank you, Professor Gench." He reflected a moment. "I have not heard any report on the condition of 'Big Blue'. It seems precariously balanced, but on the other hand it has remained in stasis for thousands of years. I wonder if there has been any decision as to the feasibility of boarding this ship?" He peered toward the engineers.

Director Drewe responded: "I don't think there has been any definite verdict here. For the present I think we had better stand clear of it."

"Unfortunate," said Kosmin. "It appears that the damage suffered by Big Purple destroyed that chamber which served as a repository of written materials. The corresponding location of Big Blue by some freak is quite undamaged, and I am anxious to investigate."

Gench sat kneading his long chin.

"In due course, in due course," said Drewe. "Yes, Professor Gench?"

Gench frowned down at his hands. He spoke slowly. "It may interest the commission to learn that aboard Sea Cow B, the ship north of Big Purple, I have located just such a repository of Sea Cow documents, though I haven't checked the contents yet. This repository is in Room 11 on the second deck from ground level and seems to be the only such repository undamaged."

"Interesting news," said Drewe, squinting sidelong toward Gench. "Interesting indeed. Well, then, on to the drive technicians: what, offhand, do you make of the Wasp and Sea Cow space-drives, vis-à-vis each other and our own?"

The meeting lasted another hour. Director Drewe made a final announcement. "Our primary goal has almost been achieved, and unless there is a pressing reason to the contrary, I think that we will start back to Earth in two days. Kindly base your thinking upon this timetable."

VI

The following morning Professor Gench continued his investigations aboard Sea Cow B. At lunch he appeared highly excited. "I believe I have located a Wasp–Sea Cow compendium in Room 11 of Sea Cow B! An amazing document! This afternoon I must check Sea Cow E for a similar store-room."

Professor Kosmin, sitting two tables distant, lowered his head over his plate.

VII

Gench seemed somewhat nervous, and his fingers trembled as he zipped himself into his out-suit. He stepped out upon the plain. Directly overhead glittered Sulwen's Star; the wrecked ships stood like models, without human reality or relevance.

Sea Cow E lay a mile to the south. Gench marched stiffly across the plain, from time to time glancing back at other personnel, unidentifiable in out-suits. His course took him past Big Blue and he veered so as to pass close under the great broken ship. He turned another quick glance over his shoulder: no one in his field of vision. He glanced up at the precariously balanced hulk. "Safe? Safe as jelly-bread." He stepped through a gap in the hull, into a picturesque tangle of girders, plates, membranes and fibers.

Professor Kosmin, watching Gench veer toward Big Blue, nodded: three jerks of the massive head. "Well, then. Now we shall see." He walked north toward Sea Cow B, and presently stood by the crushed hull. "The entrance? Yes…To the second deck then…Surprising architecture. What peculiar coloring…Hmm. Room Eleven. The numerals are clear enough. This is the '1', the single bar. And here the '2'." Kosmin proceeded along the corridor. "'6'…'7'…Strange. '10'. Where is '8' and '9'? Well, no matter. Unlucky numbers perhaps. Here is '10', and here '11'. Aha." Kosmin pushed aside the panel and entered Chamber 11.

VIII

Sulwen's Star slanted down to the gray horizon and past; darkness came instantly to the plain. Neither Gench nor Kosmin appeared for the evening meal. The steward called Director Drewe's attention to the fact.

Drewe considered the two empty seats. "I suppose we must send out to find them. Professor Gench will no doubt be exploring 'Big Blue'. I presume we will find Professor Kosmin hard at work in Sea Cow B."

IX

Professor Gench had suffered a broken collar-bone, contusions and shock from the blow of the heavy beam which Professor Kosmin — so Gench claimed — had arranged to fall upon whoever might enter Big Blue's control cabin.

"Not so!" boomed Professor Kosmin, both of whose legs had been broken as a result of his fall through the floor of Chamber 11 on the second deck of Sea Cow B. "You were warned expressly not to set foot in Big Blue. How could I set a trap in a place you were forbidden to visit? What of the detestable pitfall by which you hoped to kill me? Aha, but I am too strong for you! I caught the floor and broke my fall! I survived your worst!"

"You survive your own stupidity," sneered Gench. "Sea Cows, with two fingers on each of four arms, use base eight in their enumerations. You went into Chamber 9, not Chamber 11. A person as obtuse and as murderous as yourself has no place in the field of science! I am lucky to be alive!"

"Were my legs still sound I would tread upon you for the roach you are!" shouted Professor Kosmin.

Director Drewe intervened. "Gentlemen, calm yourselves. Reproaches are futile; remorse is more appropriate. You must realize that neither of you will head the decipherment program."

"Indeed? And why not?" snorted Gench.

"Under the circumstances I fear that I can recommend neither of you."

"Then who will be appointed?" demanded Kosmin. "The field is not crowded with able men."

Drewe shrugged. "As a mathematician, I may say that deciphering appeals to me as a fascinating exercise in logic. I might be persuaded to accept the post myself. To be candid, it is probably my only chance for continued association with the project." Director Drewe bowed politely and left the room.

Professor Gench and Professor Kosmin were silent for several minutes. Then Gench said, "Peculiar. Very peculiar indeed. I arranged no pitfall in Chamber 9. I admit I had noted that the panel could be opened from one direction only, from the corridor... A person venturing into Chamber 9 might find himself in a humiliating position... Strange."

"Hmm," rumbled Kosmin. "Strange indeed..."

There was another period of silence as the two men reflected. Then Kosmin said, "Of course I am not altogether innocent. I conceived that if you ventured into 'Big Blue' against orders you would incur a reprimand. I propped up no beam."

"Most peculiar," said Professor Gench. "A puzzling situation... A possibility suggests itself—"

"Yes?"

"Why kill us?"

"To the mathematical mind the most elegant solution is the simplest," reflected Professor Kosmin.

"A canceling of the unknowns," mused Professor Gench.

RUMFUDDLE

I

From *Memoirs and Reflections*,
by Alan Robertson:

> Often I hear myself declared humanity's preeminent benefactor, though the jocular occasionally raise a claim in favor of the original Serpent. After all circumspection, I really cannot dispute the judgment. My place in history is secure; my name will persist as if it were printed indelibly across the sky. All of which I find absurd but understandable. For I have given wealth beyond calculation. I have expunged deprivation, famine, over-population, territorial constriction: all the first-order causes of contention have vanished. My gifts go freely and carry with them my personal joy, but as a reasonable man (and for lack of other restrictive agency), I feel that I cannot relinquish all control, for when has the human animal ever been celebrated for abnegation and self-discipline?
>
> We now enter an era of plenty and a time of new concerns. The old evils are gone; we must resolutely prohibit a flamboyant and perhaps unnatural set of new vices.

THE THREE GIRLS GULPED down breakfast, assembled their homework and departed noisily for school.

Elizabeth poured coffee for herself and Gilbert. He thought she seemed pensive and moody. Presently she said, "It's so beautiful here... We're very lucky, Gilbert."

"I never forget it."

Elizabeth sipped her coffee and mused a moment, following some vagrant train of thought. She said, "I never liked growing up. I always felt strange — different from the other girls. I really don't know why."

"It's no mystery. Everyone for a fact is different."

"Perhaps…But Uncle Peter and Aunt Emma always acted as if I were more different than usual. I remember a hundred little signals. And yet I was such an ordinary little girl…Do you remember when you were little?"

"Not very well." Duray looked out the window he himself had glazed, across green slopes and down to the placid water his daughters had named the Silver River. The Sounding Sea was thirty miles south; directly behind the house stood the first trees of the Robber Woods.

Duray considered his past. "Bob owned a ranch in Arizona during the 1870s: one of his fads. The Apaches killed my father and mother. Bob took me to the ranch, and then when I was three he brought me to Alan's house in San Francisco and that's where I was brought up."

Elizabeth sighed. "Alan must have been wonderful. Uncle Peter was so grim. Aunt Emma never told me anything. Literally, not anything! They never cared the slightest bit for me, one way or the other…I wonder why Bob brought the subject up — about the Indians and your mother and father being scalped and all…He's such a strange man."

"Was Bob here?"

"He looked in a few minutes yesterday to remind us of his 'Rumfuddle'. I told him I didn't want to leave the girls. He said to bring them along."

"Hah!"

"I told him I didn't want to go to his damn Rumfuddle with or without the girls. In the first place, I don't want to see Uncle Peter, who's sure to be there…"

II

From *Memoirs and Reflections*:

I insisted then and I insist now that our dear old Mother Earth, so soiled and toil-worn, never be neglected. Since I pay the piper (in a manner of speaking) I call the tune, and to my secret amusement I am heeded most briskly the world around, in the manner of bellboys jumping to the command of an irascible old gentleman who is known to be a good tipper. No one dares to defy me. My whims become actualities; my plans progress.

Paris, Vienna, San Francisco, St. Petersburg, Venice, London, Dublin surely will persist, gradually to become idealized essences of their former selves, as wine in due course becomes the soul of the grape. What of the old vitality? The shouts and curses, the neighborhood quarrels, the raucous music, the vulgarity? Gone, all gone! (But easy of reference at any of the cognates.) Old Earth is to be a gentle, kindly world, rich in treasures and artifacts, a world of old places: old inns, old roads, old forests, old palaces, where folk come to wander and dream, to experience the best of the past without suffering the worst.

Material abundance can now be taken for granted: our resources are infinite. Metal, timber, soil, rock, water, air: free for anyone's taking. A single commodity remains in finite supply: human toil.

Gilbert Duray, the informally adopted grandson of Alan Robertson, worked on the Urban Removal Program. Six hours a day, four days a week, he guided a trashing-machine across deserted Cupertino, destroying tract houses, service stations and supermarkets. Knobs and toggles controlled a steel hammer at the end of a hundred-foot boom; with a twitch of the finger Duray toppled power-poles, exploded picture-windows, smashed siding and stucco, pulverized concrete. A disposal rig crawled fifty feet behind. The detritus was clawed upon a conveyor-belt, carried to a twenty-foot orifice and dumped with a rush and a rumble into the Apathetic Ocean. Aluminum siding, asphalt shingles, corrugated fiber-glass, TVs and barbeques, Swedish Modern furniture, Book-of-the-Month selections, concrete patio-tiles, finally the sidewalk and street itself: all to the bottom of the Apathetic Ocean. Only the trees remained: a strange eclectic forest stretching as far as the eye could reach: liquidambar and Scotch pine; Chinese pistachio, Atlas cedar and gingko; white birch and Norway maples.

At one o'clock Howard Wirtz emerged from the caboose, as they called the small locker room at the rear of the machine. Wirtz had homesteaded a Miocene world; Duray, with a wife and three children, had preferred the milder environment of a contemporary semi-cognate: the popular Type A world on which man had never evolved.

Duray gave Wirtz the work schedule. "More or less like yesterday; straight out Persimmon to Walden, then right a block and back."

Wirtz, a dour and laconic man, acknowledged the information with a jerk of the head. On his Miocene world he lived alone, in a houseboat on a mountain lake. He harvested wild rice, mushrooms and berries; he shot geese, ground-fowl, deer, young bison, and had once informed Duray that after his five year work-time he might just retire to his lake and never appear on Earth again, except maybe to buy clothes and ammunition. "Nothing here I want, nothing at all."

Duray gave a derisive snort. "And what will you do with all your time?"

"Hunt, fish, eat and sleep, maybe sit on the front deck."

"Nothing else?"

"I just might learn to fiddle. Nearest neighbor is fifteen million years away."

"You can't be too careful, I suppose."

Duray descended to the ground and looked over his day's work: a quarter-mile swath of desolation. Duray, who allowed his subconscious few extravagances, nevertheless felt a twinge for the old times, which, for all their disadvantages, at least had been lively. Voices, bicycle bells, the barking of dogs, the slam of doors, still echoed along Persimmon Avenue. The former inhabitants presumably preferred their new homes. The self-sufficient had taken private worlds, the more gregarious lived in communities on worlds of every description: as early as the Carboniferous, as current as the Type A. A few had even returned to the now uncrowded cities. An exciting era to live in: a time of flux. Duray, thirty-four years old, remembered no other way of life; the old existence, as exemplified by Persimmon Avenue, seemed antique, cramped, constricted.

He had a word with the operator of the trashing-machine; returning to the caboose he paused to look through the orifice across the Apathetic Ocean. A squall hung black above the southern horizon, toward which a trail of broken lumber drifted, to wash ultimately up on some unknown pre-Cambrian shore. There never would be an inspector sailing forth to protest; the world knew no life other than molluscs and algae, and all the trash of Earth would never fill its submarine gorges. Duray tossed a rock through the gap and watched the alien water splash up and subside. Then he turned away and entered the caboose.

Along the back wall were four doors. The second from the left was marked G. DURAY. He unlocked the door, pulled it open, and stopped short, staring in astonishment at the blank back wall. He lifted the transparent plastic flap which functioned as an air-seal and brought out the collapsed metal ring which had been the flange surrounding his passway. The inner surface was bare metal; looking through he saw only the interior of the caboose.

A long minute passed. Duray stood staring at the useless ribbon as if hypnotized, trying to grasp the implications of the situation. To his knowledge no passway had ever failed, unless it had been purposefully closed. Who would play him such a spiteful idiotic trick? Certainly not his wife Elizabeth. She detested practical jokes, and, if anything, like Duray himself, was perhaps a trifle too intense and literal-minded. He jumped down from the caboose and strode off across Cupertino forest: a sturdy heavy-shouldered man of about average stature. His features were rough and uncompromising; his brown hair was cut crisply short; his eyes glowed golden-brown and exerted an arresting force. Straight heavy eyebrows crossed his long thin nose like the bar of a T; his mouth, compressed against some strong inner urgency, formed a lower horizontal bar. All in all, not a man to be trifled with, or so it would seem.

He trudged through the haunted grove, preoccupied by the strange and inconvenient event which had befallen him. What had happened to the passway? Unless Elizabeth had invited friends out to Home, as

they called their world, she was alone, with the three girls at school…
Duray came out upon Stevens Creek Road. A farmer's pick-up truck
halted at his signal and took him into San Jose, now little more than a
country town.

At the transit center he dropped a coin in the turnstile and entered
the lobby. Four portals designated 'Local', 'California', 'North America',
'World', opened in the walls, each portal leading to a hub on Utilis*.

Duray passed into the 'California' hub, found the 'Oakland' portal,
returned to the Oakland Transit Center on Earth, passed back through
the 'Local' portal to the 'Oakland' hub on Utilis, returned to Earth
through the 'Montclair West' portal to a depot only a quarter-mile
from Thornhill School†, to which Duray walked.

In the office Duray identified himself to the clerk and requested the
presence of his daughter Dolly.

The clerk sent forth a messenger who, after an interval, returned
alone. "Dolly Duray isn't at school."

Duray was surprised; Dolly had been in good health and had set off
to school as usual. He said, "Either Joan or Ellen will do as well."

The messenger again went forth and again returned. "Neither one is
in their classrooms, Mr. Duray. All three of your children are absent."

"I can't understand it," said Duray, now fretful. "All three set off to
school this morning."

"Let me ask Miss Haig. I've just come on duty." The clerk spoke into

---

* Utilis: a world cognate to Palaeocene Earth, where, by Alan Robertson's
decree, all the industries, institutions, warehouses, tanks, dumps and
commercial offices of old Earth were now located. The name 'Utilis', so it had
been remarked, accurately captured the flavor of Alan Robertson's pedantic,
quaint and idealistic personality.

† Alan Robertson had proposed another specialized world, to be known as
'Tutelar', where the children of all the settled worlds should receive their
education in a vast array of pedagogical facilities. To his hurt surprise, he
encountered a storm of wrathful opposition from parents. His scheme was
termed mechanistic, vast, dehumanizing, repulsive. What better world for
schooling than old Earth itself? Here was the source of all tradition; let Earth
become 'Tutelar'! So insisted the parents and Alan Robertson had no choice
but to agree.

a telephone, listened, then turned back to Duray. "The girls went home at ten o'clock. Mrs. Duray called for them and took them back through the passway."

"Did she give any reason whatever?"

"Miss Haig says no; Mrs. Duray just told her she needed the girls at home."

Duray stifled a sigh of baffled irritation. "Could you take me to their locker? I'll use their passway to get home."

"That's contrary to school regulations, Mr. Duray. You'll understand, I'm sure."

"I can identify myself quite definitely," said Duray. "Mr. Carr knows me well. As a matter of fact, my passway collapsed and I came here to get home."

"Why don't you speak to Mr. Carr?"

"I'd like to do so."

Duray was conducted into the principal's office where he explained his predicament. Mr. Carr expressed sympathy and made no difficulty about taking Duray to the children's passway.

They went to a hall at the back of the school and found the locker numbered '382'. "Here we are," said Carr. "I'm afraid that you'll find it a tight fit." He unlocked the metal door with his master key and threw it open. Duray looked inside and saw only the black metal at the back of the locker. The passway, like his own, had been closed.

Duray drew back and for a moment could find no words.

Carr spoke in a voice of polite amazement. "How very perplexing! I don't believe I've ever seen anything like it before! Surely the girls wouldn't play such a silly prank?"

"They know better than to touch the passway," Duray said gruffly. "Are you sure that this is the right locker?"

Carr indicated the card on the outside of the locker, where three names had been typed: *Dorothy Duray, Joan Duray, Ellen Duray.* "No mistake," said Carr, "and I'm afraid that I can't help you any further. Are you in common residency?"

"It's our private homestead."

Carr nodded with lips judiciously pursed, to suggest that such insistence upon privacy seemed eccentric. He gave a deprecatory little chuckle. "I suppose if you isolate yourself to such an extent, you more or less must expect a series of emergencies."

"To the contrary," Duray said crisply. "Our life is uneventful, because there's no one to bother us. We love the wild animals, the quiet, the fresh air. We wouldn't have it any differently."

Carr smiled a dry smile. "Mr. Robertson has certainly altered the lives of us all. I understand that he is your grandfather?"

"I was raised in his household. I'm his nephew's foster son. The blood relationship isn't all that close."

III

From *Memoirs and Reflections*:

I early became interested in magnetic fluxes and their control. After taking my degree I worked exclusively in this field, studying all varieties of magnetic envelopes and developing controls over their formation. For many years my horizons were thus limited, and I lived a placid existence.

Two contemporary developments forced me down from my 'ivory castle'. First: the fearful overcrowding of the planet and the prospect of worse to come. Cancer already was an affliction of the past; heart diseases were under control; I feared that in another ten years immortality might be a practical reality for many of us, with a consequent augmentation of population pressure.

Secondly, the theoretical work done upon 'black holes' and 'white holes' suggested that matter compacted in a 'black hole' broke through a barrier to spew forth from a 'white hole' in another universe. I calculated pressures and considered the self-focusing magnetic sheaths, cones and whorls with which I was experimenting. Through their innate properties, these entities constricted themselves to apices of a cross-section indistinguishable from a geometric point. What if two or more cones (I asked myself) could be arranged in contraposition to produce an equilibrium? In this condition charged particles must be accelerated to near light speed and at the mutual focus constricted and impinged together. The pressures thus created, though of small scale, would be far in excess of those characteristic of the 'black holes': to unknown effect. I can now report that the mathematics of the multiple focus are a most improbable thicket, and the useful service I enforced upon what I must call a set of absurd contradictions is one of my secrets. I know that thousands of scientists, at home and abroad, are attempting to duplicate my work; they are welcome to the effort. None will succeed. Why do I speak so positively? This is my other secret.

Duray marched back to the Montclair West depot in a state of angry puzzlement. There had been four passways to Home, of which two were closed. The third was located in his San Francisco locker: the 'front door', so to speak. The last and the original orifice was cased, filed and indexed in Alan Robertson's vault.

Duray tried to deal with the problem in rational terms. The girls would never tamper with the passways. As for Elizabeth, no more than the girls would she consider such an act. At least Duray could imagine no reason which would so urge or impel her. Elizabeth, like himself a foster-child, was a beautiful passionate woman, tall, dark-haired, with lustrous dark eyes and a wide mouth which tended to curve in an endearingly crooked grin. She was also responsible, loyal, careful, industrious; she loved her family and Riverview Manor. The theory of erotic intrigue seemed to Duray as incredible as the fact of the closed passways. Though, for a fact Elizabeth was prone to wayward and incomprehensible moods. Suppose Elizabeth had received a visitor, who for some sane or insane purpose had forced her to close the passway?...Duray shook his head in frustration, like a harassed bull. The matter no doubt had some simple cause. Or on the other hand, Duray reflected, the cause might be complex and intricate. The thought by some obscure connection brought before him the image of his nominal foster-father, Alan Robertson's nephew, Bob Robertson. Duray gave his head a nod of gloomy asseveration, as if to confirm a fact he long ago should have suspected. He went to the phone booth and called Bob Robertson's apartment in San Francisco. The screen glowed white and an instant later displayed Bob Robertson's alert, clean and handsome face. "Good afternoon, Gil. Glad you called; I've been anxious to get in touch with you."

Duray became warier than ever. "How so?"

"Nothing serious, or so I hope. I dropped by your locker to leave off some books that I promised Elizabeth, and I noticed through the glass that your passway is closed. Collapsed. Useless."

"Strange," said Duray. "Very strange indeed. I can't understand it. Can you?"

"No... Not really."

Duray thought to detect a subtlety of intonation. His eyes narrowed in concentration. "The passway at my rig was closed. The passway at the girls' school was closed. Now you tell me that the downtown passway is closed."

Bob Robertson grinned. "That's a pretty broad hint, I would say. Did you and Elizabeth have a row?"

"No."

Bob Robertson rubbed his long aristocratic chin. "A mystery. There's probably some very ordinary explanation."

"Or some very extraordinary explanation."

"True. Nowadays a person can't rule out anything. By the way, tomorrow night is the Rumfuddle, and I expect both you and Elizabeth to be on hand."

"As I recall," said Duray, "I've already declined the invitation." The 'Rumfuddlers' were a group of Bob's cronies. Duray suspected that their activities were not altogether wholesome. "Excuse me; I've got to find an open passway or Elizabeth and the kids are marooned."

"Try Alan," said Bob. "He'll have the original in his vault."

Duray gave a curt nod. "I don't like to bother him, but that's my last hope."

"Let me know what happens," said Bob Robertson. "And if you're at loose ends, don't forget the Rumfuddle tomorrow night. I mentioned the matter to Elizabeth and she said she'd be sure to attend."

"Indeed. And when did you consult Elizabeth?"

"A day or so ago. Don't look so damnably gothic, my boy."

"I'm wondering if there's a connection between your invitation and the closed passways. I happen to know that Elizabeth doesn't care for your parties."

Bob Robertson laughed with easy good grace. "Reflect a moment. Two events occur. I invite you and wife Elizabeth to the Rumfuddle. This is event one. Your passways close up, which is event two. By a feat of structured absurdity you equate the two and blame me. Now is that fair?"

"You call it 'structured absurdity'," said Duray. "I call it instinct."

Bob Robertson laughed again. "You'll have to do better than that. Consult Alan and if for some reason he can't help you, come to the Rumfuddle. We'll rack our brains and either solve your problem, or come up with new and better ones." He gave a cheery nod and before Duray could roar an angry expostulation the screen faded.

Duray stood glowering at the screen, convinced that Bob Robertson knew much more about the closed passways than he admitted. Duray went to sit on a bench … If Elizabeth had closed him away from Home, her reasons must have been compelling indeed. But, unless she intended to isolate herself permanently from Earth, she would leave at least one passway ajar, and this must be the master orifice in Alan Robertson's vault.

Duray rose to his feet, somewhat heavily, and stood a moment, head bent and shoulders hunched. He gave a surly grunt and returned to the phone booth, where he called a number known to not more than a dozen persons.

The screen glowed white, while the person at the other end of the line scrutinized his face…The screen cleared, revealing a round pale face from which pale blue eyes stared forth with a passionless intensity. "Hello, Ernest," said Duray. "Is Alan busy at the moment?"

"I don't think he's doing anything particular — except resting."

Ernest gave the last two words a meaningful emphasis.

"I've got some problems," said Duray. "What's the best way to get in touch with him?"

"You'd better come up here. The code is changed. It's MHF now."

"I'll be there in a few minutes."

Back in the 'California' hub on Utilis, Duray went into a side chamber lined with private lockers, numbered and variously marked with symbols, names, colored flags, or not marked at all. Duray went to

Locker 122, and ignoring the key-hole, set the code lock to the letters MHF. The door opened; Duray stepped into the locker and through the passway to the High Sierra headquarters of Alan Robertson.

IV

From *Memoirs and Reflections*:

If one Basic Axiom controls the cosmos, it must be this: *In a situation of infinity, every possible condition occurs, not once, but an infinite number of times.*

There is no mathematical nor logical limit to the number of dimensions. Our perceptions assure us of three only, but many indications suggest otherwise: parapsychic occurrences of a hundred varieties, the 'white holes', the seemingly finite state of our own universe, which by corollary, asserts the existence of others.

Hence, when I stepped behind the lead slab and first touched the button I felt confident of success; failure would have surprised me!

But (and here lay my misgivings) what sort of success might I achieve?

Suppose I opened a hole into the interplanetary vacuum?

The chances of this were very good indeed; I surrounded the machine in a strong membrane, to prevent the air of Earth from rushing off into the void.

Suppose I discovered a condition totally beyond imagination?

My imagination yielded no safeguards.

I proceeded to press the button.

Duray stepped out into a grotto under damp granite walls. Sunlight poured into the opening from a dark blue sky. This was Alan Robertson's link to the outside world; like many other persons, he disliked a passway opening directly into his home. A path led fifty yards across bare granite mountainside to the lodge. To the west spread a great vista of diminishing ridges, valleys and hazy blue air; to the east rose a pair of granite crags with snow caught in the saddle between. Alan Robertson's lodge was built just below the timberline, beside a small lake fringed with tall dark firs. The lodge was built of rounded granite stones, with a wooden porch across the front; at each end rose a massive chimney.

Duray had visited the lodge on many occasions; as a boy he had scaled both of the crags behind the house, to look wondering off across the stillness, which on old Earth had a poignant breathing quality different from the uninhabited solitudes of worlds such as Home.

Ernest came to the door: a middle-aged man with an ingenuous face, small white hands and soft damp mouse-colored hair. Ernest disliked the lodge, the wilderness and solitude in general; he never-theless would have suffered tortures before relinquishing his post as subaltern to Alan Robertson. Ernest and Duray were almost antipodal in outlook; Ernest thought Duray brusque, indelicate, a trifle coarse and probably not disinclined to violence as an argumentative adjunct. Duray considered Ernest, when he thought of him at all, as the kind of man who takes two bites out of a cherry. Ernest had never married; he showed no interest in women, and Duray, as a boy, had often fretted at Ernest's over-cautious restrictions.

In particular Ernest resented Duray's free and easy access to Alan Robertson. The power to restrict or admit those countless persons who demanded Alan Robertson's attention was Ernest's most cherished per-quisite, and Duray denied him the use of it by simply ignoring Ernest and all his regulations. Ernest had never complained to Alan Robertson for fear of discovering that Duray's influence exceeded his own. A wary truce existed between the two, each conceding the other his privileges.

Ernest performed a polite greeting and admitted Duray into the lodge. Duray looked around the interior, which had not changed during his lifetime: varnished plank floors with red, black and white Navaho rugs, massive pine furniture with leather cushions, a few shelves of books, a half-dozen pewter mugs on the mantle over the big fireplace: a room almost ostentatiously bare of souvenirs and mementos. Duray turned back to Ernest: "Whereabouts is Alan?"

"On his boat."

"With guests?"

"No," said Ernest, with a faint sniff of disapproval. "He's alone, quite alone."

"How long has he been gone?"

"He just went through an hour ago. I doubt if he's left the dock yet. What is your problem, if I may ask?"

"The passways to my world are closed. All three. There's only one left, in the vault."

Ernest arched his flexible eyebrows. "Who closed them?"

"I don't know. Elizabeth and the girls are alone, so far as I know."

"Extraordinary," said Ernest, in a flat metallic voice. "Well then, come along." He led the way down a hall to a back room. With his hand on the knob Ernest paused and looked back over his shoulder. "Did you mention the matter to anyone? Robert, for instance?"

"Yes," said Duray curtly, "I did. Why do you ask?"

Ernest hesitated a fraction of a second. "No particular reason. Robert occasionally has a somewhat misplaced sense of humor, he and his 'Rumfuddlers'." He spoke the word with a hiss of distaste.

Duray said nothing of his own suspicions. Ernest opened the door; they entered a large room illuminated by a skylight. The only furnishing was a rug on the varnished floor. Into each wall opened four doors. Ernest went to one of these doors, pulled it open and made a resigned gesture. "You'll probably find Alan at the dock."

Duray looked into the interior of a rude hut with palm-frond walls, resting on a platform of poles. Through the doorway he saw a path leading under sunlit green foliage toward a strip of white beach. Surf sparkled below a layer of dark blue ocean and a glimpse of the sky. Duray hesitated, rendered wary by the events of the morning. Anyone and everyone was suspect, even Ernest, who now gave a quiet sniff of contemptuous amusement. Through the foliage Duray glimpsed a spread of sail; he stepped through the passway.

V

From *Memoirs and Reflections*:

> Man is a creature whose evolutionary environment has been the open air. His nerves, muscles and senses have developed across three million years in intimate contiguity with natural earth, crude stone,

live wood, wind and rain. Now this creature is suddenly—on the geologic scale, instantaneously—shifted to an unnatural environment of metal and glass, plastic and plywood, to which his psychic substrata lack all compatibility. The wonder is not that we have so much mental instability but so little. Add to this, the weird noises, electrical pleasures, bizarre colors, synthetic foods, abstract entertainments! We should congratulate ourselves on our durability.

I bring this matter up because, with my little device, so simple, so easy, so flexible, I have vastly augmented the load upon our poor primeval brains, and for a fact many persons find the instant transition from one locale to another unsettling, and even actively unpleasant.

Duray stood on the porch of the cabin, under a vivid green canopy of sunlit foliage. The air was soft and warm and smelled of moist vegetation. Duray stood listening. The mutter of the surf came to his ears and from a far distance a single bird-call.

Duray stepped down to the ground and followed the path under tall palm trees to a river-bank. A few yards downstream, beside a rough pier of poles and planks, floated a white and blue trimaran ketch, sails hoisted and distended to a gentle breeze. On the deck stood Alan Robertson, on the point of casting off the mooring lines. Duray hailed him; Alan Robertson turned in surprise and vexation, which vanished when he recognized Duray. "Hello Gil; glad you're here! For a moment I thought it might be someone to bother me. Jump aboard; you're just in time for a sail."

Duray somberly joined Alan Robertson on the boat. "I'm afraid I am here to bother you."

"Oh?" Alan Robertson raised his eyebrows in instant solicitude. He was a man of no great height, thin, nervously active. Wisps of rumpled white hair fell over his forehead; mild blue eyes inspected Duray with concern, all thought of sailing forgotten. "What in the world has happened?"

"I wish I knew. If it were something I could handle myself I wouldn't bother you."

"Don't worry about me; there's all the time in the world for sailing. Now tell me what's happened."

"I can't get through to Home. All the passways are closed off: why and how I have no idea. Elizabeth and the girls are out there alone; at least I think they're out there."

Alan Robertson rubbed his chin. "What an odd business! I can certainly understand your agitation…You think Elizabeth closed the passways?"

"It's unreasonable — but there's no one else."

Alan Robertson turned Duray a shrewd kindly glance. "No little family upsets? Nothing to cause her despair and anguish?"

"Absolutely nothing. I've tried to reason things out, but I draw a blank. I thought that maybe someone — a man — had gone through to visit her and decided to take over — but if this were the case, why did she come to the school for the girls? That possibility is out. A secret love affair? Possible but so damn unlikely. Since she wants to keep me off the planet, her only motive could be to protect me, or herself, or the girls from danger of some sort. Again this means that another person is concerned in the matter. Who? How? Why? I spoke to Bob. He claims to know nothing about the situation, but he wants me to come to his damned 'Rumfuddle' and he hints very strongly that Elizabeth will be on hand. I can't prove a thing against Bob, but I suspect him. He's always had a taste for odd jokes."

Alan Robertson gave a lugubrious nod. "I won't deny that." He sat down in the cockpit and stared off across the water. "Bob has a complicated sense of humor, but he'd hardly close you away from your world…I hardly think that your family is in actual danger, but of course we can't take chances. The possibility exists that Bob is not responsible, that something uglier is afoot." He jumped to his feet. "Our obvious first step is to use the master-orifice in the vault." He looked a shade regretfully toward the ocean. "My little sail can wait…A lovely world this: not fully cognate with Earth — a cousin, so to speak. The fauna and flora are roughly contemporary except for man. The hominids have never developed."

The two men returned up the path, Alan Robertson chatting light-heartedly: "— thousands and thousands of worlds I've visited, and looked into even more, but do you know I've never hit upon a good system of classification? There are exact cognates — of course we're never sure exactly *how* exact they are. These cases are relatively simple, but then the problems begin... Bah! I don't think about such things any more. I know that when I keep all the nominates at zero the cognates appear. Over-intellectualizing is the bane of this, and every other era. Show me a man who deals only with abstraction and I'll show you the dead futile end of evolution..." Alan Robertson chuckled. "If I could control the machine tightly enough to produce real cognates, our troubles would be over... Much confusion of course. I might step through into the cognate world immediately as a true cognate Alan Robertson steps through into our world, with net effect of zero. An amazing business, really; I never tire of it..."

They returned to the transit room of the mountain lodge. Ernest appeared almost instantly. Duray suspected he had been watching through the passway.

Alan Robertson said briskly, "We'll be busy for an hour or two, Ernest. Gilbert is having difficulties and we've got to set things straight."

Ernest nodded somewhat grudgingly, or so it seemed to Duray. "The progress report on the Ohio Plan has arrived. Nothing particularly urgent."

"Thank you, Ernest, I'll see to it later. Come along, Gilbert; let's get to the bottom of this affair." They went to Door No. 1, and passed through to the Utilis hub. Alan Robertson led the way to a small green door with a three-dial coded lock, which he opened with a flourish. "Very well; in we go." He carefully locked the door behind them and they walked the length of a short hall. "A shame that I must be so cautious," said Alan Robertson. "You'd be astonished at the outrageous requests otherwise sensible people make of me. I sometimes become exasperated... Well, it's understandable, I suppose."

At the end of the hall Alan Robertson worked the locking dials of a red door. "This way, Gilbert; you've been through before." They stepped through a passway into a hall, which opened into a circular concrete chamber fifty feet in diameter, located, so Duray knew, deep under the Mad Dog Mountains of the Mojave Desert. Eight halls extended away into the rock; each hall communicated with twelve aisles. The center of the chamber was occupied by a circular desk twenty feet in diameter: here six clerks in white smocks worked at computers and collating machines. In accordance with their instructions they gave Alan Robertson neither recognition nor greeting.

Alan Robertson went up to the desk, at which signal the chief clerk, a solemn young man bald as an egg came forward. "Good afternoon, sir."

"Good afternoon, Harry. Find me the index for 'Gilbert Duray', on my personal list."

The clerk bowed smartly. He went to an instrument and ran his fingers over a bank of keys; the instrument ejected a card which Harry handed to Alan Robertson. "There you are, sir."

Alan Robertson showed the card to Duray, who saw the code: '4:8:10/6:13:29'.

"That's your world," said Alan Robertson. "We'll soon learn how the land lies. This way, to Radiant 4." He led the way down the hall, turned into the aisle numbered "8", and proceeded to Stack 10. "Shelf 6," said Alan Robertson. He checked the card. "Drawer 13...Here we are." He drew forth the drawer, ran his fingers along the tabs. "Item 29. This should be Home." He brought forth a metal frame four inches square, and held it up to his eyes. He frowned in disbelief. "We don't have anything here either." He turned to Duray a glance of dismay. "This is a serious situation!"

"It's no more than I expected," said Duray tonelessly.

"All this demands some careful thought." Alan Robertson clicked his tongue in vexation. "Tst, tst, tst..." He examined the identification plaque at the top of the frame. "4:8:10/6:13:29," he read. "There seems to be no question of error." He squinted carefully at the numbers, hesitated, then slowly replaced the frame. On second thought he took the frame forth once more. "Come along, Gilbert," said Alan Robertson. "We'll have a cup of coffee and think this matter out."

The two returned to the central chamber, where Alan Robertson gave the empty frame into the custody of Harry the clerk. "Check the records, if you please," said Alan Robertson. "I want to know how many passways were pinched off the master."

Harry manipulated the buttons of his computer. "Three only, Mr. Robertson."

"Three passways and the master — four in all?"

"That's right, sir."

"Thank you, Harry."

VI

From *Memoirs and Reflections*:

> I recognized the possibility of many cruel abuses, but the good so outweighed the bad that I thrust aside all thought of secrecy and exclusivity. I consider myself not Alan Robertson, but, like Prometheus, an archetype of Man, and my discovery must serve all men.
>
> But caution, caution, caution!

> I sorted out my ideas. I myself coveted the amplitude of a private, personal, world; such a yearning was not ignoble, I decided. Why should not everyone have the same if he so desired, since the supply was limitless? Think of it! The wealth and beauty of an entire world: mountains and plains, forests and flowers, ocean cliffs and crashing seas, winds and clouds — all beyond value, yet worth no more than a few seconds of effort and a few watts of energy.
>
> I became troubled by a new idea. Would everyone desert old Earth and leave it a vile junk-heap? I found the concept intolerable… I exchange access to a world for three to six years of remedial toil, depending upon occupancy.

A lounge overlooked the central chamber. Alan Robertson gestured Duray to a seat and drew two mugs of coffee from a dispenser. Settling in a chair, he turned his eyes up to the ceiling. "We must collect our thoughts. The circumstances are somewhat unusual; still, I have lived with unusual circumstances for almost fifty years.

"So then: the situation. We have verified that there are only four passways to Home. These four passways are closed, though we must accept Bob's word in regard to your downtown locker. If this is truly the case, if Elizabeth and the girls are still on Home, you will never see them again."

"Bob is mixed up in this business. I could swear to nothing but —"

Alan Robertson held up his hand. "I will talk to Bob; this is the obvious first step." He rose to his feet and went to the telephone in the corner of the lounge. Duray joined him. Alan spoke into the screen. "Get me Robert Robertson's apartment in San Francisco."

The screen glowed white. Bob's voice came from the speaker. "Sorry; I'm not at home. I have gone out to my world Fancy, and I cannot be reached. Call back in a week, unless your business is urgent, in which case call back in a month."

"Mmph," said Alan Robertson returning to his seat. "Bob is sometimes a trifle too flippant. A man with an under-extended intellect…" He drummed his fingers on the arm of his chair. "Tomorrow night is his party? What does he call it… A Rumfuddle?"

"Some such nonsense. Why does he want me? I'm a dull dog; I'd rather be home building a fence."

"Perhaps you had better plan to attend the party."

"That means, submit to his extortion."

"Do you want to see your wife and family again?"

"Naturally. But whatever he has in mind won't be for my benefit, or Elizabeth's."

"You're probably right there. I've heard one or two unsavory tales regarding the Rumfuddlers…The fact remains that the passways are closed. All four of them."

Duray's voice became harsh. "Can't you open a new orifice for us?"

Alan Robertson gave his head a sad shake. "I can tune the machine very finely. I can code accurately for the 'Home' class of worlds, and as closely as necessary approximate a particular world-state. But at each setting, no matter how fine the tuning, we encounter an infinite number of worlds. In practice, inaccuracies in the machine, back-lash, the gross size of electrons, the very difference between one electron and another, make it difficult to tune with absolute precision. So even if we tuned exactly to the 'Home' class, the probability of opening into your particular Home is one in an infinite number: in short, negligible."

Duray stared off across the chamber. "Is it possible that a space once entered might tend to open more easily a second time?"

Alan Robertson smiled. "As to that, I can't say. I suspect not, but I really know so little. I see no reason why it should be so."

"If we can open into a world precisely cognate, I can at least learn why the passways are closed."

Alan Robertson sat up in his chair. "Here is a valid point. Perhaps we can accomplish something in this regard." He glanced humorously sidewise at Duray. "On the other hand — consider this situation. We create access into a 'Home' almost exactly cognate to your own — so nearly identical that the difference is not readily apparent. You find there an Elizabeth, a Dolly, a Joan and an Ellen indistinguishable from your own, and a Gilbert marooned on Earth. You might even convince yourself that this is your very own Home."

"I'd know the difference," said Duray shortly, but Alan Robertson seemed not to hear.

"Think of it! An infinite number of Homes isolated from Earth, an infinite number of Elizabeths, Dollys, Joans and Ellens marooned; an infinite number of Gilbert Durays trying to regain access…The sum effect might be a wholesale reshuffling of families with everyone more or less good-natured about the situation. I wonder if this could be Bob's idea of a joke to share with his Rumfuddlers."

Duray looked sharply at Alan Robertson, wondering whether the man were serious. "It doesn't sound funny, and I wouldn't be very good-natured."

"Of course not," said Alan Robertson hastily. "An idle thought — in rather poor taste, I'm afraid."

"In any event, Bob hinted that Elizabeth would be at his damned Rumfuddle. If that's the case she must have closed the passways from this side."

"A possibility," Alan Robertson conceded, "but unreasonable. Why should she seal you away from Home?"

"I don't know but I'd like to find out."

Alan Robertson slapped his hands down upon his thin shanks and jumped to his feet, only to pause once more. "You're sure you want to look into these cognates? You might see things you wouldn't like."

"So long as I know the truth, I don't care whether I like it or not."

"So be it."

The machine occupied a room behind the balcony. Alan Robertson surveyed the device with pride and affection. "This is the fourth model, and probably optimum; at least I don't see any place for significant improvement. I use a hundred and sixty-seven rods converging upon the center of the reactor sphere. Each rod produces a quantum of energy, and is susceptible to several types of adjustment, to cope with the very large number of possible states. The number of particles to pack the universe full is on the order of ten raised to the power of sixty; the possible permutations of these particles would number two raised to the power of ten raised to the power of sixty. The universe of course is built of many different particles, which makes the final number of possible, or let us say, thinkable states a number like two raised to the power of ten raised to the power of sixty, all times 'x', where 'x' is the number of particles under consideration. A large unmanageable number, which we need not consider because the conditions we deal with — the possible variations of planet Earth — are far fewer."

"Still a very large number," said Duray.

"Indeed yes. But again the sheer unmanageable bulk is cut away by a self-normalizing property of the machine. In what I call 'floating neutral' the machine reaches the closest cycles, which is to say, that infinite class of perfect cognates. In practice, because of infinitesimal inaccuracies, 'floating neutral' reaches cognates more or less imperfect, perhaps by no more than the shape of a single grain of sand. Still 'floating neutral' provides a natural base, and by adjusting the controls we reach cycles at an ever greater departure from Base. In practice I search out a good cycle, and strike a large number of passways, as many as a hundred thousand. So now to our business." He went to a console at the side. "Your code number, what was it now?"

Duray brought forth the card and read the numbers: "4:8:10/6:13:29."

"Very good. I give the code to the computer, which searches the files and automatically adjusts the machine. Now then, step over here; the process releases dangerous radiation."

The two stood behind lead slabs. Alan Robertson touched a button;

watching through a periscope Duray saw a spark of purple light, and heard a small groaning rasping sound seeming to come from the air itself.

Alan Robertson stepped forth and walked to the machine. In the delivery tray rested an extensible ring. He picked up the ring, looked through the hole. "This seems to be right." He handed the ring to Duray. "Do you see anything you recognize?"

Duray put the ring to his eye. "That's Home."

"Very good. Do you want me to come with you?"

Duray considered. "The time is Now?"

"Yes. This is a time-neutral setting."

"I think I'll go alone."

Alan Robertson nodded. "Whatever you like. Return as soon as you can, so I'll know you're safe."

Duray frowned at him sidewise. "Why shouldn't I be safe? No one is there but my family."

"Not *your* family. The family of a cognate Gilbert Duray. The family may not be absolutely identical. The cognate Duray may not be identical. You can't be sure exactly what you will find — so be careful."

VII

From *Memoirs and Reflections*:

> When I think of my machine and my little forays in and out of infinity, an idea keeps recurring to me which is so rather terrible that I close it out of my mind, and I will not even mention it here.

Duray stepped out upon the soil of Home, and stood appraising the familiar landscape. A vast meadow drenched in sunlight rolled down to wide Silver River. Above the opposite shore rose a line of low bluffs, with copses of trees in the hollows. To the left, landscape seemed to extend indefinitely and at last become indistinct in the blue haze of distance. To the right, the Robber Woods ended a quarter-mile from where Duray stood. On a flat beside the forest, on the bank of a small stream, stood a house of stone and timber: a sight which seemed to Duray the most beautiful he had ever seen. Polished glass windows sparkled in the sunlight; banks of geraniums glowed green and red. From the chimney rose a wisp of smoke. The air smelled cool and sweet, but seemed — so Duray imagined — to carry a strange tang, different — so he imagined — from the meadow-scent of his own Home. Duray started forward, then halted. The world was his own, yet not his own. If he had not been conscious of the fact, would he have recognized the strangeness? Nearby rose an outcrop of weathered gray field-rock: a rounded mossy pad on which he had sat only two days before, contemplating the building of a dock. He walked over and looked down at the stone. Here he had sat, here were the impressions of his heels in the soil; here was the pattern of moss from which he had absently scratched a fragment. Duray bent close. The moss was whole. The man who had sat here, the cognate Duray, had not scratched at the moss. So then: the world was perceptibly different from his own.

Duray was relieved and yet vaguely disturbed. If the world had been the exact simulacrum of his own, he might have been subjected to unmanageable emotions — which still might be the case. He walked toward the house, along the path which led down to the river. He stepped up to the porch. On a deck chair was a book: *Down There, A Study in Satanism*, by J. K. Huysmans. Elizabeth's tastes were eclectic. Duray had not previously seen the book; was it perhaps that Bob Robertson had put through the parcel delivery?

Duray went into the house. Elizabeth stood across the room. She had evidently watched him coming up the path. She said nothing; her face showed no expression.

Duray halted, somewhat at a loss as to how to address this woman. "Good afternoon," he said at last.

Elizabeth allowed a wisp of a smile to show. "Hello, Gilbert."

At least, thought Duray, on cognate worlds the same language was spoken. He studied Elizabeth. Lacking prior knowledge would he have perceived her to be someone different from his own Elizabeth? Both were beautiful women: tall and slender, with curling black shoulder-length hair, worn without artifice. Their skins were pale with a dusky undertone; their mouths were wide, passionate, stubborn. Duray knew his Elizabeth to be a woman of inexplicable moods, and this Elizabeth was doubtless no different — yet somehow a difference existed, which Duray could not define, deriving perhaps from the strangeness of her atoms, the stuff of a different universe. He wondered if she sensed the same difference in him.

He asked, "Did you close off the passways?"

Elizabeth nodded, without change of expression.

"Why?"

"I thought it the best thing to do," said Elizabeth in a soft voice.

"That's no answer."

"I suppose not. How did you get here?"

"Alan made an opening."

Elizabeth raised her eyebrows. "I thought that was impossible."

"True. This is a different world to my own. Another Gilbert Duray built this house. I'm not your husband."

Elizabeth's mouth drooped in astonishment. She swayed back a step and put her hand up to her neck: a mannerism Duray could not recall in his own Elizabeth. The sense of strangeness came ever more strongly upon him. He felt an intruder. Elizabeth was watching him with a wide-eyed fascination. She said in a hurried mutter: "I wish you'd leave; go back to your own world; do!"

"If you've closed off all the passways, you'll be isolated," growled Duray. "Marooned, probably forever."

"Whatever I do," said Elizabeth, "it's not your affair."

"It is my affair, if only for the sake of the girls. I won't allow them to live and die alone out here."

"The girls aren't here," said Elizabeth in a flat voice. "They are where neither you nor any other Gilbert Duray will find them. So now go back to your own world, and leave me in whatever peace my soul allows me."

Duray stood glowering at the fiercely beautiful woman. He had never heard his own Elizabeth speak so wildly. He wondered if on his own world another Gilbert Duray similarly confronted his own Elizabeth, and as he analyzed his feelings toward this woman before him he felt a throb of annoyance. A curious situation. He said in a quiet voice, "Very well. You, and my own Elizabeth, have decided to isolate yourselves. I can't imagine your reasons."

Elizabeth gave a wild laugh. "They're real enough."

"They may be real now, but ten years from now, or forty years from now, they may seem unreal. I can't give you access to your own Earth, but if you wish, you can use the passway to the Earth from which I've just come, and you need never see me again."

Elizabeth turned away and went to look out over the valley. Duray spoke to her back. "We've never had secrets between us, you and I — or I mean, Elizabeth and I. Why now? Are you in love with some other man?"

Elizabeth gave a snort of sardonic amusement. "Certainly not … I'm disgusted with the entire human race."

"Which presumably includes me."

"It does indeed, and myself as well."

"And you won't tell me why?"

Elizabeth, still looking out the window, wordlessly shook her head.

"Very well," said Duray in a cold voice. "Will you tell me where you've sent the girls? They're mine as much as yours, remember."

"These particular girls aren't yours at all."

"That may be, but the effect is the same."

Elizabeth said tonelessly: "If you want to find your own particular girls, you'd better find your own particular Elizabeth and ask her. I can only speak for myself … To tell you the truth I don't like being part of a composite person, and I don't intend to act like one. I'm just me. You're you, a stranger, whom I've never seen before in my life. So I wish you'd leave."

Duray strode from the house, out into the sunlight. He looked once around the wide landscape, then gave his head a surly shake and marched off along the path.

VIII

From *Memoirs and Reflections*:

> The past is exposed for our scrutiny; we can wander the epochs like lords through a garden, serene in our purview. We argue with the noble sages, refuting their laborious concepts, should we be so

unkind. Remember (at least) two things. First: the more distant from Now, the less precise our conjunctures, the less our ability to strike to any given instant. We can break in upon yesterday at a stipulated second; during the Eocene plus or minus ten years is the limit of our accuracy; as for the Cretaceous or earlier, an impingement within three hundred years of a given date can be considered satisfactory. Secondly: the past we broach is never our own past, but at best the past of a cognate world, so that any illumination cast upon historical problems is questionable and perhaps deceptive. We cannot plumb the future; the process involves a negative flow of energy, which is inherently impractical. An instrument constructed of anti-matter has been jocularly recommended, but would yield no benefit to us. The future, thankfully, remains forever shrouded.

"Aha, you're back!" exclaimed Alan Robertson. "What did you learn?"

Duray described the encounter with Elizabeth. "She makes no excuse for what she's done; she shows hostility which doesn't seem real, especially since I can't imagine a reason for it."

Alan Robertson had no comment to make.

"The woman isn't my wife, but their motivations must be the same. I can't think of one sensible explanation for conduct so strange, let alone two."

"Elizabeth seemed normal this morning?" asked Alan Robertson.

"I noticed nothing unusual."

Alan Robertson went to the control panel of his machine. He looked over his shoulder at Duray.

"What time do you leave for work?"

"About nine."

Alan Robertson set one dial, turned two others until a ball of green light balanced wavering precisely half-way along a glass tube. He signaled Duray behind the lead slab and touched the button. From the center of the machine came the impact of one hundred and sixty-seven colliding nodules of force, and the groan of rending dimensional fabric.

Alan Robertson brought forth the new passway. "The time is morning. You'll have to decide for yourself how to handle the situation. You can try to watch without being seen; you can say that you have paper-work to catch up on, that Elizabeth should ignore you and go about her normal routine, while you unobtrusively see what happens."

Duray frowned. "Presumably for each of these worlds there is a Gilbert Duray who finds himself in my fix. Suppose each tries to slip inconspicuously into someone else's world to learn what is happening. Suppose each Elizabeth catches him in the act and furiously accuses the man she believes to be her husband of spying on her — this in itself might be the source of Elizabeth's anger."

"Well, be as discreet as you can. Presumably you'll be several hours, so I'll go back to the boat and putter about. Locker Five in my private hub yonder; I'll leave the door open."

Once again Duray stood on the hillside above the river, with the rambling stone house built by still another Gilbert Duray two hundred yards along the slope. From the height of the sun, Duray judged local time to be about nine o'clock: somewhat earlier than necessary. From the chimney of the stone house rose a wisp of smoke; Elizabeth had built a fire in the kitchen fireplace. Duray stood reflecting. This morning in his own house Elizabeth had built no fire. She had been on the point of striking a match and then had decided that the morning was already warm. Duray waited ten minutes, to make sure that the local Gilbert Duray had departed, then set forth toward the house. He paused by the big flat stone to inspect the pattern of moss. The crevice seemed narrower than he remembered, and the moss was dry and discolored. Duray took a deep breath. The air, rich with the odor of grasses and herbs, again seemed to carry an odd unfamiliar scent. Duray proceeded slowly to the house, uncertain whether, after all, he were engaged in a sensible course of action.

He approached the house. The front door was open. Elizabeth came to look out at him in surprise. "That was a quick day's work!"

Duray said lamely, "The rig is down for repairs. I thought I'd catch up on some paperwork. You go ahead with whatever you were doing."

Elizabeth looked at him curiously. "I wasn't doing anything in particular."

He followed Elizabeth into the house. She wore soft black slacks and an old gray jacket; Duray tried to remember what his own Elizabeth had worn, but the garments had been so familiar that he could summon no recollection.

Elizabeth poured coffee into a pair of stoneware mugs and Duray took a seat at the kitchen table, trying to decide how this Elizabeth differed from his own — if she did. This Elizabeth seemed more subdued and meditative; her mouth might have been a trifle softer. "Why are you looking at me so strangely?" she asked suddenly.

Duray laughed. "I was merely thinking what a beautiful girl you are."

Elizabeth came to sit in his lap and kissed him, and Duray's blood began to flow warm. He restrained himself; this was not his wife; he wanted no complications. And if he yielded to temptations of the moment, might not another Gilbert Duray visiting his own Elizabeth do the same?...He scowled.

Elizabeth, finding no surge of ardor, went to sit in the chair opposite. For a moment she sipped her coffee in silence. Then she said, "Just as soon as you left Bob called through."

"Oh?" Duray was at once attentive. "What did he want?"

"That foolish party of his — the Rubble-menders or some such thing. He wants us to come."

"I've already told him no three times."

"I told him no again. His parties are always so peculiar. He said he wanted us to come for a very special reason, but he wouldn't tell me the reason. I told him thank you but no."

Duray looked around the room. "Did he leave any books?"

"No. Why should he leave me books?"

"I wish I knew."

"Gilbert," said Elizabeth, "you're acting rather oddly."

"Yes, I suppose I am." For a fact Duray's mind was whirling. Suppose now he went to the school passway, brought the girls home from school, then closed off all the passways, so that once again he had an Elizabeth and three daughters, more or less his own; then the conditions he had encountered would be satisfied. And another Gilbert Duray, now happily destroying the tract houses of Cupertino would find himself bereft...Duray recalled the hostile conduct of the previous Elizabeth. The passways in that particular world had certainly not been closed off by an intruding Duray…A startling possibility came to his mind. Suppose a Duray had come to the house and succumbing to temptation had closed off all passways except that one communicating with his own world; suppose then that Elizabeth, discovering the imposture, had killed him…The theory had a grim plausibility, and totally extinguished whatever inclination Duray might have had for making the world his home.

Elizabeth said, "Gilbert, why are you looking at me with that strange expression?"

Duray managed a feeble grin. "I guess I'm just in a bad mood this morning. Don't mind me. I'll go make out my report." He went into the wide cool living room, at once familiar and strange, and brought out the work-records of the other Gilbert Duray…He studied the handwriting: like his own, firm and decisive, but in some indefinable way, different — perhaps a trifle more harsh and angular. The three Elizabeths were not identical, nor were the Gilbert Durays.

An hour passed. Elizabeth occupied herself in the kitchen; Duray pretended to write a report.

A bell sounded. "Somebody at the passway," said Elizabeth.

Duray said, "I'll take care of it."

He went to the passage room, stepped through the passway, looked through the peep-hole — into the large bland sun-tanned face of Bob Robertson.

Duray opened the door. For a moment he and Bob Robertson confronted each other. Bob Robertson's eyes narrowed. "Why hello, Gilbert. What are you doing at home?"

Duray pointed to the parcel Bob Robertson carried. "What do you have there?"

"Oh these?" Bob Robertson looked down at the parcel as if he had forgotten it. "Just some books for Elizabeth."

Duray found it hard to control his voice. "You're up to some mischief, you and your Rumfuddlers. Listen, Bob: keep away from me and Elizabeth. Don't call here, and don't bring around any books. Is this definite enough?"

Bob raised his sun-bleached eyebrows. "Very definite, very explicit. But why the sudden rage? I'm just friendly old Uncle Bob."

"I don't care what you call yourself; stay away from us."

"Just as you like, of course. But do you mind explaining this sudden decree of banishment?"

"The reason is simple enough. We want to be left alone."

Bob made a gesture of mock despair. "All this over a simple invitation to a simple little party, which I'd really like you to come to."

"Don't expect us. We won't be there."

Bob's face suddenly went pink. "You're coming a very high horse over me my lad, and it's a poor policy. You might just get hauled up with a jerk. Matters aren't all the way you think they are."

"I don't care a rap one way or another," said Duray. "Goodbye."

He closed the locker door and backed through the passway. He returned into the living room. Elizabeth called from the kitchen. "Who was it, dear?"

"Bob Robertson, with some books."

"Books? Why books?"

"I didn't trouble to find out. I told him to stay away. After this, if he's at the passway, don't open it."

Elizabeth looked at him intently. "Gil — you're so strange today! There's something about you that almost scares me."

"Your imagination is working too hard."

"Why should Bob trouble to bring me books? What sort of books? Did you see?"

"Demonology. Black magic. That sort of thing."

"Mmf. Interesting — but not all that interesting... I wonder if a world like ours, where no one has ever lived, would have things like goblins and ghosts?"

"I suspect not," said Duray. He looked toward the door. There was nothing more to be accomplished here and it was time to return to his own Earth. He wondered how to make a graceful departure. And what would occur when the Gilbert Duray now working his rig came home?

Duray said, "Elizabeth, sit down in this chair here."

Elizabeth slowly slid into the chair at the kitchen table and watched him with a puzzled gaze.

"This may come as a shock," he said. "I am Gilbert Duray, but not your personal Gilbert Duray. I'm his cognate."

Elizabeth's eyes widened to lustrous dark pools.

Duray said, "On my own world Bob Robertson caused me and my Elizabeth trouble. I came here to find out what he had done and why, and to stop him from doing it again."

Elizabeth asked, "What has he done?"

"I still don't know. He probably won't bother you again. You can tell your personal Gilbert Duray whatever you think best, or even complain to Alan."

"I'm bewildered by all this!"

"No more so than I." He went to the door. "I've got to leave now. Goodby."

Elizabeth jumped to her feet and came impulsively forward. "Don't say goodby. It has such a lonesome sound, coming from you … It's like my own Gilbert saying goodby."

"There's nothing else to do. Certainly I can't follow my inclinations and move in with you. What good are two Gilberts? Who'd get to sit at the head of the table?"

"We could have a round table," said Elizabeth. "Room for six or seven. I like my Gilberts."

"Your Gilberts like their Elizabeths." Duray sighed and said, "I'd better go now."

Elizabeth held out her hand. "Goodby, cognate Gilbert."

IX

From *Memoirs and Reflections*:

The Oriental world-view differs from our own — specifically my own — in many respects, and I was early confronted with a whole set of dilemmas. I reflected upon Asiatic apathy and its obverse, despotism; warlords and brain-laundries; indifference to disease, filth and suffering; sacred apes and irresponsible fecundity.

I also took note of my resolve to use my machine in the service of all men.

In the end I decided to make the 'mistake' of many before me; I proceeded to impose my own ethical point of view upon the

Oriental life-style. Since this was precisely what was expected of me; since I would have been regarded as a fool and a mooncalf had I done otherwise; since the rewards of cooperation far exceeded the gratifications of obduracy and scorn: my programs are a wonderful success, at least to the moment of writing.

Duray walked along the riverbank toward Alan Robertson's boat. A breeze sent twinkling cat's-paws across the water and bellied the sails which Alan Robertson had raised to air; the boat tugged at the mooring lines.

Alan Robertson, wearing white shorts and a white hat with a loose flapping brim, looked up from the eye he had been splicing at the end of a halyard. "Aha, Gil! you're back. Come aboard, and have a bottle of beer."

Duray seated himself in the shade of the sail and drank half the beer at a gulp. "I still don't know what's going on — except that one way or another Bob is responsible. He came while I was there. I told him to clear out. He didn't like it."

Alan Robertson heaved a melancholy sigh. "I realize that Bob has the capacity for mischief."

"I still can't understand how he persuaded Elizabeth to close the passways. He brought out some books, but what effect could they have?"

Alan Robertson was instantly interested. "What were the books?"

"Something about satanism, black magic; I couldn't tell you much else."

"Indeed, indeed!" muttered Alan Robertson. "Is Elizabeth interested in the subject?"

"I don't think so. She's afraid of such things."

"Rightly so. Well, well, that's disturbing." Alan Robertson cleared his throat and made a delicate gesture, as if beseeching Duray to geniality and tolerance. "Still, you mustn't be too irritated with Bob. He's prone to his little mischiefs, but —"

"'Little mischiefs'!" roared Duray. "Like locking me out of my home and marooning my wife and children? That's going beyond mischief!"

Alan Robertson smiled. "Here; have another beer; cool off a bit. Let's reflect. First, the probabilities. I doubt if Bob has really marooned Elizabeth and the girls, or caused Elizabeth to do so."

"Then why are all the passways broken?"

"That's susceptible to explanation. He has access to the vaults; he might have substituted a blank for your master orifice. There's one possibility, at least."

Duray could hardly speak for rage. At last he cried out: "He has no right to do this!"

"Quite right, in the largest sense. I suspect that he only wants to induce you to his 'Rumfuddle'."

"And I don't want to go, especially when he's trying to put pressure on me."

"You're a stubborn man, Gil. The easy way, of course, would be to relax and look in on the occasion. You might even enjoy yourself."

Duray glared at Alan Robertson. "Are you suggesting that I attend the affair?"

"Well — no. I merely proposed a possible course of action."

Duray drank more beer and glowered out across the river. Alan Robertson said, "In a day or so, when this business is clarified, I think that we — all of us — should go off on a lazy cruise, out there among the islands. Nothing to worry us, no bothers, no upsets. The girls would love such a cruise."

Duray grunted. "I'd like to see them again before I plan any cruises. What goes on at these Rumfuddler events?"

"I've never attended. The members laugh and joke and eat and drink, and gossip about the worlds they've visited and show each other movies: that sort of thing. Why don't we look in on last year's party? I'd be interested myself."

Duray hesitated. "What do you have in mind?"

"We'll set the dials to a year-old cognate to Bob's world Fancy, and see precisely what goes on. What do you say?"

"I suppose it can't do any harm," said Duray grudgingly.

Alan Robertson rose to his feet. "Help me get these sails in."

X

From *Memoirs and Reflections*:

The problems which long have harassed historians have now been resolved. Who were the Cro-Magnons; where did they evolve? Who were the Etruscans? Where were the legendary cities of the proto-Sumerians before they migrated to Mesopotamia? Why the identity between the ideographs of Easter Island and Mohenjo Daro? All these fascinating questions have now been settled and reveal to us the full scope of our early history. We have preserved the library at old Alexandria from the Mohammedans and the Inca codices from the Christians. The Guanches of the Canaries, the Ainu of Hokkaido, the Mandans of Missouri, the blond Kaffirs of Bhutan: all are now known to us. We can chart the development of every language syllable by syllable, from earliest formulation to the present. We have identified the Hellenic heroes, and I myself have searched the haunted forests of the ancient North and, in their own stone keeps, met face to face those mighty men who generated the Norse myths.

Standing before his machine, Alan Robertson spoke in a voice of humorous self-deprecation. "I'm not as trusting and forthright as I would like to be; in fact I sometimes feel shame for my petty subterfuges; and now I speak in reference to Bob. We all have our small faults, and Bob certainly does not lack his share. His imagination is perhaps his greatest curse: he is easily bored, and sometimes tends to over-reach himself. So while I deny him nothing, I also make sure that I am in a position to counsel or even remonstrate, if need be. Whenever I open a passway to one of his formulae, I unobtrusively strike a duplicate which I keep in my private file. We will find no difficulty in visiting a cognate to Fancy."

Duray and Alan Robertson stood in the dusk, at the end of a pale white beach. Behind them rose a low basalt cliff. To their right the ocean reflected the afterglow and a glitter from the waning moon; to the left palms stood black against the sky. A hundred yards along the beach dozens of fairy lamps had been strung between the trees to illuminate a long table laden with fruit, confections, punch in crystal bowls. Around the table stood several dozen men and women in animated conversation; music and the sounds of gaiety came down the beach to Duray and Alan Robertson.

"We're in good time," said Alan Robertson. He reflected a moment. "No doubt we'd be quite welcome, still it's probably best to remain inconspicuous. We'll just stroll unobtrusively down the beach, in the shadow of the trees. Be careful not to stumble or fall, and no matter what you see or hear, do nothing! Discretion is essential; we want no awkward confrontations."

Keeping to the shade of the foliage, the two approached the merry group. Fifty yards distant, Alan Robertson held up his hand to signal a halt. "This is as close as we need approach; most of the people you know, or more accurately, their cognates. For instance, there is Royal Hart, and there is James Parham and Elizabeth's aunt, Emma Bathurst, and her uncle Peter, and Maude Granger, and no end of other folk."

"They all seem very gay."

"Yes; this is an important occasion for them. You and I are surly outsiders who can't understand the fun."

"Is this all they do, eat and drink and talk?"

"I think not," said Alan Robertson. "Notice yonder; Bob seems to be preparing a projection screen. Too bad that we can't move just a bit closer." Alan Robertson peered through the shadows. "But we'd better take no chances; if we were discovered everyone would be embarrassed."

They watched in silence. Presently Bob Robertson went to the projection equipment and touched a button. The screen became alive with vibrating rings of red and blue. Conversations halted; the group turned toward the screen. Bob Robertson spoke, but his words were inaudible to the two who watched from the darkness. Bob Robertson gestured to the screen, where now appeared the view of a small country town, as if seen from an airplane. Surrounding was flat farm country, a land of wide horizons; Duray assumed the location to be somewhere in the

Middle West. The picture changed, to show the local high school, with students sitting on the steps. The scene shifted to the football field, on the day of a game: a very important game to judge from the conduct of the spectators. The local team was introduced; one by one the boys ran out on the field to stand blinking into the autumn sunlight; then they ran off to the pre-game huddle.

The game began; Bob Robertson stood by the screen in the capacity of an expert commentator, pointing to one or another of the players, analyzing the play. The game proceeded, to the manifest pleasure of the Rumfuddlers. At half-time the bands marched and counter-marched, then play resumed. Duray became bored and made fretful comments to Alan Robertson who only said: "Yes, yes; probably so," and "My word, the agility of that halfback!" and "Have you noticed the precision of the line-play? Very good indeed!" At last the final quarter ended; the victorious team stood under a sign reading:

THE SHOWALTER TORNADOES
Champions of Texas
1951

The players came forward to accept trophies; there was a last picture of the team as a whole, standing proud and victorious; then the screen burst out into a red and gold starburst and went blank. The Rumfuddlers rose to their feet and congratulated Bob Robertson who laughed modestly, and went to the table for a goblet of punch.

Duray said disgustedly, "Is this one of Bob's famous parties? Why does he make such a tremendous occasion of the affair? I expected some sort of debauch."

Alan Robertson said, "Yes, from our standpoint at least the proceedings seem somewhat uninteresting. Well, if your curiosity is satisfied, shall we return?"

"Whenever you like."

Once again in the lounge under the Mad Dog Mountains, Alan Robertson said: "So now and at last we've seen one of Bob's famous Rumfuddles. Are you still determined not to attend the occasion of tomorrow night?"

Duray scowled. "If I have to go to reclaim my family, I'll do so. But I just might lose my temper before the evening is over."

"Bob has gone too far," Alan Robertson declared. "I agree with you there. As for what we saw tonight, I admit to a degree of puzzlement."

"Only a degree? Do you understand it at all?"

Alan Robertson shook his head with a somewhat cryptic smile. "Speculation is pointless. I suppose you'll spend the night with me at the lodge?"

"I might as well," grumbled Duray. "I don't have anywhere else to go."

Alan Robertson clapped him on the back. "Good lad! We'll put some steaks on the fire and turn our problems loose for the night."

XI

From *Memoirs and Reflections*:

When I first put the Mark I machine into operation I suffered great fears. What did I know of the forces which I might release?…With all adjustments at dead neutral, I punched a passway into a cognate Earth. This was simple enough; in fact, almost anti-climactic…Little by little I learned to control my wonderful toy; our own world and all its past phases became familiar to me. What of other worlds? I am sure that in due course we will move instantaneously from world to world, from galaxy to galaxy, using a special space-traveling hub on Utilis. At the moment I am candidly afraid to punch through passways at blind random. What if I opened into the interior of a sun? Or into the center of a black hole? Or into an anti-matter universe? I would certainly destroy myself and the machine and conceivably Earth itself.

Still, the potentialities are too entrancing to be ignored. With painstaking precautions and a dozen protective devices, I will attempt to find my way to new worlds, and for the first time interstellar travel will be a reality.

Alan Robertson and Duray sat in the bright morning sunlight beside the flinty blue lake. They had brought their breakfast out to the table and now sat drinking coffee. Alan Robertson made cheerful conversation for the two of them. "These last few years have been easier on me; I've relegated a great deal of responsibility. Ernest and Henry know my policies as well as I do, if not better; and they're never frivolous or inconsistent." Alan Robertson chuckled. "I've worked two miracles: first, my machine, and second, keeping the business as simple as it is. I refuse to keep regular hours; I won't make appointments; I don't keep records; I pay no taxes; I exert great political and social influence, but only informally; I simply refuse to be bothered with administrative detail, and consequently I find myself able to enjoy life."

"It's a wonder some religious fanatic hasn't assassinated you," said Duray sourly.

"No mystery there! I've given them all their private worlds, with my best regards, and they have no energy left for violence! And as you know, I walk with a very low silhouette. My friends hardly recognize me on the street." Alan Robertson waved his hand. "No doubt you're more concerned with your immediate quandary. Have you come to a decision regarding the Rumfuddle?"

"I don't have any choice," Duray muttered. "I'd prefer to wring Bob's neck. If I could account for Elizabeth's conduct, I'd feel more comfortable. She's not even remotely interested in black magic. Why did Bob bring her books on Satanism?"

"Well — the subject is inherently fascinating," Alan Robertson suggested, without conviction. "The name 'Satan' derives from the Hebrew word for 'adversary'; it never applied to a real individual. Zeus of course was an Aryan chieftain of about 3500 B.C., while 'Woden' lived somewhat later. He was actually 'Othinn', a shaman of enormous personal force, who did things with his mind that I can't do with the machine... But again I'm rambling."

Duray gave a silent shrug.

"Well then, you'll be going to the Rumfuddle," said Alan Robertson, "by and large the best course, whatever the consequences."

"I believe that you know more than you're telling me."

Alan Robertson smiled and shook his head. "I've lived with too much uncertainty among my cognate and near-cognate worlds. Nothing is sure; surprises are everywhere. I think the best plan is to fulfill Bob's requirements. Then, if Elizabeth is indeed on hand, you can discuss the event with her."

"What of you? Will you be coming?"

"I am of two minds. Would you prefer that I came?"

"Yes," said Duray. "You have more control over Bob than I do."

"Don't exaggerate my influence! He is a strong man, for all his idleness. Confidentially, I'm delighted that he occupies himself with games rather than..." Alan Robertson hesitated.

"Rather than what?"

"Than that his imagination should prompt him to less innocent games. Perhaps I have been over-ingenuous in this connection. We can only wait and see."

XII

From *Memoirs and Reflections*:

> If the Past is a house of many chambers, then the Present is the most recent coat of paint.

At four o'clock Duray and Alan Robertson left the lodge and passed through Utilis to the San Francisco depot. Duray had changed into a somber dark suit; Alan Robertson wore a more informal costume: blue jacket and pale gray trousers. They went to Bob Robertson's locker, to find a panel with the sign:

NOT HOME!

FOR THE RUMFUDDLE GO TO ROGER WAILLE'S LOCKER, RC3-96
AND PASS THROUGH TO EKSHAYAN!

The two went on to Locker RC3-96 where a sign read:

RUMFUDDLERS, PASS! ALL OTHERS: AWAY!

Duray shrugged contemptuously and parting the curtain looked through the passway, into a rustic lobby of natural wood, painted in black, red, yellow, blue and white floral designs. An open door revealed an expanse of open land and water glistening in the afternoon sunlight. Duray and Alan Robertson passed through, crossed the foyer and looked out upon a vast slow river flowing from north to south. A rolling plain spread eastward away and over the horizon. The western bank of the river was indistinct in the afternoon glitter. A path led north to a tall house of eccentric architecture. A dozen domes and cupolas stood against the sky; gables and ridges created a hundred unexpected angles. The walls showed a fish-scale texture of hand-hewn shingles; spiral columns supported the second- and third-story entablatures, where wolves and bears carved in vigorous curves and masses snarled, fought, howled and danced. On the side overlooking the river a pergola clothed with vines cast a dappled shade; here sat the Rumfuddlers.

Alan Robertson looked at the house, up and down the river, across the plain. "From the architecture, the vegetation, the height of the sun, the characteristic haze, I assume the river to be either the Don or the Volga, and yonder the steppes. From the absence of habitation, boats and artifacts, I would guess the time to be early historic — perhaps 2,000 or 3,000 B.C., a colorful era. The inhabitants of the steppes are nomads; Scyths to the east, Celts to the west, and to the north the homeland of the Germanic and Scandinavian tribes; and yonder the mansion of Roger Waille, and very interesting too, after the extravagant fashion of the Russian Baroque. And, my word! I believe I see an ox on the spit! We may even enjoy our little visit!"

"You do as you like," muttered Duray, "I'd just as soon eat at home."

Alan Robertson pursed his lips. "I understand your point of view, of course, but perhaps we should relax a bit. The scene is majestic, the house is delightfully picturesque; the roast beef is undoubtedly delicious; perhaps we should meet the situation on its own terms."

Duray could find no adequate reply, and kept his opinions to himself.

"Well then," said Alan Robertson, "equability is the word. So now let's see what Bob and Roger have up their sleeves." He set off along the path to the house, with Duray sauntering morosely a step or two behind.

Under the pergola a man jumped to his feet and flourished his hand;

Duray recognized the tall spare form of Bob Robertson. "Just in time," Bob called jocosely. "Not too early, not too late. We're glad you could make it!"

"Yes, we found we could accept your invitation after all," said Alan Robertson. "Let me see, do I know anyone here? Roger, hello!…And William…Ah! the lovely Dora Gorski!…Cypriano…" He looked around the circle of faces, waving to his acquaintants.

Bob clapped Duray on the shoulder. "Really pleased you could come! What'll you drink? The locals distill a liquor out of fermented mare's milk, but I don't recommend it."

"I'm not here to drink," said Duray. "Where's Elizabeth?"

The corners of Bob's wide mouth twitched. "Come now, old man; let's not be grim. This is the Rumfuddle! A time for joy and self-renewal! Go dance about a bit! Cavort! Pour a bottle of champagne over your head! Sport with the girls!"

Duray looked into the blue eyes for a long second. He strained to keep his voice even. "Where is Elizabeth?"

"Somewhere about the place. A charming girl, your Elizabeth! We're delighted to have you both!"

Duray swung away. He walked to the dark and handsome Roger Waille. "Would you be good enough to take me to my wife?"

Waille raised his eyebrows as if puzzled by Duray's tone of voice. "She's in primping and gossiping. If necessary I suppose I could pull her away for a moment or two."

Duray began to feel ridiculous, as if he had not been locked away from his world, subjected to harassments and doubts, and made the butt of some obscure joke. "It's necessary," he said. "We're leaving."

"But you've just arrived!"

"I know."

Waille gave a shrug of amused perplexity, and turned away toward the house. Duray followed. They went through a tall narrow doorway into an entry-hall paneled with a beautiful brown-gold wood, which Duray automatically identified as chestnut. Four high panes of tawny glass turned to the west filled the room with a smoky half-melancholy light. Oak settees, upholstered in leather, faced each other across a black, brown and gray rug. Tabourets stood at each side of the settees, and each supported an ornate golden candelabra in the form of conventionalized stag's-heads. Waille indicated these last. "Striking, aren't they? The Scythians made them for me. I paid them in iron knives. They think I'm a great magician; and for a fact, I am." He reached into the air and plucked forth an orange, which he tossed upon a settee. "Here's Elizabeth now, and the other maenads as well."

Into the chamber came Elizabeth, with three other young women whom Duray vaguely recalled having met before. At the sight of Duray, Elizabeth stopped short. She essayed a smile, and said in a light strained voice, "Hello, Gil. You're here after all." She laughed nervously and, Duray felt, unnaturally. "Yes, of course you're here. I didn't think you'd come."

Duray glanced toward the other women, who stood with Waille watching half-expectantly. Duray said, "I'd like to speak to you alone."

"Excuse us," said Waille. "We'll go on outside."

They departed. Elizabeth looked longingly after them, and fidgeted with the buttons of her jacket.

"Where are the children?" Duray demanded curtly.

"Upstairs, getting dressed." She looked down at her own costume, the festival raiment of a Transylvanian peasant girl: a green skirt embroidered with red and blue flowers, a white blouse, a black velvet vest, glossy black boots.

Duray felt his temper slipping; his voice was strained and fretful. "I don't understand anything of this. Why did you close the passways?"

Elizabeth attempted a flippant smile. "I was bored with routine."

"Oh? Why didn't you mention it to me yesterday morning? You didn't need to close the passways."

"Gilbert, please. Let's not discuss it."

Duray stood back, tongue-tied with astonishment. "Very well," he said at last. "We won't discuss it. You go up and get the girls. We're going home."

Elizabeth shook her head. In a neutral voice she said, "It's impossible. There's only one passway open. I don't have it."

"Who does? Bob?"

"I guess so; I'm not really sure."

"How did he get it? There were only four, and all four were closed."

"It's simple enough. He moved the downtown passway from our locker to another, and left a blank in its place."

"And who closed off the other three?"

"I did."

"Why?"

"Because Bob told me to. I don't want to talk about it; I'm sick to death of the whole business." And she half-whispered: "I don't know what I'm going to do with myself."

"I know what I'm going to do," said Duray. He turned toward the door.

Elizabeth held up her hands and clenched her fists against her breast. "Don't make trouble please! He'll close our last passway!"

"Is that why you're afraid of him? If so — don't be. Alan wouldn't allow it."

Elizabeth's face began to crumple. She pushed past Duray and walked quickly out upon the terrace. Duray followed, baffled and furious. He looked back and forth across the terrace. Bob was not to be seen. Elizabeth had gone to Alan Robertson; she spoke in a hushed urgent voice. Duray went to join them. Elizabeth became silent and turned away, avoiding Duray's gaze.

Alan Robertson spoke in a voice of easy geniality. "Isn't this a lovely spot? Look how the setting sun shines on the river!"

Roger Waille came by rolling a cart with ice, goblets and a dozen bottles. Now he said: "Of all the places on all the Earths this is my favorite. I call it 'Ekshayan', which is the Scythian name for this district."

A woman asked, "Isn't it cold and bleak in the winter?"

"Frightful!" said Waille. "The blizzards howl down from the north; then they stop and the land is absolutely still. The days are short and the sun comes up red as a poppy. The wolves slink out of the forests, and at dusk they circle the house. When a full moon shines, they howl like banshees, or maybe the banshees are howling! I sit beside the fireplace, entranced."

"It occurs to me," said Manfred Funk, "that each person, selecting a site for his home, reveals a great deal about himself. Even on old Earth, a man's home was ordinarily a symbolic simulacrum of the man himself; now, with every option available, a person's house is himself."

"This is very true," said Alan Robertson, "and certainly Roger need not fear that he has revealed any discreditable aspects of himself by showing us his rather grotesque home on the lonely steppes of prehistoric Russia."

Roger Waille laughed. "The grotesque house isn't me; I merely felt that it fitted its setting... Here, Duray, you're not drinking. That's chilled vodka; you can mix it or drink it straight in the time-tested manner."

"Nothing for me, thanks."

"Just as you like. Excuse me; I'm wanted elsewhere." Waille moved away, rolling the cart. Elizabeth leaned as if she wanted to follow him, then remained beside Alan Robertson, looking thoughtfully over the river.

Duray spoke to Alan Robertson as if she were not there. "Elizabeth refuses to leave. Bob has hypnotized her."

"That's not true," said Elizabeth softly.

"Somehow, one way or another, he's forced her to stay. She won't tell me why."

"I want the passway back," said Elizabeth. But her voice was muffled and uncertain.

Alan Robertson cleared his throat. "I hardly know what to say. It's a very awkward situation. None of us wants to create a disturbance —"

"There you're wrong," said Duray.

Alan Robertson ignored the remark. "I'll have a word with Bob after the party. In the meantime I don't see why we shouldn't enjoy the company of our friends, and that wonderful roast ox! Who is that turning the spit? I know him from somewhere."

Duray could hardly speak for outrage. "After what he's done to us?"

"He's gone too far, much too far," Alan Robertson agreed. "Still, he's a flamboyant feckless sort and I doubt if he understands the full inconvenience he's caused you."

"He understands well enough. He just doesn't care."

"Perhaps so," said Alan Robertson sadly. "I had always hoped — but that's neither here nor there. I still feel that we should act with restraint. It's much easier not to do than to undo."

Elizabeth abruptly crossed the terrace and went to the front door of the tall house, where her three daughters had appeared: Dolly, 12;

Joan, 10; Ellen, 8: all wearing green, white and black peasant frocks and glossy black boots. Duray thought they made a delightful picture. He followed Elizabeth across the terrace.

"It's Daddy," screamed Ellen, and threw herself in his arms. The other two, not to be outdone, did likewise.

"We thought you weren't coming to the party," cried Dolly. "I'm glad you did though." "So'm I." "So'm I."

"I'm glad I came too, if only to see you in these pretty costumes. Let's go see Grandpa Alan." He took them across the terrace, and after a moment's hesitation, Elizabeth followed. Duray became aware that everyone had stopped talking to look at him and his family, with, so it seemed, an extraordinary, even avid, curiosity, as if in expectation of some entertaining extravagance of conduct. Duray began to burn with emotion. Once, long ago, while crossing a street in downtown San Francisco, he had been struck by an automobile, suffering a broken leg and a fractured clavicle. Almost as soon as he had been knocked down, pedestrians came pushing to stare down at him, and Duray, looking up in pain and shock had seen only the ring of white faces and intent eyes, greedy as flies around a puddle of blood. In hysterical fury he had staggered to his feet, striking out into every face within reaching distance, man and woman alike. He hated them more than the man who had run him down: the ghouls who had come to enjoy his pain. Had he the miraculous power, he would have crushed them into a screaming bale of detestable flesh, hurled the bundle twenty miles out into the Pacific Ocean... Some faint shadow of this emotion affected him now, but today he would provide them no unnatural pleasure. He turned a single glance of cool contempt around the group, then took his three eager-faced daughters to a bench at the back of the terrace. Elizabeth followed, moving like a mechanical object. She seated herself at the end of the bench and looked off across the river. Duray stared heavily back at the Rumfuddlers, compelling them to shift their gazes, to where the ox roasted over a great bed of coals. A young man in a white jacket turned the spit; another basted the meat with a long-handled brush. A pair of Orientals carried out a carving table; another brought a carving set; a fourth wheeled out a cart laden with salads, round crusty loaves, trays of cheese and herrings. A fifth man, dressed as a Transylvanian gypsy, came from the house with a violin. He went to the corner of the terrace and began to play melancholy music of the steppes.

Bob Robertson and Roger Waille inspected the ox, a magnificent sight indeed. Duray attempted a stony detachment, but his nose was under no such strictures; the odor of the roast meat, garlic and herbs tantalized him unmercifully. Bob Robertson returned to the terrace and held up his hands for attention; the fiddler put down his instrument. "Control your appetites; there'll still be a few minutes, during which we can discuss our next Rumfuddle. Our clever colleague Bernard Ulman recommends a hostelry in the Adirondacks: the Sapphire Lake Lodge. The hotel was built in 1902, to the highest standards of Edwardian comfort. The clientele is derived from the business community of New York. The cuisine is kosher; the management maintains an atmosphere of congenial gentility; the current date is 1930. Bernard has furnished photographs. Roger, if you please..."

Waille drew back a curtain to reveal a screen. He manipulated the projection machine and the hotel was displayed on the screen: a rambling half-timbered structure overlooking several acres of park and a smooth lake.

"Thank you, Roger. I believe that we also have a photograph of the staff..."

On the screen appeared a stiffly posed group of about thirty men and women, all smiling with various degrees of affability. The Rumfuddlers were amused; some among them tittered.

"Bernard gives a very favorable report as to the cuisine, the amenities and the charm of the general area. Am I right, Bernard?"

"In every detail," declared Bernard Ulman. "The management is attentive and efficient; the clientele is well-established."

"Very good," said Bob Robertson. "Unless someone has a more entertaining idea, we will hold our next Rumfuddle at the Sapphire Lake Lodge. And now I believe that the roast beef should be ready: done to a turn as the expression goes."

"Quite right," said Roger Waille. "Tom, as always, has done an excellent job at the spit."

The ox was lifted to the table. The carver set to work with a will. Duray went to speak to Alan Robertson, who blinked uneasily at his approach. Duray asked, "Do you understand the reason for these parties? Are you in on the joke?"

Alan Robertson spoke in a precise manner: "I certainly am not 'in on the joke', as you put it." He hesitated, then said: "The Rumfuddlers will never again intrude upon your life or that of your family. I am sure of this. Bob became over-exuberant; he exercised poor judgment, and I intend to have a quiet word with him. In fact, we have already exchanged certain opinions. At the moment your best interests will be served by detachment and unconcern."

Duray spoke with sinister politeness: "You feel then that I and my family should bear the brunt of Bob's jokes?"

"This is a harsh view of the situation, but my answer must be 'yes'."

"I'm not so sure. My relationship with Elizabeth is no longer the same. Bob has done this to me."

"To quote an old apothegm: 'Least said, soonest mended'."

Duray changed the subject. "When Waille showed the photograph of the hotel staff, I thought some of the faces were familiar. Before I could be quite sure the picture was gone."

Alan Robertson nodded unhappily. "Let's not develop the subject, Gilbert. Instead —"

"I'm into the situation too far," said Duray. "I want to know the truth."

"Very well then," said Alan Robertson hollowly, "your instincts are accurate. The management of the Sapphire Lake Lodge, in cognate circumstances, has achieved an unsavory reputation. As you have guessed, they comprise the leadership of the National Socialist Party during 1938 or thereabouts. The manager of course is Hitler, the desk clerk is Goebbels, the head-waiter is Goering, the bellboys are Himmler and Hess, and so on down the line. They are of course not aware of the activities of their cognates on other worlds. The hotel's clientele is for the most part Jewish, which brings a macabre humor to the situation."

"Undeniably," said Duray. "What of that Rumfuddlers party that we looked in on?"

"You refer to the high-school football team? The 1951 Texas champions as I recall." Alan Robertson grinned. "And well they should be. Bob identified the players for me. Are you interested in the line-up?"

"Very much so."

Alan Robertson drew a sheet of paper from his pocket. "I believe —
yes, this is it." He handed the sheet to Duray, who saw a schematic
line-up:

LE	LT	LG	C	RG	RT	RE
Achilles	Charle-magne	Hercules	Goliath	Samson	Richard the Lion Hearted	Billy the Kid

Q
Machiavelli

LHB   RHB
Sir Galahad   Geronimo

FB
Cuchullain

Duray returned the paper. "You approve of this?"

"I had best put it like this," said Alan Robertson, a trifle uneasily.
"One day, chatting with Bob, I remarked that much travail could be
spared the human race if the most notorious evil-doers were early in
their lives shifted to environments which afforded them constructive
outlets for their energies. I speculated that having the competence
to make such changes it was perhaps our duty to do so. Bob became
interested in the concept and formed his group, the Rumfuddlers, to
serve the function I had suggested. In all candor I believe that Bob and
his friends have been attracted more by the possibility of entertainment
than by altruism, but the effect has been the same."

"The football players aren't evil-doers," said Duray. "Sir Galahad,
Charlemagne, Samson, Richard the Lion Hearted…"

"Exactly true," said Alan Robertson, "and I made this point to Bob.
He asserted that all were brawlers and bully-boys, with the possible
exception of Sir Galahad; that Charlemagne, for example, had conquered
much territory to no particular achievement; that Achilles, a national
hero to the Greeks, was a cruel enemy to the Trojans; and so forth. His
justifications are somewhat specious perhaps… Still these young men
are better employed making touchdowns than breaking heads."

After a pause Duray asked: "How are these matters arranged?"

"I'm not entirely sure. I believe that by one means or another, the desired babies are exchanged with others of similar appearance. The child so obtained is reared in appropriate circumstances."

"The jokes seem elaborate and rather tedious."

"Precisely!" Alan Robertson declared. "Can you think of a better method to keep someone like Bob out of mischief?"

"Certainly," said Duray. "Fear of the consequences." He scowled across the terrace. Bob had stopped to speak to Elizabeth. She and the three girls rose to their feet.

Duray strode across the terrace. "What's going on?"

"Nothing of consequence," said Bob. "Elizabeth and the girls are going to help serve the guests." He glanced toward the serving table, then turned back to Duray. "Would you help with the carving?"

Duray's arm moved of its own volition. His fist caught Bob on the angle of the jaw, and sent him reeling back into one of the white-coated Orientals, who carried a tray of food. The two fell into an untidy heap. The Rumfuddlers were shocked and amused, and watched with attention.

Bob rose to his feet gracefully enough and gave a hand to the Oriental. Looking toward Duray he shook his head ruefully. Meeting his glance, Duray noted a pale blue glint; then Bob once more became bland and debonair.

Elizabeth spoke in a low despairing voice: "Why couldn't you have done as he asked? It would have all been so simple."

"Elizabeth may well be right," said Alan Robertson.

"Why should she be right?" demanded Duray. "We are his victims! You've allowed him a taste of mischief, and now you can't control him!"

"Not true!" declared Alan. "I intend to impose rigorous curbs upon the Rumfuddlers, and I will be obeyed."

"The damage is done, so far as I am concerned," said Duray bitterly. "Come along, Elizabeth, we're going home."

"We can't go home. Bob has the passway."

Alan Robertson drew a deep sigh, and came to a decision. He crossed to where Bob stood with a goblet of wine in one hand, massaging his jaw with the other. Alan Robertson spoke to Bob politely, but with authority. Bob was slow in making reply. Alan Robertson spoke again, sharply. Bob only shrugged. Alan Robertson waited a moment, then returned to Duray, Elizabeth and the three children.

"The passway is at his San Francisco apartment," said Alan Robertson in a measured voice. "He will give it back to you after the party. He doesn't choose to go for it now."

Bob once more commanded the attention of the Rumfuddlers. "By popular request we replay the record of our last but one Rumfuddle, contrived by one of our most distinguished, diligent and ingenious Rumfuddlers, Manfred Funk. The locale is the Red Barn, a roadhouse twelve miles west of Urbana, Illinois; the time is the late summer of 1926; the occasion is a Charleston dancing contest. The music is provided by the legendary Wolverines, and you will hear the fabulous cornet of Leon Bismarck Beiderbecke." Bob gave a wry smile, as if the music were not to his personal taste. "This was one of our most rewarding occasions, and here it is again."

The screen showed the interior of a dance-hall, crowded with excited young men and women. At the back of the stage sat the Wolverines, wearing tuxedos; to the front stood the contestants: eight dapper young men and eight pretty girls in short skirts. An announcer stepped forward and spoke to the crowd through a megaphone: "Contestants are numbered one through eight! Please, no encouragement from the audience. The prize is this magnificent trophy and fifty dollars cash; the presentation will be made by last year's winner Boozy Horman. Remember, on the first number we eliminate four contestants, on the second number two; and after the third number we select our winner. So then: Bix and the Wolverines, and *Sensation Rag!*"

From the band came music, from the contestants agitated motion. Duray asked, "Who are these people?"

Alan Robertson replied in an even voice: "The young men are locals and not important. But notice the girls: no doubt you find them attractive. You are not alone. They are Helen of Troy, Deirdre, Marie Antoinette, Cleopatra, Salome, Lady Godiva, Nefertiti and Mata Hari."

Duray gave a dour grunt. The music halted; judging applause from the audience, the announcer eliminated Marie Antoinette, Cleopatra, Deirdre, Mata Hari, and their respective partners. The Wolverines played *Fidgety Feet*; the four remaining contestants danced with verve and dedication; but Helen and Nefertiti were eliminated. The Wolverines played *Tiger Rag*. Salome and Lady Godiva and their young men performed with amazing zeal. After carefully appraising the volume of applause, the announcer gave his judgment to Lady Godiva and her partner. Large on the screen appeared a close-up view of the two happy faces; in an excess of triumphant joy they hugged and kissed each other. The screen went dim; after the vivacity of the Red Barn the terrace above the Don seemed drab and insipid.

The Rumfuddlers shifted in their seats. Some uttered exclamations to assert their gaiety; others stared out across the vast empty face of the river.

Duray glanced toward Elizabeth; she was gone. Now he saw her circulating among the guests with three other young women, pouring wine from Scythian decanters.

"It makes a pretty picture, does it not?" said a calm voice. Duray turned to find Bob standing behind him; his mouth twisted in an easy half-smile but his eyes glinting pale blue.

Duray turned away. Alan Robertson said, "This is not at all a pleasant situation, Bob, and in fact completely lacks charm."

"Perhaps at future Rumfuddles, when my face feels better, the charm will emerge... Excuse me; I see that I must enliven the meeting." He stepped forward. "We have a final pastiche: oddments and improvisations, vignettes and glimpses, each in its own way entertaining and instructive. Roger; start the mechanism, if you please."

Roger Waille hesitated and glanced sidelong toward Alan Robertson.

"The item number is sixty-two, Roger," said Bob in a calm voice. Roger Waille delayed another instant then shrugged and went to the projection machine.

"The material is new," said Bob, "hence I will supply a commentary. First we have an episode in the life of Richard Wagner, the dogmatic and occasionally irascible composer. The year is 1843; the place is Dresden. Wagner sets forth on a summer night to attend a new opera *Der Sängerkrieg* by an unknown composer. He alights from his carriage before the hall; he enters; he seats himself in his loge. Notice the dignity of his posture; the authority of his gestures! The music begins: listen!"

From the projector came the sound of music. "It is the overture," stated Bob. "But notice Wagner: why is he stupefied? Why is he overcome with wonder? He listens to the music as if he has never heard it before. And in fact he hasn't; he has only just yesterday set down a few preliminary notes for this particular opus, which he planned to call *Tannhäuser*; today, magically, he hears it in its final form. Wagner will walk home slowly tonight, and perhaps in his abstraction he will kick the dog Schmutzi... Now, to a different scene: St. Petersburg in the year 1880 and the stables in back of the Winter Palace. The ivory and gilt carriage rolls forth to convey the Czar and the Czarina to a reception at the British Embassy. Notice the drivers: stern, well-groomed, intent at their business. Marx's beard is well-trimmed; Lenin's goatee is not so pronounced. A groom comes to watch the carriage roll away. He has a kindly twinkle in his eye, does Stalin." The screen went dim once more, then brightened to show a city street lined with automobile showrooms and used car lots. "This is one of Shawn Henderson's projects. The four used-car lots are operated by men who in other circumstances were religious notables: prophets and so forth. That alert keen-featured man in front of 'Quality Motors', for instance, is Mohammed. Shawn is conducting a careful survey, and at our next Rumfuddle he will report upon his dealings with these four famous figures."

Alan Robertson stepped forward, somewhat diffidently. He cleared his throat. "I don't like to play the part of spoil-sport, but I'm afraid I have no choice. There will be no further Rumfuddles. Our original goals have been neglected and I note far too many episodes of purposeless frivolity and even cruelty. You may wonder at what seems a sudden decision, but I have been considering the matter for several days. The Rumfuddles have taken a turn in an unwholesome direction, and conceivably might become a grotesque new vice, which of course is far from our original ideal. I'm sure that every sensible person, after a few moments' reflection, will agree that now is the time to stop. Next week you may return to me all passways except those to worlds where you maintain residence."

The Rumfuddlers sat murmuring together. Some turned resentful glances toward Alan Robertson; others served themselves more bread and meat. Bob came over to join Alan and Duray. He spoke in an easy manner. "I must say that your admonitions arrive with all the delicacy of a lightning bolt. I can picture Jehovah smiting the fallen angels in a similar style."

Alan Robertson smiled. "Now then, Bob, you're talking nonsense. The situations aren't at all similar. Jehovah struck out in fury; I impose my restrictions in all good will, in order that we can once again turn our energies to constructive ends."

Bob threw back his head and laughed. "But the Rumfuddlers have lost the habit of work. We only want to amuse ourselves, and after all, what is so noxious in our activities?"

"The trend is menacing, Bob." Alan Robertson's voice was reasonable. "Unpleasant elements are creeping into your fun, so stealthily that you yourself are unaware of them. For instance, why torment poor Wagner? Surely there was gratuitous cruelty, and only to provide you a few instants of amusement. And, since the subject is in the air, I heartily deplore your treatment of Gilbert and Elizabeth. You have brought them both an extraordinary inconvenience, and in Elizabeth's case, actual suffering. Gilbert got something of his own back, and the balance is about even."

"Gilbert is far too impulsive," said Bob. "Self-willed and egocentric, as he always has been."

Alan held up his hand. "There is no need to go further into the subject, Bob. I suggest that you say no more."

"Just as you like, though the matter, considered as practical rehabilitation, isn't irrelevant. We can amply justify the work of the Rumfuddlers."

Duray asked quietly, "Just how do you mean, Bob?"

Alan Robertson made a peremptory sound, but Duray said, "Let him say what he likes, and make an end to it. He plans to do so anyway."

There was a moment of silence. Bob looked across the terrace to where the three Orientals were transferring the remains of the beef to a service cart.

"Well?" Alan Robertson asked softly. "Have you made your choice?"

Bob held out his hands in ostensible bewilderment. "I don't understand you! I want only to vindicate myself and the Rumfuddlers. I think we have done splendidly. Today we have allowed Torquemada to roast a dead ox instead of a living heretic; the Marquis de Sade has fulfilled his obscure urges by caressing seared flesh with a basting brush, and did you notice the zest with which Ivan the Terrible hacked up the carcass? Nero, who has real talent, played his violin; Attila, Genghis Khan, and Mao Tse Tung efficiently served the guests. Wine was poured by Messalina, Lucrezia Borgia, Delilah, and Gilbert's charming wife Elizabeth. Only Gilbert failed to demonstrate his rehabilitation, but at least he provided us a touching and memorable picture: Gilles de Rais, Elizabeth Báthory and their three virgin daughters. It was sufficient. In every case we have shown that rehabilitation is not an empty word."

"Not in every case," said Alan Robertson, "specifically that of your own."

Bob looked at him askance. "I don't follow you."

"No less than Gilbert, are you ignorant of your background. I will now reveal the circumstances so that you may understand something of yourself and try to curb the tendencies which have made your cognate an exemplar of cruelty, stealth and treachery."

Bob laughed: a brittle sound like cracking ice. "I admit to a horrified interest."

"I took you from a forest a thousand miles north of this very spot, while I traced the phylogeny of the Norse gods. Your name was Loki. For reasons which are not now important I brought you back to San Francisco and there you grew to maturity."

"So I am Loki."

"No. You are Bob Robertson, just as this is Gilbert Duray, and here is his wife Elizabeth. Loki, Gilles de Rais, Elizabeth Báthory: these are names applied to human material which has not functioned quite as well. Gilles de Rais, judging from all evidence, suffered from a brain tumor; he fell into his peculiar vices after a long and honorable career. The case of Princess Elizabeth Báthory is less clear, but one might suspect syphilis and consequent cerebral lesions."

"And what of poor Loki?" inquired Bob with exaggerated pathos.

"Loki seemed to suffer from nothing except a case of old-fashioned meanness."

Bob seemed concerned. "So that these qualities apply to me?"

"You are not necessarily identical to your cognate. Still, I advise you to take careful stock of yourself, and, so far as I am concerned, you had best regard yourself as on probation."

"Just as you say." Bob looked over Alan Robertson's shoulder. "Excuse me; you've spoiled the party and everybody is leaving. I want a word with Roger."

Duray moved to stand in his way, but Bob shouldered him aside and strode across the terrace, with Duray glowering at his back.

Elizabeth said in a mournful voice, "I hope we're at the end of all this."

Duray growled, "You should never have listened to him."

"I didn't listen; I read about it in one of Bob's books; I saw your picture; I couldn't —"

Alan Robertson intervened. "Don't harass poor Elizabeth; I consider her both sensible and brave; she did the best she could."

Bob returned. "Everything taken care of," he said cheerfully. "All except one or two details."

"The first of these is the return of the passway. Gilbert and Elizabeth, not to mention Dolly, Joan and Ellen, are anxious to return home."

"They can stay here with you," said Bob. "That's probably the best solution."

"I don't plan to stay here," said Alan Robertson in mild wonder. "We are leaving at once."

"You must change your plans," said Bob. "I have finally become bored with your reproaches. Roger doesn't particularly care to leave his home, but he agrees that now is the time to make a final disposal of the matter."

Alan Robertson frowned in displeasure. "The joke is in very poor taste, Bob."

Roger Waille came from the house, his face somewhat glum. "They're all closed. Only the main gate is open."

Alan Robertson said to Gilbert: "I think that we will leave Bob and Roger to their Rumfuddle fantasies. When he returns to his senses we'll get your passway. Come along then, Elizabeth! Girls!"

"Alan," said Bob gently. "You're staying here. Forever. I'm taking over the machine."

Alan Robertson asked mildly: "How do you propose to restrain me? By force?"

"You can stay here alive or dead; take your choice."

"You have weapons then?"

"I certainly do." Bob displayed a pistol. "There are also the servants. None have brain tumors or syphilis, they're all just plain bad."

Roger said in an awkward voice, "Let's go and get it over."

Alan Robertson's voice took on a harsh edge. "You seriously plan to maroon us here, without food?"

"Consider yourself marooned."

"I'm afraid that I must punish you, Bob, and Roger as well."

Bob laughed gaily. "You yourself are suffering from brain disease — megalomania. You haven't the power to punish anyone."

"I still control the machine, Bob."

"The machine isn't here. So now —"

Alan Robertson turned and looked around the landscape, with a frowning air of expectation. "Let me see: I'd probably come down from the main gate; Gilbert and a group from behind the house. Yes; here we are."

Down the path from the main portal, walking jauntily, came two Alan Robertsons with six men armed with rifles and gas grenades. Simultaneously from behind the house appeared two Gilbert Durays and six more men, similarly armed.

Bob stared in wonder. "Who are these people?"

"Cognates," said Alan smiling. "I told you I controlled the machine, and so do all my cognates. As soon as Gilbert and I return to our Earth, we must similarly set forth and in our turn do our part on other worlds cognate to this... Roger, be good enough to summon your servants. We will take them back to Earth. You and Bob must remain here."

Waille gasped in distress. "Forever?"

"You deserve nothing better," said Alan Robertson. "Bob perhaps deserves worse." He turned to the cognate Alan Robertsons. "What of Gilbert's passway?"

Both replied, "It's in Bob's San Francisco apartment, in a box on the mantelpiece."

"Very good," said Alan Robertson. "We will now depart. Goodby,

Bob. Goodby, Roger. I am sorry that our association ended on this rather unpleasant basis."

"Wait!" cried Roger. "Take me back with you!"

"Goodby," said Alan Robertson. "Come along then, Elizabeth. Girls! Run on ahead!"

XIII

Elizabeth and the children had returned to Home; Alan Robertson and Duray sat in the lounge above the machine. "Our first step," said Alan Robertson, "is to dissolve our obligation. There are of course an infinite number of Rumfuddles at Ekshayans and an infinite number of Alans and Gilberts. If we visited a single Rumfuddle, we would, by the laws of probability, miss a certain number of the emergency situations. The total number of permutations, assuming that an infinite number of Alans and Gilberts makes a random choice among an infinite number of Ekshayans, is infinity raised to the infinite power. What percentage of this number yields blanks for any given Ekshayan, I haven't calculated. If we visited Ekshayans until we had by our own efforts rescued at least one Gilbert and Alan set, we might be forced to scour fifty or a hundred worlds, or more. Or we might achieve our rescue on the first visit. The wisest course, I believe, is for you and I to visit, say, twenty Ekshayans. If each of the Alan and Gilbert sets does the same, then the chances for any particular Alan and Gilbert to be abandoned are one in twenty times nineteen times eighteen times seventeen, etcetera. Even then I think I will arrange that an operator check another five or ten thousand worlds to gather up that one lone chance…"

JACK VANCE was born in 1916 to a well-off California family that, as his childhood ended, fell upon hard times. As a young man he worked at a series of unsatisfying jobs before studying mining engineering, physics, journalism and English at the University of California Berkeley. Leaving school as America was going to war, he found a place as an ordinary seaman in the merchant marine. Later he worked as a rigger, surveyor, ceramicist, and carpenter before his steady production of sf, mystery novels, and short stories established him as a full-time writer.

His output over more than sixty years was prodigious and won him three Hugo Awards, a Nebula Award, a World Fantasy Award for lifetime achievement, as well as an Edgar from the Mystery Writers of America. The Science Fiction and Fantasy Writers of America named him a grandmaster and he was inducted into the Science Fiction Hall of Fame.

His works crossed genre boundaries, from dark fantasies (including the highly influential *Dying Earth* cycle of novels) to interstellar space operas, from heroic fantasy (the *Lyonesse* trilogy) to murder mysteries featuring a sheriff (the Joe Bain novels) in a rural California county. A Vance story often centered on a competent male protagonist thrust into a dangerous, evolving situation on a planet where adventure was his daily fare, or featured a young person setting out on a perilous odyssey over difficult terrain populated by entrenched, scheming enemies.

Late in his life, a world-spanning assemblage of Vance aficionados came together to return his works to their original form, restoring material cut by editors whose chief preoccupation was the page count of a pulp magazine. The result was the complete and authoritative *Vance Integral Edition* in 44 hardcover volumes. Spatterlight Press is now publishing the VIE texts as ebooks, and as print-on-demand paperbacks.

Colophon

This book was printed using Adobe Arno Pro as the primary text font, with NeutraFace used on the cover.

This title was created from the digital archive of the Vance Integral Edition, a series of 44 books produced under the aegis of the author by a worldwide group of his readers. The VIE project gratefully acknowledges the editorial guidance of Norma Vance, as well as the cooperation of the Department of Special Collections at Boston University, whose John Holbrook Vance collection has been an important source of textual evidence.

Special thanks to R.C. Lacovara, Patrick Dusoulier, Koen Vyverman, Paul Rhoads, Chuck King, Gregory Hansen, Suan Yong, and Josh Geller for their invaluable assistance preparing final versions of the source files.

Source: Paul Rhoads, Norma Vance, Harrison Watson, Jr.; Digitize: Donna Adams, Derek W. Benson, Richard Chandler, Joel Hedlund, Alun Hughes, David Mortimore, Joe Ormond, Paul Rhoads, Thomas Rydbeck, Bill Schmaltz, Gan Uesli Starling, Billy Webb, Dave Worden; Format: John A. D. Foley, R.C. Lacovara, Bill Schmaltz; Diff: John A. D. Foley, Rob Gerrand, Damien G. Jones, David A. Kennedy, R.C. Lacovara, Paul Rhoads, Thomas Rydbeck, Suan Hsi Yong; Diff-Merge: Steve Sherman; Tech Proof: Rob Friefeld, Peter Ikin, Bob Moody, Errico Rescigno, Hans van der Veeke, Matt Westwood; Text Integrity: Patrick Dusoulier, Rob Friefeld, Helmut Hlavacs, David A. Kennedy, R.C. Lacovara, Paul Rhoads, Kenneth Roberts, Thomas Rydbeck, John A. Schwab, Steve Sherman, Tim Stretton; Implement: Donna Adams, Derek W. Benson, Mike Dennison, Patrick Dusoulier, Damien G. Jones, John McDonough, Paul Rhoads, Hans van der Veeke; Security: Paul Rhoads, Tim Stretton; Compose: Andreas Irle; Comp Review: Andreas Björklind, Christian J. Corley, Marcel van Genderen, Brian Gharst, Charles King, Per Kjellberg, Stephane Leibovitsch, Bob Luckin, Paul Rhoads, Robin L. Rouch; Update Verify: Andreas Björklind, Top Changwatchai, John A. D. Foley, Rob Friefeld, Marcel van Genderen, Charles King, Bob Luckin, Robert Melson, Paul Rhoads, Robin L. Rouch; RTF-Diff: Mark Bradford, Patrick Dusoulier, Charles King, Errico Rescigno, Bill Schaub, Hans van der Veeke; Textport: Patrick Dusoulier, Charles King, Steve Sherman; Proofread: Erik Arendse, Michel Bazin, Derek W. Benson, Alan Bird, Andreas Björklind, Carina Björklind, Malcolm Bowers, Mark Bradford, Foppe Brolsma, Graziano Carlon, John H. Chalmers, Top Changwatchai, Deborah Cohen, Christian J. Corley, Michael Duncan, John A. D. Foley, Marcel van Genderen, Rob Gerrand, Carl Goldman, Ed Gooding, Yannick Gour, Erec Grim, Jasper Groen, Evert Jan de Groot, Charles Hardin, Marc Herant, Brent Heustess, Patrick Hudson, Peter Ikin, Lucie Jones, Jurriaan Kalkman, Karl Kellar,

David A. Kennedy, A.G. Kimlin, Charles King, Per Kjellberg, John Kleeman, R.C. Lacovara, Stephane Leibovitsch, Bob Luckin, Betty Mayfield, Chris McCormick, Robert Melson, Bob Moody, David Mortimore, Till Noever, Jim Pattison, Dave Peters, Simon Read, David Reitsema, Paul Rhoads, Joel Riedesel, John Robinson Jr., Robin L. Rouch, Jeffrey Ruszczyk, Thomas Rydbeck, Bill Schaub, Bill Sherman, Michael J. Smith, Gabriel Stein, Mark J. Straka, Hans van der Veeke, Russ Wilcox

Artwork (maps based on original drawings by Jack and Norma Vance):

Paul Rhoads, Christopher Wood

Book Composition and Typesetting: Joel Anderson

Art Direction and Cover Design: Howard Kistler

Proofing: Steve Sherman, Dave Worden

Jacket Blurb: John Vance

Management: John Vance, Koen Vyverman

Made in United States
Troutdale, OR
12/18/2023

16034560R00148